SUNRISE IN THE WEST

Glen Natalier

Published in Australia by Sid Harta Publishers Pty Ltd,
ABN: 46 119 415 842
23 Stirling Crescent, Glen Waverley, Victoria 3150 Australia
Telephone: +61 3 9560 9920, Facsimile: +61 3 9545 1742
E-mail: author@sidharta.com.au

First published in Australia 2017
This edition published 2018
Copyright © Glen Natalier 2017
Cover design, typesetting: WorkingType (www.workingtype.com.au)

This book is a work of fiction. It is however based on the actual experiences of Franz and
Helena Natalier and their family members in Germany who fled their home in Rucken.
Franz Natalier's cousins, Frank and Henry Natalier and their families did live in Australia.
Known historical figures have been represented in their actual roles. Other characters
are the author's creation and any similarities to that of people living or dead are purely
coincidental.

Natalier, Glen
Sunrise in the West
ISBN: 978-1-925230-05-5
pp304

About the Author

Glen Natalier was born into a closely knit rural community in the Lockyer Valley in Queensland, Australia. He chose not to stay on the family farm but completed the necessary studies to become a high school teacher of geography and German language. During these teaching years he wrote a number of  geography text books directed towards the syllabus requirements at that time. This allowed him to travel widely collecting, first hand, material and photographs to be used in the books. Years of teaching have left him with a love of learning and he finds that writing helps detract from the cares and worries which always seem to arise.

The tennis and footballs of previous years have morphed into golf balls which bring great pleasure when seen against the green of the centre of a fairway.

Now retired, he lives with his wife, Jill, caring for a teen-age grandson. They live in a town just over a few hills from where he was born. Their four children and their families are scattered around Australia.

Remembering
Franz, Helena, Ruth and Edith.

Author's Notes and Acknowledgments

At the end of the nineteenth century, my grandfather, Friedrich Natalier (known as Fritz), emigrated to Australia from a region in the far eastern extremities of the German Empire known as the Memelland. He came alone and left behind his own family and many relatives. Over time, and especially as a result of World War I, contact between him and his family in Australia and those of his homeland was lost.

During the last stages of World War II, members of the Natalier families in the Memelland had to flee their homes in the face of an advancing, avenging Russian army. Some died during the flight and others reached the relative safety of areas occupied by the more considerate Western Allies. In their poverty in a destroyed nation, life became a struggle to stay alive. Many of these displaced German refugees sought help from relatives who they knew were living in Australia and other countries.

Through the Red Cross Franz Natalier, the protagonist of this story, was put into contact with his cousins Frank and Henry in Australia. In a letter written to them in 1947, Franz briefly described some of the experiences of their escape. This letter has survived and I have used it as the basis of this story.

There have been shoves and pushes, hands of help and encouragement from numerous people who have aided me in expanding the few pages of Franz' letter. These include members of the Natalier relationship here in Australia who wanted to know more about their long-lost cousins on the other side of the world. Especially I would single out my wife, Jill, whose claim that I often don't get around to finishing things is probably true. It was she who supplied the necessary push, and then later suggestions and proof-reading which helped make the book what it is.

I want to record a word of thanks and gratitude to the two daughters of the story, Ruth and Edith, and their husbands Michael Martini and Enno Eden, who later showed great love and hospitality to me and my family when visiting Germany.

Many thanks to Gary Natalier and Terry McIvor who turned my mud maps into something more legible. Thanks also for the courage and help shown by members of the Sidharta Publishing organisation who transformed my Word document into something which can proudly take its place on a bookshelf or coffee table.

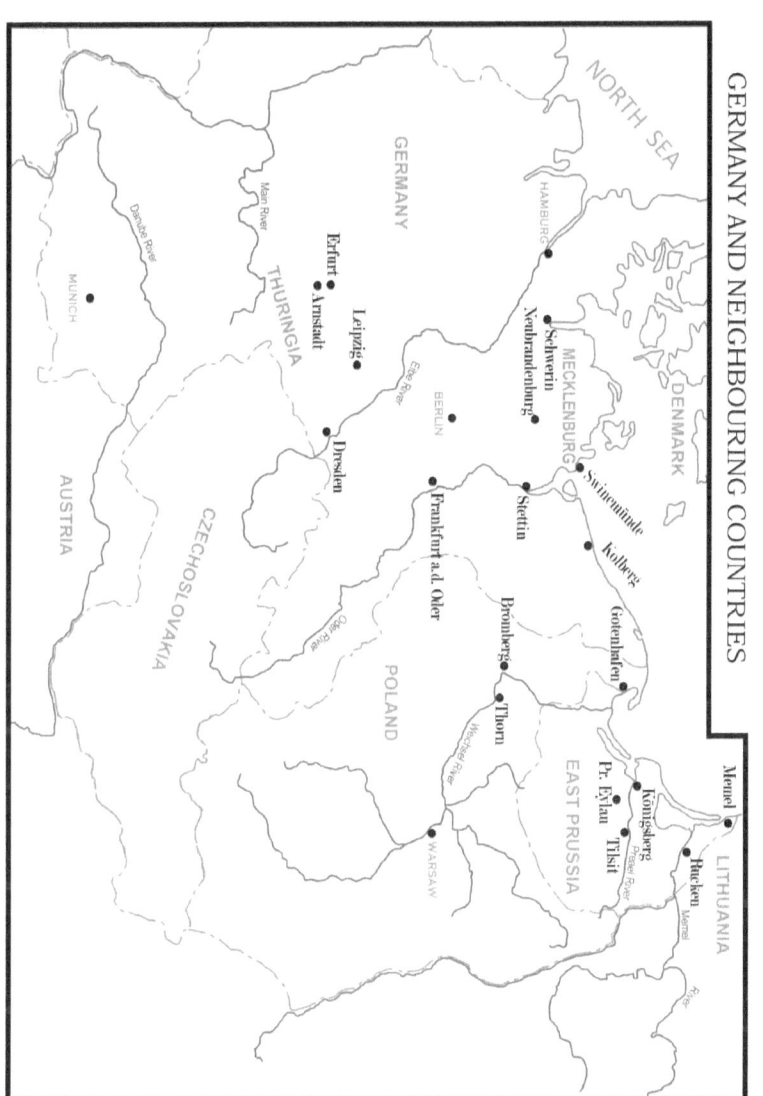

GERMANY AND NEIGHBOURING COUNTRIES

NORTH SEA

GERMANY

HAMBURG

Danube River

Main River

MUNICH

Erfurt
Arnstadt

THURINGIA

Leipzig

Elbe River

Dresden

AUSTRIA

CZECHOSLOVAKIA

BERLIN

Schwerin
Neubrandenburg

MECKLENBURG

DENMARK

Swinemünde

Stettin

Kolberg

Frankfurt a.d. Oder

Oder River

POLAND

Bromberg

Gotenhafen

Thorn

Vistula River

WARSAW

Pr. Eylau

EAST PRUSSIA

Königsberg

Tilsit

Pregel River

Memel

Rucken

LITHUANIA

Memel

River

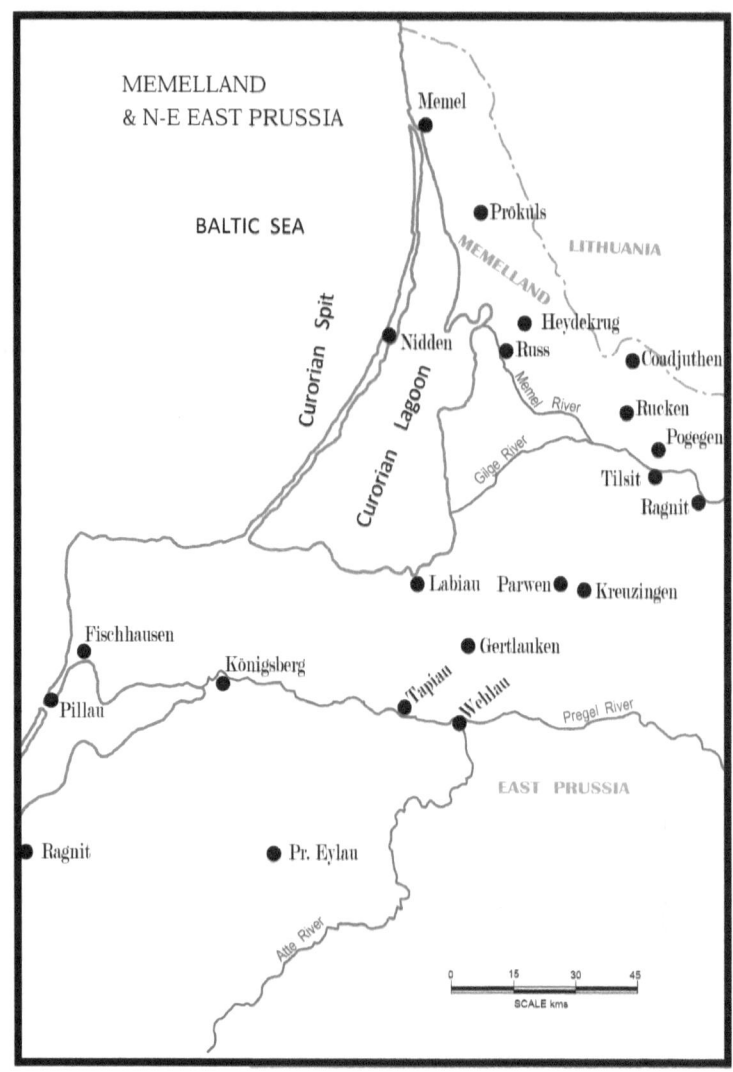

Preface

Die Heimat

(The homeland)

Memelland. This small fleck of land touching the Baltic
Sea is where our story begins. It is called after the Memel,
the German name of a river which flows into the Baltic at this
point. This is the *German* name, for it has been given a variety of
names over the ages depending on which language was claiming
ownership. It has also been called the Njemen, the Neuman,
Njoman, Neman and Nieman and probably many others. This
changing of names would seem to indicate that this was a very
confused and unsettled area. It was. The German people who
once lived here, who called this their *Heimat* — their homeland
— solved the problem by simply calling it *der Fluss* (the River).

This linguistic approach may have solved the nomenclature
of this multi-lingual river but it did little to solve the frequent
complex, upsetting political situations which would arise in this
region. This small corner of the world has often been the pawn in
the games that powerful, victorious governments play, especially
in, and after, times of hostility. The various nations which at
one time and another exercised their power here bear witness to
this. It was once Lithuanian, for long centuries German, briefly
French, then independent (but not really), German again (very
briefly), Russian and now once again Lithuanian.

It has its tales to tell and its sufferings to share. There have
been moments of pride and also of shame. It had its simple

1

farming folk who were only intent on earning a livelihood, and for them life moved along in rhythm with the seasonal changes. Then there were other times when distant political drums rolled, unrest and persecution became not uncommon and innocent lives were at risk. All of this, and more, has been recorded in the history books, unheeded by the Memel (or Njemen, or Neuman, or let's just say the River!) which slowly winds its final one hundred kilometres to the coast.

History can be cold and impersonal, often detached from those who form the human face of what can be merely a short reference in some scholar's tome. These faces generally remain unknown and unsung — the cannon fodder of history.

But each is the face of a human being, of an individual who has been born to be loved and to love, to laugh and to cry, to hope and to strive towards enjoying that gift called life. These are the people who stoically pursue their lot in life, who work to have food to eat, who strive to bring joy and contentment to themselves and who live to give help and friendship to their acquaintances. These people form community. They come together to celebrate and share their joys; but also at times to mourn their sorrows. They meet to socialise and enjoy each other's company, and also to meditate on spiritual matters; to worship.

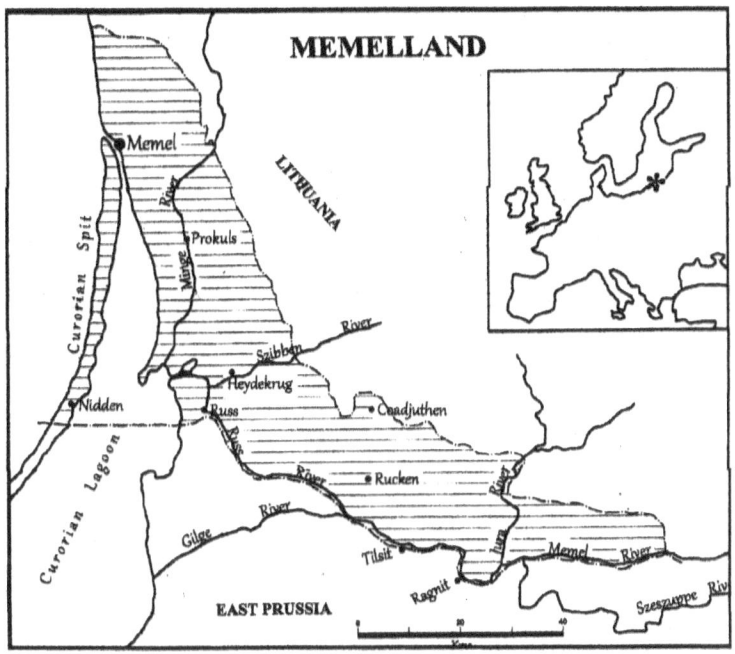

The previous German region of Memelland was situated at the southern end of the present Baltic country of Lithuania. The locations shown here with their German names now all have Lithuanian names. Rucken, for example, where this story begins, is now known as Rukai.

Chapter 1

Es kam schon wieder zum Krieg

(War broke out again.)

It was Sunday, 23rd July 1944, and a vicious war was still raging throughout Europe. Ever since September, 1939, when Nazi Germany invaded Poland the continent was in a state of war. For the first three years of conflict, the German war machine swept across the landscape overcoming all the resistance in its way. This was not just a thrust in one direction but Germany and her allies spread war and destruction in all directions. It reached a point of total warfare throughout Europe where not only military personnel were involved but civilians were also drawn into the conflict and suffered greatly.

But the tide of battle had turned. The swift advances of the *Wehrmacht* had been arrested. By the end of 1942 the German armies were suffering defeat in many areas and a determined opponent was pushing them back towards their homeland. The Battle of El Alamein in Egypt, in November 1942, began the demise of the German forces in Northern Africa. By the middle of 1943 allied forces were landing in Sicily and Italy. After five months, bloody fighting in Stalingrad the Germans were forced to retreat and abandon their push towards the Russian capital. The eastern front began moving westward. Then on D-Day, 6th June 1944, the invasion at Normandy saw the establishment of an allied foothold in Northern Europe. The German army was in no position to stop an advancing enemy and by the middle of 1944 defeat was closing in on Germany from all directions. The German people were facing a conquering army and the accompanying suffering. The Nazi propaganda machine tried to convince the people differently but most could no longer be persuaded to accept what they knew were blatant mistruths.

For one group of people in the small village of Rucken in the Memelland however, the terrors of war had been briefly forgotten in the peacefulness of their church.

Sunday church service had just concluded at the Evangelical Lutheran Church. It stood solidly just on the edge of the farming community of Rucken where the Schillgallen Road met the *Memeler Chaussee*, the main road running through the district. It was nearing midday and the late summer sun still radiated enough energy to cause the Sunday-best dressed parishioners to seek the shade of the leafy elms. The emerging worshippers had quickly formed into groups of differing sizes, drawn together by habit, by relationship and often by mutual affinity for the recent gossip. Other groups were clusters of old friends who had always lived in the village and who enjoyed their Sunday chat. They were not embarrassed to admit that they looked forward to going to church. One should not delve too deeply into their motives. However, Pfarrer Joneleit was well aware of this and he also looked forward to joining in their discussions.

This Sunday morning routine represented a pattern that had not changed in decades. The same people would attend this local church with attendances remaining fairly constant. Older worshippers would die but their place would be taken by babies born to excited young couples. It was noticeable that the last few years had seen a decrease in attendance. This was not because of a waning of faith within the community. There were spaces within the family groups and everyone was very aware of these gaps, knowing that some would never be filled again. The Muller's son Heinz would not be seen in his too tight shirt, often with a button missing. His body would remain buried somewhere on the plains of the Ukraine, unmarked. Rudi Wagner was studying philosophy in Königsberg when he was called up to help defend the fatherland. His parents know where their much-loved family member was buried, as do also a number of other grieving folk who had been notified of the death of a son, a father, a husband or brother.

Teenager Anna, would spend most of the time during the Pfarrer's address staring at the empty space between Mr and Mrs Freund. Emil should be sitting there. Her prayers are always for him only. Will that space be filled again? All in the congregation hope that it will be. Many are also realists and inwardly know that with the state of the war as it is, his return is doubtful. Attendance at the church service can be a sad reminder of absent congregation members for those who are now present. Pfarrer Joneleit is aware of this too and always attempts to lift the mood of his flock and emphasise the message of hope and the joy that faith in a Creator God can ignite. In this way, he attempts to be positive, and the worshippers can leave a little uplifted.

Outside the church most tried to keep war topics well in the background. In one group, half a dozen local farmers, friends from their youth, were gathered discussing those topics God-fearing souls would find most appropriate after divine worship — the weather, condition of their crops, the weather, and occasionally a comment on the Pfarrer's sermon. Conversation was well under way, often loud with two or three making quite different points at the same time. This was normal. Complete agreement would often be followed by stunned silence. Agreeing with someone was no way to promote discussion.

Franz Natalier was less forthcoming with his contributions today. He stood there, occasionally nodding, often staring into space. He could have been mistaken for a retiring, quiet thinker. His friends knew that this was not the normal Franz. His eyes lacked the usual sparkle that denoted an alert, mostly amusing story-teller.

'What's wrong, Franz? You're quiet today.'

'You know me, Brothers, I never have much to say.'

'Nah! Get away with you! You look as though your workhorses have swallowed their feed bags. Can be true sometimes, but mention horses and you can go on and on. But tell us, how is that prize foal you are always talking about?'

'Well seeing that you want to know, he's doing fine and his mother! You can see that the young mare is so very proud of him. You should see her. It's unbelievable.' Franz was clearly warming to his memories. One hand had even come off his walking stick and he was waving it around illustrating his enthusiasm. 'When I go up to give him a scratch between the ears, she trots over and gives me a gentle nuzzle in the back. "That's my young boy," she seems to be saying.' His hearty manner quickly took on a more sombre vein as he continued, 'But I'm worried. I'm really worried.'

The eyes which had wandered to the empty stork's nest on top of the church tower when he began talking about his prize mare and her foal, and others which were watching a group of young boys chasing one another, refocused on Franz Natalier when it was clear that he had problems. It was accepted here that light-hearted banter be returned in like manner, but any hint of seriousness in a conversation would result in respectful attention. They were quietly waiting for him to continue.

Franz was a very well respected member, not only of the German-speaking fraternity of Rucken, but of the whole community. He was a mere child of six when the red brick church had been erected and he had been associated with it ever since. It was here that he had received his first communion at the age of fourteen. Although still unwell, suffering the after-effects of war service, he had helped in repairing the damage done to the church by Russian artillery during the Great War. It was here that he and his beloved Helena had been married in 1924. She had been widowed by the Great War and brought three young boys into the marriage. He had readily accepted them as his own. For years he had sat on the Church's Board of Elders. He was loved and respected. Over the years people had learnt that his advice was well thought out and inwardly verified. Folks would listen to him. He was to be trusted.

'Not about your horses, then?' from his neighbour, Walter Kreise.

'If only it were as simple as that. No, I'm worried about where this war is headed and what will happen to us all.' Franz was never one to bring up the topic of war after church. His friends knew his attitude to what had happened and he regarded church as a place to escape the cares and worries of everyday life. Like his friend the Pfarrer Joneleit he wished a church service to be optimistic and uplifting for his life. Today, however, his attitude called for some explanation.

'We all are worried to some extent, Franz, but Gauleiter Keller says that the Party has things under control, and that we should not believe all those stories to the contrary.'

'Keller! I don't take much notice of what he says. We all know that he only ever has one answer to everything — the official line. He's just a Nazi yes man. No, Helena's boy, Fritz, says how things are falling apart in the west on the fronts there, and that our army has no hope of holding back the enemy forces. He says it's just a matter of time and they will be marching into Berlin itself.'

'Helena's boy Fritz, had better watch what he says or he will find himself in trouble and you and your wife will be getting a visit from Gauleiter Keller,' warned Alfred Hensleit, whose Nazi sympathies could often be discerned, especially in this remote area where Berlin politics were often discounted and strong political feelings seldom revealed; but unerringly read.

'Oh, come on Alfred. It's time you see Keller for what he really is. Brothers, let's be honest. We have already lost this foolish war. Surely our leaders can see that. Why don't they accept the fact, call a halt to all the fighting and save lives instead of sacrificing them. The enemy is closing in. We're being squashed. Life is being squeezed out of us. And it's not the Yanks or Tommies that I'm worrying about, but the Asian hordes coming in on the east wind.'

'Our boys will be able to stop them, won't they?'

'That's just the point, we have no chance. Ever since we failed to take Leningrad they have been pushing us back. You've seen what's moving down the main road from Heydekrug recently — a broken, defeated army. What reinforcements have you seen going the other way? But it's what I hear people around here saying that has me worried. And it's mainly coming from our Lithuanian friends. They say the Russian army is intent on cleaning out all the German people in these eastern regions. And that's us! Mark my words. The Russians are coming and our lives are at stake. If we are still here when they arrive, we are dead men. That's what's worrying me.'

Franz's waving hand had found its way back to the handle of his walking stick. He was now leaning forward on the stick and this posture seemed to give added emphasis to his premonitions. There was a pause in the conversation. It was one of those moments which seemed to denote general agreement. These were men not wanting to disagree with Franz. They also had been aware of what was happening. A couple of the heads were nodding their agreement.

There was a realisation that they could soon all be caught up in the fury of battle even thought they were civilians. Up until recently their remoteness had basically isolated these people from the reality of combat. News bulletins, sons home on leave and propaganda had kept them aware of the war surrounding their homeland, but fighting on the Rhine, around Milan or in Stalingrad was not personal. It was something happening to other people far away. It was similar to the feeling of many bomber pilots. Dropping bombs from a great height on a city was not really killing people. It was remote and impersonal. Reality strikes when blazing infernos, screaming mothers and blackened bodies come to the fore.

Franz and his companions were now contemplating this reality.

'Papa.' This caused Franz to straighten and turn around. A slight, blond-haired teenager had tapped him on the right shoulder.

'Good heavens, Edith. Don't creep up on me like that!'

'I didn't creep up, Papa. You were so busy talking that you didn't hear me. Mama says she's ready to go home and to tell you that Ruth and I are going to Aunty Therese for lunch.'

'That's fine. Tell Mama that I'm coming.' And then to his circle of friends, 'It seems that I have to be off. But as from now, I'm not going to sit and do nothing. I am going to start getting ready to leave the farm before the Russians arrive. My advice is that you all do the same. God be with us all.'

After bidding his friends farewell, Franz made his way to the front gate where his wife, Helena, was watching him approach, worrying that his slight limp seemed worse than usual.

Chapter 2

Church at Ten O'clock

On this July day also, fifteen thousand kilometres away on the other side of the world in the Ropeley district in Australia, most of the local farmers and their families were heading towards their usual Sunday morning destination. It was not yet nine o'clock in the morning and these country folk were on their way to their church service which began at ten. A casual observer might think that they had a long way to travel seeing that they were on the road so early. That was not really the case, but it was important to get there early so that there was plenty of time for a good yarn before the bell rang and everyone had to move into the pews.

The really early birds were already in their regular spots. Old Emil Hoger and Henry Natalier were two of these. They were two of the elders of the congregation and always had a small amount of organisation to do before the service began. Actually, these jobs would normally take about five minutes but they used this as an excuse to arrive very early. This allowed even more time to chat.

'Hello, Emil. How goes it?'

' G'day Henry. Nah! Not so good.'

'What's worrying you? Is Bertha still crook?'

'Na, Bertha is feeling much better. She should be up and about in a few days. No, it's Stumpy.'

'Stumpy. Your old blue cattle dog? What's the matter with him?'

'Found him stone cold dead this morning when I went out to

get the cows. Had to bring the blighters in by myself. And they were in the far paddock where they shouldn't have been. Don't know where the other dogs were. That's always been the trouble. When Stumpy isn't around they skulk off somewhere to get out of a bit of work. I think that black snake in the wood heap got him. We know there's one in there but we can't catch the bugger.'

'That's tough, Emil. Old Stumpy was your best dog too. What are you going to do?'

'I want to catch Gus Krenske when he gets here. See if he still has any of those pups left that he wants to get rid of. I know their mother is a good worker.'

Here at Ropeley, a rural community hidden in a creek valley west of Brisbane in Australia, the local church was an important social centre. It was an important part of the Sunday routine for all but a few residents in the two adjacent valleys of Ropeley and Tent Hill. This would be up at sunrise, milk the small herd of dairy cows, complete the other essential morning jobs, have breakfast and then start getting ready for church. The church service always commenced at ten o'clock.

And that ten o'clock start was fixed in stone here at the Immanuel Lutheran Church. This allowed the congregation members time to do their morning jobs before arriving at church in time to sit down and talk to one another. This talking had to take place before the church service, for there was little time after service to stand around. Lunch for these hard-working farmers was at twelve o'clock, midday. It was at twelve o'clock during the week so why should their stomach juices be upset on Sundays by having to wait longer for food? Pastor Koehler was well aware of this, so he would make sure that the last hymn was finished by 11.30am. Then all roads would lead from the church, home to the dinner table.

He well remembers that shortly after arriving at this place, his first posting as an ordained minister, he conducted a service that lasted almost two hours and went on till midday. It was a special day with a couple of baptisms and a longer communion service. Being new to the district, he was unaware of the traditional time constraints. It had only happened that one time however, for immediately after the service he was approached by two of the elders who told him what was expected. On thinking back, he could see a feeling of restlessness during the last half hour of that service. He now understood why that was.

After service, the large weather-board church was soon alone with its pine trees, fig trees and eucalypts. Before service on the other hand, the church yard was abuzz with groups catching up on the previous week's events. The corrugated, galvanised-iron shelter shed orientated to catch the winter sun and protect from the cold winter westerly winds was where the older married men would meet. Here the seats — hand adzed, ironbark planks — were smooth and shiny, the result of years of polishing by the seats of Sunday suits. Here the old pioneers could find shade from the scorching summer sun, protection from rain and a sunny spot on chilly winter mornings. An hour yarning here and everyone would be up with what was happening in the district.

Unlike the men, the women of the congregation were more migratory in their pre-service manoeuvres. Immediately on arriving at the church many would be seen walking next door to the pastor's residence, carrying "something for the pastor and Mrs Koehler". This was the generosity of these country folk. These "little somethings" would be gifts of all manner of fruit and vegetables in season, cakes and biscuits, eggs and plucked chooks and dairy produce.

Judith Hetherington had recently been appointed as teacher at the one-teacher primary school at Ropeley East. She was boarding with the Steinhardts near the school and felt obliged to go to church with them. Until coming to the school she had never really heard of the Lutheran Church and now she was living in a district where almost everyone attended a Lutheran church. The practices and traditions were new and intriguing to her but she felt that it would aid her in her job if she, as she put it, joined in with the locals.

This morning she approached the mother of one of her pupils. 'So, Mrs Hahn, why are you women always keeping the pastor's larder full? Doesn't he get paid?'

'Yes, he does get paid, but it probably is not as much as he deserves.'

'Why all the goodies then and not just pay him a few more pounds every week?'

'As you know, Miss Hetherington, all of us live on farms of one sort or another and we all benefit from having this fresh produce, so why shouldn't the pastor and his family benefit as well?'

'I think it's a wonderful thing that you are all doing. I'm sure it is not like this down in Brisbane; not that I'd really know I'm ashamed to say. Is this a new thing or has it always been like this?'

'As long as I can remember. My old mum says that when the church first started the gifts were the pastor's main income. And it was much harder for the members then. Many were struggling to get their farms producing. And we're not the only ones who do this. All the country churches around here look after their pastors quite well.'

They headed back to Mrs Hahn's car where she deposited the cake tin which had contained last week's gift. Others on returning from the manse would head towards whomever they wanted to gossip with. This would usually vary from week to week. Their conversation would concentrate around house and family matters. Combine this with what the men had been talking about and it is seen that the families would be well aware of what was happening in the district. Miss church and you were in danger of missing out on the weekly news.

The young lads would congregate around the different vehicles in the parking area, especially with the appearance of a new addition — brand new or second hand. No, the young girls would not be near the cars and the boys. They would be sharing their thoughts and dreams under the spreading fig trees to the side of the church. Which leaves the children and there were plenty of these. Yes, they were left to amuse themselves. They were everywhere — under the trees, around the trees and in the trees; under the church hall, around the hall, but not in the hall. They would go there later for Sunday School. Before the church service began they were never in one place for very long. This great expenditure of energy was probably to prepare them for their time in church ahead when they would have to sit quietly beside or between, their parents.

Going to church was a busy Sunday outing for the whole family. A happy day out. A time to put on one's Sunday clothes. For many children, a time to put on shoes for the only time in the week. This Sunday in 1944 had nothing special to mark it out from the many other Sundays in the life of this country church. A few years ago, there would have been anxiety of the faces of many of the parishioners who had friends in Darwin when it was bombed by the Japanese. Then when the southward push of the Japanese was halted by the Battle of the Coral Sea many expressed a feeling of relief. But in recent times, with the Pacific war retreating from Australian regions, talk about war practically disappeared. Very few in the congregation were personally involved, for in this farming community the young men were required to work producing food and hence were not conscripted. And it must not be forgotten that the many hundreds of people turned up at Immanuel Lutheran Church to practise their religion, to worship God. It was not only a community social gathering.

The Rev. A.H.Koehler was the much loved and highly respected pastor of this rural congregation. He had arrived at this community in 1936 after completing his theological studies at a seminary in distant Adelaide, three thousand kilometres away. He had no trouble fitting in with the conservative church-going people who formed the congregation. Initially, his main problem was getting to know the four hundred and fifty individuals he was to serve. More difficult perhaps was getting to know who was related to whom.

The congregation owed its establishment to the wave of German settlers who came to the district during the latter half of the nineteenth century. Previously the land had been owned and operated as large estates, but after it was sub-divided into smaller holdings the newly-arrived migrants were able to become small landholders.

The migrants were Protestant Christians coming mainly from the eastern regions of the German Empire. They had a common language (well basically), a common religious belief (well basically) and a common purpose of becoming financially successful and this formed the basis of a strong community. If you were able to look down the membership list at that time, you could be excused for thinking that you were back in Germany. Here was Baltzer, Bachmann, Beck, Dionysius, Grams, Gehrke, Hermann, Hoger, Kajewski, Logan, Logan?? (Yes, Jimmy Logan married one of Wilhelm Weier's girls, so what could he do but join the flock?) Manteuffel, Natalier, Steinhardt....The list went on and on.

For many decades marriage would take place within this closely-knit group often with two or three brothers marrying girls from the same family. The families were large with ten and more children not being unusual. So, numbers at the church grew.

With the large families came the fact that age differences between siblings could be quite large. Pastor Koehler always enjoyed telling his city colleagues how in one of his families the son married his own mother's younger sister.

'Yes, it was old Mick's second marriage,' he would begin his story. 'His first wife died young, quite unexpectedly, leaving Mick with two young boys — Alf and Gustav. Then Mick married one of the older Tillack girls, Martha. Fifteen years later Alf married Martha's young sister Helen. He didn't know whether to call his mother (step-mother really) Mum or Sis. And it was strange for Mick's new wife as well, for her younger sister now became her step-daughter.'

'And they expected me to know who was who right from the beginning,' Pastor Koehler would jokingly comment. 'But they are solid, country folk. They took me under their wing and would merely laugh at my many mistakes. They were always ready to help me when I needed help. Probably the only time someone wouldn't come immediately when I needed help was when their mare was foaling or their dog was having pups.'

After the service on that windy July morning in 1944, two brothers, Frank and Henry Natalier (they had actually been baptised Franz and Heinrich), were talking as they moved to their cars to go home for dinner.

'The Rev. carried on a bit today, don't you think?'

'Yes, you could say that. When he gets on to talking about the evils of dancing he just doesn't know when to stop.'

'Do you think he was getting at Arnie because he plays the squeeze-box at the dances up the creek?'

'Maybe. I didn't think of that but believe me, if he was, you can be sure Arnie wouldn't take much notice.'

'I see Annie in the car getting a bit anxious. She wants to get straight home and make sure Roy has the vegetables on the stove. He stayed home today to look after the meal. You and Aggie are bringing the kids to dinner today, aren't you?'

'Sure. We'll go straight home, get changed and then come on up.'

With that, Frank's Oldsmobile and Henry's old Buick soon joined the stream of cars leaving the church grounds heading home for dinner.

Chapter 3

Ich hatte eine Landwirtschaft von 16 Hectare Grösse, und wir konnten ganz gut davon leben.

(I had a farm of 16 hectares and we could live quite well off it.)

With the Sunday church service over for another week, groups of worshippers were slowly making their way to their farms and homes. Franz and Helena were walking along the Schillgallen Road with their neighbours and good friends, Walter and Lotte Kreise. The two women, whose walking pace seemed to reflect the speed at which they were talking, were soon metres ahead of their husbands. They looked back to see what was holding them up and saw that the men had stopped. Franz had his walking stick in his right hand waving it in the air so as to embrace the whole landscape.

'I mean to say, Walter. Look! The land here is as flat as our kitchen table. Where on earth would we be able to set up a defensive position here?'

'I know what you mean, Franz. It's good to grow crops on but wouldn't keep an enemy at bay. We would have to pull back to the river.'

'And our places here? What would happen to them?'

'Yes, the Russians would run straight through them. And they wouldn't need to keep to the roads either. Their tanks and trucks could go anywhere here.'

'That's my point. But then when it is all boiled down we would need more than a few hills to stop this happening. As I said at church; we need to get ready to move. It would be suicide for us to stay. The Russians who are coming will not be as forgiving as those who were here last time.'

The Schillgallen Road ran in a direct line through these flat fertile plains of what could have once been described as the delta of the Memel river. In its natural state these were flat, swampy reaches which would flood periodically. Now a network of drainage canals turned the area into fertile farmland. At this time of year, the fields which came right up to the edge of the road were at their emerald best. The vegetable plots were thriving. The ears in the grain fields were swelling. A few farmers had already harvested their first crop of grass and the stooks of drying fodder dotted some paddocks. The ubiquitous storks were treading lightly through these pastures on the lookout for unwary frogs, beetles and lizards. In other fields, the yellow and white wild flowers gave a cheery feeling to the knee-high pastures. Lines of trees picked out the courses of drainage canals while clumps of trees signalled the location of ponds in the landscape.

This was the homeland to these farming families. This was the soil which gave them their livelihood. This was part of them. This was the land they loved. The quiet country road, the peaceful landscape, the gentle warm breeze, the friends walking slowly home from worshipping at their local church, how this belied the terror and the tragedies unfolding beyond the horizon to the north and east.

An hour later Franz and Helena were just finishing their light lunch. When visitors were invited or when relatives were expected to call, Helena would always make sure that their appetites were fully satisfied, but she and Franz were just as happy to eat a much lighter meal when they were by themselves.

Today they were contented to enjoy a cold bowl of pea soup with a thick slice of home-baked rye bread. Being Sunday also meant that there would be no heavy work out in the fields. It was a day of rest and Franz took that literally. He usually took the opportunity to have an afternoon nap. He was always telling people how he slept better if his stomach was not full of heavy food. Then rubbing his paunch, he would continue, 'There's enough weight there already without adding to it.'

This Sunday he remained sitting at the table with his wife rather than going off to his daytime couch. Helena looked at him with a query in her eye. Franz looked back and came out with what was on his mind, 'My dear, I don't think that we can wait any longer. It's clear to me that we will have to leave our home soon. We now have to get serious about what we should take with us when we really do have to leave.'

'What on earth do you mean? What are you talking about?'

'I'm talking about us and the war. You know what Fritz told us about the situation on the western front and how we have no hope of stopping the enemy forces pushing us back. I believe it is even worse here in the east. The Russians have stopped our advance and now our armies are retreating. If this keeps going — and I don't see how we are going to stop it — the Russians will be here in Rucken in no time. You know what everyone is saying, even the authorities? We Germans will not be safe here when the Russians arrive. We have to move out well before they get here. The problem is that they keep telling us the opposite. I don't know how that fellow Keller can say what he does. It's becoming more and more obvious why he was appointed Gauleiter. He's just here to push Nazi propaganda.'

'But he says there's no need to move yet. Our lives are at stake and surely he wouldn't be saying those things if they were not true.'

'I have no idea why he is saying what is he is and that we should not be preparing to flee. Probably that's what those fools in Berlin have told him to tell everyone. I believe that there is a need to be organised. I think we have to be ready.'

'If you think so, Franz. I agree there's no harm in spending some time now deciding what we should take and what has to stay behind.'

With that, Helena stood up from the table where they were sitting after lunch and walked over to the sideboard. She opened the middle drawer, took out a number of neatly-folded serviettes, placed them to the side and then lifted out a photo album which she carried over to her husband.

Franz was taken aback. Here they were about to discuss matters which could determine life and death and his wife wanted to look through a photo album. At least it shouldn't take too long for they did not have a large collection of photos. She sat down after drawing her chair a little closer to his.

'This has to come with us. We don't have many photos of the family after we lost all those others in our house fire. If we don't take them along with us, you have no idea what might become of them.'

And they spent the next quarter of an hour contentedly together with old memories.

Photos finished, Helena stood and set about tidying the table, cleaning the lunch dishes and generally fussing about in the kitchen.

Franz closed his eyes. Fixed in his mind was one of the postcards from Helena's album. It was a view of the sea-side town of Nidden that they had brought back with them on their trip there. OK, it wasn't a photo he had taken but it was bright and cheerful and brought back many memories of that week-end. Twelve months ago. Can it be so long? How time seems to pass so quickly. But now the whole trip was coming back to him.

Gert had come home on leave and he wanted to visit his favourite aunt who lived in Russ at the mouth of the River. That would have been the last time the family had an outing together. There was the train trip, the bus trip over to Russ and then the old steamer across the Curonian Lagoon to Nidden. It was really Aunt Ida who suggested that they go across to the sand-spit for the day. She has never changed. Even when they were still kids, big sister Ida would always be making suggestions. Giving orders would be closer to the mark! Franz smiled to himself.

After spending the rest of Saturday with her and some other friends in Russ they had caught the steamer early on Sunday morning. They were all happy that the weather promised not to spoil the day. It was one of those wonderful late summer days that only the Memelland can give you. Franz was especially pleased that the wind stayed away, for even after they had sailed past the Windenburger Corner and out of sheltered waters the lagoon was calm. Only recently there had been another drowning there. People just didn't realise how the wind could change so quickly and the water of the lagoon can become very dangerous for small craft. Franz had never liked the sea and boats and was so happy that the crossing was so calm. He was happier still when they berthed in Nidden.

Yes, it all turned out to be so pleasant. Even Gert seemed to forget the war and his involvement in it as he raced his sisters up the big dune to be first at the look-out point. Looking out over the expanse of sand dunes, the peacefulness and the beauty made one forget the hatred that was being enacted on the plains of Latvia a short distance to the north.

The view of calm and peace completely belied the strength of the wind down on the beach. The wind off the Baltic was strong and cold even on that warm summer day. Not surprising when Franz thought about it, for a storm had made its presence felt just a few days before. In spite of the cold wind whistling along the beach, the girls thought that all their Christmases had come at once. First it was Edith who picked up a crystal-clear piece of golden amber. Then Ruth spotted a couple more pieces. The storm must have washed them ashore and the scavengers who always emerge after a storm had obviously missed these few pieces. It was their lucky day. The next half hour spent looking for more proved to be a waste of time.

Franz and Helena strolled slowly along the beach, past the beach baskets which were facing away from the water on a day such as this. Most held would-be bathers who were escaping the wind. Then came the small dressing sheds. Nidden was a popular holiday resort and in the summer months was generally crowded with visitors. Many would come and spend longer periods of time there. For Franz and Helena this was just a short break from the jobs waiting back at home. But even in their contentment Franz could feel that Helena was missing her three sons. His peace and contentment in married life came at great expense for her and her first family. Willy, her first husband, had not survived the Great War and lost his life near Memel — fighting to defend his homeland. Now two of her sons were away in the German army and the other, Kurt, was working on the railways.

His brothers would often tease Kurt about how lucky he was to be working on the railways. Franz was not so sure. Trains and train depots were prime targets for bombing raids. He already had had a few near misses. How the mind wanders when it is given free rein and how a simple postcard can lead a tired, relaxed man down so many paths.

Franz had drifted into a light sleep and his mind was still on the beach in Nidden. A fishing boat had just tied up and the girls had gone down to watch the fishermen unload their catch. What she had seen was not clear, but Edith was coming running back shouting.

'Papa, Papa! It's so horrible. I just can't believe it! Papa! Papa, wake up!'

Franz' head jerked up after having drooped down onto his chest.

'Oh, dear. I must have dozed off. What's the matter child? Why are you so upset?' He quickly realised he was in his favourite chair at home and not on a sand dune. 'What's Aunty Therese been telling you?'

'It's not Aunty Therese. It's Katie. She turned up while we were there, and oh, what she has been saying is so horrible. I just can't believe it.'

His young daughter was becoming more and more worked up, and talking faster and faster, louder and louder. Franz, ever slow and considered in his speech, interrupted her.

'Edith, calm down and a little slower and quieter, please. I may have been having a little nap, but I'm awake now and I'm not deaf. What's this about Katie? I had no idea she was back home. I thought that she was still working with that family somewhere up there near Riga.' And turning to his other daughter he added, 'Ruth, what has happened?'

'Oh, Papa. Edith is right. Everything is so horrible. Katie had to flee for her life. Luckily her boss had to go to Memel on business and he gave her a ride to there. Then she had to walk the rest of the way here.'

'Had to flee. Why? And walked from Memel. That's over one hundred kilometres from here.'

'There were no trains running so what could she do? She couldn't stay there, and she wanted to get home. She knew a school friend living in Prokuls so she stayed with her the first night. She was lucky they were still there. They were packing and were planning to leave as soon as everything was organized. Then she walked to Heydekrug and stayed in the church there with a whole lot of other people who were fleeing. Then today she walked down from Heydekrug.'

'It seems as though it's even worse than I ever thought it would be.' Although he didn't realize it then Franz's comment was an insightful, albeit dire, prediction of what was ahead for his own family.

Edith couldn't hold back with her unsettling news. 'They're murdering all the German people they come to. And I don't mean just the soldiers. Everybody. No one is safe. Those beasts are raping the girls and women and then shooting them. How can they do things like that? Why don't the officers stop them? Why do they hate us so much? Papa, what are we going to do?'

'We will have to leave here too, girls. I've seen this coming for some time. Your mother and I were just talking about this before I had my nap. We started to work out what to pack to take with us and we were going through the photo album. Remember our trip to Nidden? That was a year ago now. The post-card of the boat harbour there got me thinking about it all once again. That was the last time we had Gert with us. Now with your shocking news it's time that we did more than just think about what to do.'

The restful Sunday afternoon had come to an abrupt end as a result of the alarming news brought by the girls. But even so, an afternoon nap must come to an end. Some work on the farm never waits until tomorrow and now it was time to move on to attacking those chores that needed to be attended to, Sunday or not. The six cows had to be milked, pigs fed and horses stabled.

They all shared in the work that had to be done. Edith's job was to ensure that the poultry was well cared for. This feathered flock she regarded as her friends and family. Old Hermie, the drake, would always waddle over to get a pat on the head as well as getting more than his share of the grain which Edith was scattering around. She would always collect more eggs than they needed, but her aunties welcomed what she took around to them each week.

The geese, all four of them, did not make an attempt to become friendly. They remained aloof. Their one concession was that they did not honk alarmingly when she approached as they still did to her father. This didn't endear them to him and so it caused him no distress when the time came round every so often on very special occasions when he had to kill one and prepare it for the oven. In actual fact he only chopped the head off. Helena had to do everything else. She plucked it, keeping the softer down to make into feather beds and pillows. And it was she who prepared it for the oven and finally served it up to friends at that time.

Ruth helped Franz milk the cows, all six of which were being milked at the moment. They were still out in the field closest to the house. But autumn was approaching and it would soon be time for them to spend the evenings in shelter. For now it was a short walk with bucket and stool in hand to reach them. It had always amazed Ruth how these huge black and white beasts would stand contentedly allowing themselves to be milked. They would put up with all the squeezing and pulling with only the occasional switch of the tail and a backward glance at the human calves who were easing their tight udders.

Cows milked, pigs fed and then there was time for Franz to spend with his horses. Work horses all three, but for the foal. This young colt also could look forward to a pleasant life on the farm, well fed, well cared for and kindly used like the older working horses. When there were fields to be ploughed, it was the horses who pulled the plough. When bags of grain were to be taken to the railway station it was the horses who pulled the wagon. It was in Franz's nature to believe that a creature which supplies so much help without complaint should be treated kindly. He was known to have reprimanded his neighbour further down the road, who was less considerate of his animals.

The evening approached and Franz and Helena with their two daughters, Ruth and Edith were ready to rest from the fortunes and the labours of the day. They gathered in the comfort of their home to ponder the wide range of emotions that had been experienced on that Sunday. On that peaceful summer evening however there was a feeling in the air that the chill of autumn was approaching.

Chapter 4

Sunday Dinner on the Farm

'Come, Lord Jesus, be our guest, and let these gifts to us be blessed. Amen.'

At around twelve o'clock on this Sunday, as indeed at each mealtime on every day of the week, this simple prayer of thanksgiving could be heard rising from the district's farmsteads, finding its way to ever attentive divine ears. Frank Natalier's home was no exception. As a child, he had learnt to sit at the table and wait patiently until his father offered a prayer of thanks for the meal about to be eaten. It was the same prayer Frank now offered, except then it would have been said in his father's native German language: *Komm Herr Jesus, sei unser Gast und segne, was du uns bescheret hast. Amen.* Now he also insisted that his family (and guests who were joining them) wait until he had said grace.

Henry Natalier and his family had come to share Sunday dinner with his brother. Both families were standing around talking, waiting for lunch to begin. When Annie and son, Roy, in the kitchen saw that everything was ready they said that everyone could take a seat. There was a little shuffling and shifting about until all those present were seated.

'Who else is there to come?' asked Henry when he noticed one set place still unoccupied.

'That's Mervyn's. He's still trying to wash the grease off himself after spending all morning tinkering with his bike,' replied Annie.

'What! Is he AWOL again?'

'No,' replied Frank, 'it's legitimate this time. They've given him a job in Brisbane teaching officers how to ride. He likes that; telling officers what to do.'

The whole district knew of Mervyn's on-going fight with the army. He was Frank and Annie's oldest son, a tall, strapping, healthy young man and the only one of the family to be called up to do compulsory military service. But he was shy and as he put it "reluctant to shoot at people he did not know in a war he did not start." For twelve months, he had played hide and seek with army police. When first drafted he was being sent to Townsville, 1,800 kilometres from home, for basic training but he jumped train before arriving there and three weeks later turned up back at his home. Then began a cat and mouse game during which Mervyn would clear off up the mountains when word reached him that the military police were on their way.

This could not go on indefinitely and finally when it was realised that Mervyn was an expert bike rider and mechanic he was given a job training army riders. With this all were contented and so he spent his army days well away from enemy danger. 'But not from danger,' he was always quick to add when talking about his role in the war. 'It's pretty dangerous teaching those drongo officers to ride a bike. They're likely to run you down if you don't watch.'

In a short while he arrived and lunch could begin. As he sat down, Merle, the only daughter in both these families, when she saw the hands beside her fiddling with the cutlery, felt it her duty to kick her little brother, Glen, under the table and say, 'Wait until Uncle Frank says grace.'

'What did you kick me for, Sis? I was only straightening my pudding spoon.'

'Well you should have your hands folded waiting for grace rather than playing with your spoons.'

'I didn't see your hands folded!'

Then once table grace was completed, often with everyone joining in, all were free to enjoy the Sunday roast dinner set before them.

Already on coming through the back kitchen door, everyone became aware that there would be roast duck for dinner. Those brown, crackling aromas seeping from the door of the Crown wood stove were easily recognisable. Even before then, most would have anticipated roast duck for dinner. The majority of farmsteads in the district had a poultry flock in which the hens provided the eggs and the ducks the Sunday roast dinner. The crisp-skinned flesh and a slice of richly spiced stuffing would be liberally surrounded by a variety of vegetables all grown in the home garden or as part of the farm's production — potatoes, pumpkin, beans and carrots. And to top it all off there would be a covering of rich gravy.

The full, rich savour of the meal won by the toil of the farmers and prepared by the hand of grateful family members joined with the simple prayer of these people and rose on high as a fragrant offering of thanksgiving for the blessings bestowed on those who worked the soil.

'Hey, Aunty Annie, did you cook the gizzards?'

'Well, Glen, yes and no,' replied Anna.

'I don't understand you. Did you or didn't you?'

'I didn't cook them separately, but I minced them up with some other bits and pieces and put that in the stuffing.'

'Oh, that's a pity. I like the gizzards,' continued Glen, a little disappointed.

'Glen, don't be such a pill,' came in sister Merle who was always on the lookout for occasions when she might comment on her little brother's behaviour. 'You don't like the gizzards at all. You never eat them at home even when Mum does give them to you. Here, do you want the parson's nose instead? You never want that at home either.'

'Yes I do. But I only like it when it's nice and crispy. Do you know that eating the parson's nose will make you run faster? If you eat enough of them you might even be able to catch me.'

'Don't be ridiculous. Where did you get a silly idea like that from?'

'Well try and see. You might even win the race by a nose.'

The dinner around the large table was a happy, friendly affair. Frank and Annie's large dining table had been extended by the addition of a table normally kept on the veranda. With this extension, all the fourteen members of the two families could sit together, albeit a little crowded.

The two brothers, Frank and Henry, had always retained a close relationship. Frank, the oldest of the family had been born eighteen months after their father, Friedrich and future wife Maria, had migrated from Germany. Henry was the youngest, nine years younger than Frank, and the three sisters were placed at even intervals between them. The sisters had married and were living with their families some distance away and so the two brothers regularly spent time together. Unfortunately, their youngest sister, Emma, had died at a young age leaving her husband with four children. The fact that they were both farmers with similar types of farms, living only six kilometres apart made family gatherings easily arranged.

With their six strapping boys, Henry and Aggie's daughter and their three boys Hostess Annie was worried that the two large ducks might not satisfy all the hungry mouths. But heaven forbid that a country meal should stop there.

'Hey, what's for pudding, Roy?' Naturally six-year-old Glen was looking forward to something sweet. He directed his question to Roy for he knew that Roy spent a lot of time in the kitchen helping his mother provide for the other six men in the family.

'Well, young fellow, why don't you just wait and see.'

'Oh, come on. I bet it's bread pudding and boiled rice. Mum says that you are the expert at making bread pudding. Hey Sis, did you see what we are having?'

'No, I did not,' answered Merle, 'and if you don't finish your cabbage and pumpkin you mightn't be getting any anyway.'

Conversation kept bouncing around the table as the meal was enjoyed. Both sets of parents occupied one end of the table and so they were happy to talk among themselves. For the boys, it was a free-for-all. How are the cabbages coming on? How are you getting on with that girl next door, Alan? Who was the red head I saw you talking to in Gatton at last week's cattle sales? How's the new bike going? Did you go to the pictures last night? Who won the tennis between you and College View? The topics were of work, of entertainment, friendships and leisure. These were questions that portrayed the daily life of young farming lads in the district. Questions whose answers rarely took one out of the district in which they lived and worked.

Finally, the time had come. Perhaps not quickly enough for those keen on a good plate of pudding; but it had come.

Merle and Glen got up from their places and went into the kitchen ostensibly to help hand the plates around, but really to quickly satisfy their curiosity as to what would be served up. They joined Roy and brother Reg who, while listening to the radio from which Bing Crosby was crooning *I'll Be Seeing You*, were doing the serving out.

'Angel's food! Did you make that Roy?'

'No, Merle,' he replied, 'that's Mum's specialty.'

'And green jelly,' shouted Glen as he watched Reg get a large dish of shivering green out of the fridge.

'And,' continued Reg, 'that's not all. There's custard, and I'll open a couple of bottles of preserved pears that Mum did last year. That will be two fewer bottles we have to eat our way through. The tree was loaded last year and Mum did a number of batches. We've been eating preserved pears ever since.'

'I'm sure I still have room for a few, and they will help get rid of that taste of cabbage,' put in Glen, as he used his finger to wipe up a blotch of spilt custard from the kitchen table and put it into his mouth.

'Here, take these plates out to Mum and Father and make yourself useful,' said Merle, now that Roy and Reg had finished filling the fourteen bowls.

This was the nature of a Sunday lunch here. A happy occasion. It would not be complete without a liberal portion of dessert, often with the boys going back for second helpings. In this household storing the leftovers was never a problem.

Hungers satisfied, a short prayer of thanks was recited by Frank and the large gathering soon dispersed.

Frank and Annie's house was a typical Queenslander — a weatherboard house with wide verandas on two or three sides, set on high stumps. One veranda would typically face north to catch the winter sun, and it was this spot with its couch and squatter's chairs where Frank and Henry ended up after lunch. They made themselves comfortable in the chairs, pulled out their tobacco tins which held a plug of pipe tobacco and a pocket knife and cut off a filling for their pipes.

After a little sucking and puffing the two men were soon enveloped in a haze of differing aromas. Henry was the first to comment. 'That plug of yours has rather a nice smell. Do you know what brand it is? Don't know that I've smelt it before.'

Frank thought for a while as he took a few more puffs. 'Yes, I like it. Only been using it for a few weeks. I think it's called *Old*

English. The barber sells it. He put me on to it when I was having a haircut. That would have been at the last pig sales.'

'Yes, it's good out here in the open but it might be a bit strong-smelling for me if I were to smoke it all the time. I like my *Edgeworth Mild*, so I'll stick to that.' A comfortable silence reigned for a few minutes as the two brothers rested in the winter sun after their filling Sunday meal. Small puffs of smoke continued to rise from the two contented countenances.

Then Frank restarted the conversation. 'Did you see the headlines of *The Courier-Mail* yesterday?'

'No, we don't get *The Courier-Mail*. Why, what do they say?'

'There's been another attempt on Hitler's life. Wait a minute, I'll get it.' Then in a very loud voice he called out, 'Annie! Annie!' After hearing a faint, 'What do you want?' coming from the kitchen, he continued, 'Could you bring yesterday's *Courier-Mail* out here please.'

Her response was not quite audible, but soon Roy arrive with the desired newspaper.

'Thanks, Roy,' reacted Frank after his son had handed him the paper and he continued as he held it up and pointed to the bold headlines, 'Here, listen to this: **Bloodbath for Opponents of Hitler.**' Then he handed the paper to his brother who continued reading: '*Unsuccessful attempt to assassinate Hitler has precipitated the greatest bloodbath in Germany since the wholesale killings of old-guard Nazis in 1934. Himmler, new Commander-in-Chief of the German Home Front, is acting quickly and ruthlessly to crush what Goering announced as an attempt at revolt by a group of army generals. Hitler suffered burns, bruises and slight concussion when, according to his own story, a bomb exploded six feet away from him. A member of his staff was killed and others injured.*' Then after browsing a little further through the paper's report Henry said, 'I pity the poor beggars who were involved. It's a shame really.

These fellows who wanted to do what is best for the country will end up being executed, and Hitler and his thugs will stay in control.'

Frank agreed and commented, 'But if we can believe the papers it's just a matter of time before the Allies will see an end to it all. It's the same with the Japs here in the Pacific. They are being pushed back to where they belong. Then the world can start living in peaceful times again. Not that it's been a great worry for us.'

'No, that's true,' agreed Henry, and then he continued. 'Talking about the war in Europe, you know Frank, I have often wondered over the past few years whether we still have relatives there and if they are in the war fighting for the Germans.'

'I don't really know,' replied Frank. 'I do know, well you know too, that Dad had a number of brothers and sisters still living in Germany when he left to come out here. I remember him saying that his older brother had a big family. And I remember him getting the occasional letter from Germany. I used to collect the stamps off the letters. They must still be around somewhere.'

'No, I don't recall him getting any letters; but he may have and I've forgotten.'

'It was the 1914-18 war that stopped everything,' Frank remarked. 'Then he died a few years later and that was that. Since then there has been no contact.'

'After he died I made no effort to contact his family back in Germany. It didn't cross my mind,' Henry seemed quite apologetic.

'No. Well I didn't either,' consoled Frank. 'I suppose that part of Dad's life was so far away and we never really were part of it. But getting back to your question. We probably do have cousins and relatives over there and know nothing about them.'

'Those from Dad's time would be too old to be fighting in a

war but who knows what children they might have had. But I can imagine that if they did have children they would be involved somehow.'

'No. We'll probably never know. But let's hope it's soon all over.' Frank, concentrating on packing down the tobacco more firmly in his pipe, seemed to bring an end to that topic.

'You know, if it wasn't for all the Yanks you see on the roads, and those camping on my.... What the devil?' Henry's train of thought was interrupted by a loud motorbike that went roaring up the hill in front of the veranda. 'Who are those two maniacs on that bike?'

Whereas the two older men were content to sit and quietly have a pipe on the veranda in the sun, the sons had more active pursuits in mind when dinner was finished. Roy chose to help the women clean up after the meal but all the others headed outside. Alan was seen heading off across the creek towards the neighbour's house. Frank's two youngest boys, Johnny and Graham, were keen to show off their new air-rifles which they had recently purchased. So, these two, together with their cousins Ron and Glen, went to the storeroom under the house where they kept the two air-rifles.

'Shall we go up to the big pepperina tree and see if we can get a few sparrows?' suggested Ron, who prided himself on being a good shot.

'I don't think we'd better do that,' said Graham. 'If Dad hears about it we'd all get a good kick up the backside.'

'What. Even for shooting a few sparrows? They are only pests.'

'Yes,' came in Johnny, 'the Boss has made it very clear that we are not to shoot birds of any kind.'

'So, what can we do?' went on Ron. 'We just can't stand here looking at these things.'

'Well,' suggested Graham, 'first we'll get some jam tins and have some target practice. Then we can go over to the barn and see if we can get a few rats. He doesn't mind us shooting the rats.'

While these four were organising their afternoon's shooting entertainment, the older ones, lead by Mervyn, made straight for the work-shed where Mervyn kept his latest prize possession. He had always had a great interest in motor-cycles and he had just bought his latest, a second-hand BSA.

'Feast your eyes on that!' he said to his younger cousin, Terence, as he opened the door. Terence had also recently bought a motor-bike and appreciated what he saw. Whereas he was duly impressed he would not consider it appropriate to show his feelings.

'A BSA. You know what that stands for, don't you?'

'Of course. It's named after the Birmingham Small Arms Company that manufactures them. Everyone knows that. What are you getting at?'

'Well, I've heard it stands for Bloody Sore Arse,' laughed Terence.

'Get away with you. You know that your Triumph comes nowhere near this little beauty.'

The admiring and discussing continued until Terence made a suggestion that Mervyn knew would be coming. 'Let's go for a spin and see what it is worth.'

A few minutes later with Mervyn opening the throttle and Terence riding pillion they were roaring up the road in front of the house causing distress to their two fathers on the veranda.

Later in the afternoon, the family members came drifting back to the house. It went without saying that midday dinner at someone's place also included afternoon tea at 3 o'clock. The fruits of a Saturday morning in the kitchen baking would now appear on the dining room table. The mass-produced products of Arnott's and Webster's would be shunned in favour of freshly baked cakes, slices and biscuits. Indeed, it was a point of honour for both Annie and Roy that there would be a suitable selection of offerings for the visitors. Oh, the shame if a visitor should arrive to find the biscuit tins empty.

Now, armed with a huge pot of tea, and decked with sponge rolls, chocolate cake, ginger slices, jam drops and not forgetting a large slab of streusel kuchen — Annie's special — the table was ready to fill the imaginary gaps in the boys' stomachs. So, when Annie said to Roy, 'I think it's time to call everyone in for afternoon tea,' he did not have to call too loud or for too long.

The afternoon tea represented the conclusion to the social outing. Once completed, the visitors said their goodbyes and headed home, happy, contented and very satisfied with life.

Chapter 5

Ich hatte 2-3 Pferde, welche jährlich Fohlen hatten.

(I had two or three horses which would have foals every year.)

Next morning Helena was standing in the sun at the front door and saw her husband approaching from the shed and called out to him, 'Where are you going with that horse collar? You look just like one of your draughthorses with it draped over your shoulder like that.'

After the alarming news brought home by the girls yesterday Franz was even more convinced of the urgency of fleeing with his family. It would mean abandoning his home where he had lived all his life, heading west and staying in front of the advancing Russian army if at all possible. Then when the war was over they could come back and pick up the pieces.

Preparations. That was important now. They would have to go in the wagon pulled by two of his horses. The horse collar, so vital a part of the harness which allows the wagon to be pulled comfortably by the horses needs to be in good working order. He had noticed that the stitching in one of the collars was coming adrift and was in need of attention. Ordinarily this was a job which would have waited till winter when it was usual to do those less urgent jobs and the freezing weather did not allow out-door work. It had been waiting for winter.

Now with the prospect of having to use the collar on the horses day in, day out, so that they could keep moving, its repair became imperative. An ill-functioning collar rubbing the horse's shoulder would soon lead to sores and Franz loved his horses too much to allow that to happen. It must be attended to now.

He stopped now to reply to his wife. 'I'm taking the collar over to Fred Ringies at the estate to see if he has time to fix it up.'

'I thought you fixed that yourself some time ago.'

'No, I had just added it to my winter list.'

'You better have a look at the mare's halter, as well. I noticed that the stitching was coming apart on it too. You do plan to take the mare with us when we go, don't you? And probably the foal as well, if I know you.'

'Good that you reminded me. I had forgotten all about that halter. Hope Fred will have the time to help me out.'

'And find out what the people at the Manor are planning to do,' Helena called out as Franz was making his way towards the track leading over to the big house on the estate.

Schillgallen Estate was one of those larger properties which was dotted throughout the Memelland area. These estates were established by an order of German Knights many centuries before and many still existed, lying side by side with the small holdings run by individual farmers. Franz Natalier's small farm of sixteen hectares bordered the five hundred-hectare estate to the east. Over the years he had become very friendly with Franz Habedanck, the present owner.

The friendship was built probably on the fact that they both had similar political ideas and a love of horses. From the beginning, they were concerned about the direction in which the political leaders in Berlin were taking their country. They felt comfortable sharing their thoughts with one another. Both Franzes prided themselves on the fact that they could tell a really good horse when they saw one. This knowledge was the basis of many long conversations about this horse or that. The stables at the estate usually housed fifty and more quality specimens, many of them working stock but also a number of pure-bred breeding stock for the equestrian fraternity. So Franz was greeted most excitedly by his neighbour.

'Franz, you're just in time. Come and see my new stallion. It just arrived up from Trakehner. And why on earth are you dragging that collar around with you?'

'I want to see if Fred can repair some of the stitching for me,' replied Franz who was pleased to put the collar and halter down and stretch his aching shoulder. 'I've got so much I have to do at the moment and it would take me forever to get it done. Fred could do it in no time with his eyes shut.'

'That shouldn't be a problem. He's probably over in the harness room now. We'll drop your burden off there and then go on down to the other stables to see my new horse.'

They found Fred repairing some minor damage to a saddle. He was an old school mate of Franz and like many of the others in the small village of Schillgallen found full-time employment on the estate. They greeted each other like long-lost friends although they had only been speaking in the last week. Franz would have liked to stay and talk further with his old mate, which is what he had in mind when he decided to bring the collar over, but the estate boss didn't have this in mind. After explaining to Fred what he wanted they strode off to see the new Trakehner addition.

They found him in one of the new, spacious stalls that had recently been added to the complex. He was surrounded by four admiring stable boys. Franz found himself looking at sixteen hands of shining black beauty. He blurted out his uncontrolled appreciation, 'What a magnificent beast!'

'Yes,' agreed the new owner, 'this is one of the best I've had for a while. I was lucky to get hold of him. A lot of regulars are not buying stock at all these days. And look how quiet he is after moving into a new, strange stall.'

Franz took the halter off one of the lads and stroked the stallion's forehead while looking into its eyes and remarked, 'That broad forehead and fine muzzle. That's how a true Trakehner should look.'

'And not only good looks,' came back Herr Habedanck, as he patted the horse on the rump. 'Look at the strength here! And his papers can trace his bloodline back to Templehüter, a legendary sire of years past.'

'Yes. I've heard of him, but never imagined that I would see one of his progeny first hand.'

And so the two horse lovers stood admiring every feature of this new addition. There was Franz Habedanck with a stable of over fifty and money to buy top quality stock and Franz Natalier his farming neighbour who owned three horses and a foal, a couple of men whose friendship was cemented in a love of horses.

Walking back to the manor house the conversation turned to more serious matters. Franz Natalier brought up the topic which was occupying his mind so much of the time recently. 'What do you make of Gauleiter Keller and what he's been saying?'

'We all know he's a fool, but a dangerous one. What's he been saying now that's getting you so upset?'

'He claims that the Russian advances have been stopped and we have nothing to be worried about. But I just don't believe that. My sister Therese's girl Katie, has come back from her work up near Riga. Just yesterday. What she is saying is enough to make us fear for our future. She had to flee for her life and is lucky to be back here at all. She even had to walk all the way from Memel.' Franz was becoming quite worked up; something that would seldom happen.

'Slow down, old friend. What has she been saying that is

so upsetting?' It appeared that the alarming news had not yet reached the Schillgallen manor.

Franz continued, trying to be a little more in command of his emotions. 'She says that the Russian army is systematically clearing the land of all German people. Those who did not flee are taken. The women and girls are raped and then shot. The children are simply shot or bayoneted to death. The men who are not shot in front of their families are rounded up and taken... to goodness knows where. Thousands of German citizens are headed this way trying to keep in front of the Russians.'

'But haven't we been able to stop the Russian advance? Surely there is some truth in what Keller has been telling us? We still have thousands of men over there don't we?'

'I don't know what forces we have where. How are we ever to know that? All I really know is what Katie has told us from what she heard and saw up there. I'm starting to pack and get ready to go whether Keller says so or not. That's why I brought that collar around for Fred to patch up. It wouldn't do my horses much good pulling a wagon with a broken collar. It's very serious, Franz. What are you going to do about it?'

'Yes, I've always known that it would come to this. But that it should be as urgent as you say. Yes, that's a worry. I just can't go and leave everything. What would happen to it all? The horses, the cattle, the crops?'

'Who knows. The locals would probably pick through the scraps after the Russians have left. But believe me. No one would worry about burying you. As I see it, you have two choices. Either go and perhaps save your life, or stay and be shot. Either way the estate will be destroyed. And tell your German workers they have to go. They won't stand a chance if they stay.'

'Franz, my friend, I really hope everything is not as bad as you say it is,' said the owner of the estate. 'But then I would be foolish not to take seriously what you have been saying. I can remember other times when you have been proven right. I thank you for your friendship and your honest opinion whenever I asked for it. And sometimes, I might add, even when I didn't ask you for it. God be with you as you go. We can only hope that after the war we will be able to come back and continue our lives here. You go. Take Helena and the girls to safety. But be careful. Oh, and I will tell Fred to get to work on your collar and take it over to you when he has finished the job.'

And with a half-hearted wave, Franz turned to go home.

Helena saw him in the distance, head down, slowly walking along the road towards her house. She knew it was Franz but could not imagine why he looked so depressed. He soon joined her in the garden beside the house.

'What on earth has Fred been telling you to make you look like this?'

'Like what?'

'Like a week of wet Sundays. You seem to have all the cares of the country on your shoulders.'

'I took the collar and halter to Fred but didn't really get the chance to have a good yarn with him.'

'Don't tell me Fred was too busy to stop and talk to you. I've never seen the time yet when he would rather work than talk.'

'No, it's just that Franz met me and wanted me to see his new horse which had just arrived this morning.'

'What! He's still buying horses? Doesn't he have enough already?'

'I think he's foolish and I as good as told him that, but you know him. If it's about horses, he makes up his own mind. But I must admit it's a real beauty, a shiny, black Trakehner stallion. It's the sort of horse I dream about; but no good for working on the farm. He would be like a trophy to be kept on the mantle-shelf and hired out for his services.'

'Well, if you have just seen the best horse in the world why are you looking so down?'

'I have the feeling that old Franz doesn't plan to move out before the Russians arrive. I told him clearly what I thought — that if he fled he had a chance to save his life and maybe come back and get things going again; but if he stayed it would be the end of him. I pointed out how his stable of horses would be lost whatever happens. The Russians are not going to leave a stable of fit, healthy horses behind. They will be pulling wagons and guns and when they're too weak to do that they will end up in the goulash pot. But he didn't seem to see it that way.'

'Franz, he will have to make up his own mind. As long as he lets his workers go when they wish, and I'm sure that he would do that. It's not helping anyone by your worrying so much about the estate. We, as you have been telling me, have our own arrangements to see to. What about the harness?'

'Franz promised to get Fred straight on to it and bring both pieces over when he is finished.'

'That's good. Another thing we will not have to worry about. And do you know what? There are probably others, who knows how many, who haven't really seen the seriousness of the situation that lies ahead. It will do us no good worrying about everyone else.'

Chapter 6

Es kam immer zu Streitigkeiten zwischen Deutschen und Littauer.

(There were always squabbles between Germans and Lithuanians.)

It was the end of July 1944, and even a mediocre clairvoyant would have seen that a major catastrophe was bearing down on the Memelland. Had history prepared the people here sufficiently for what was about to unfold? That they had often been tested was recorded for all to read. Tribulation and challenges had appeared in many guises over the centuries. In overcoming these, many inhabitants had perished but importantly many more had also survived.

In the early eighteenth century plague had swept through the land leaving some areas so devoid of human life that migrants had to be encouraged from far afield to help bring the land back into production. The cholera epidemic of the mid-nineteenth century was so severe that 1831 became known as the Year of the Cholera. Extreme floods and devastating fires have also found their way into the pages of this region's history books.

Plague and natural disasters can be devastating but generally accepted and suffered as an act of God which could not have been avoided. Most of those who survived would shrug their shoulders, accept their loss and be thankful that they were spared. The over-religious might ask, 'Why me, God? Why my family?' but life went on. The greatest tragedies of the Memelland are those which might have been avoided. These are those calamities that have resulted from human actions.

WAR. War written in capital letters. It was war that brought untold suffering to the people. These were the conflicts not of their own making. Conflicts initiated by the powerful from afar, but which ensnared the local inhabitants and brought to them death and destruction. State rulers and their generals have always regarded the Memelland as a good area through which to march. Franz Natalier was always remembered for saying, 'God was very unkind when he gave the Memelland its place in the world.' He would have to go on and explain, 'He didn't choose an out-of-the-way, quiet spot. No, he placed us right where the opposing armies would march forward and backward.'

War had visited the Memelland frequently in the past and now it had come once more to this God-designated spot. Hearing the echo of marching feet and the rattle and rumble of heavy armament had become an almost daily experience for the quiet farming people of Rucken.

Back in March 1939, Franz had welcomed the German regiments as they marched across the Luise bridge in Tilsit to claim his homeland for Germany once again. He and his family had even travelled down to Tilsit to watch and cheer. Well, he would tell his friends, it was really Helena and the children who wanted to go. He himself would have chosen not to be there.

Edith, especially, had been so excited. 'We want to see Fritz marching.'

Helena was even more determined. Fritz was her eldest child from a previous marriage. He was part of the family living and working on the farm while he was growing up. Then he had decided to join the army. 'A mother needs to see her son and be proud of him,' she explained to her husband. So, they had joined the thousands of others who lined the roadway to welcome a new era.

It was a rousing spectacle as the band led the way across the bridge over the Memel River which connected the Memelland with Tilsit and the East Prussian territories. With regimental flags aloft and fluttering, brass instruments shining in the spring sunshine, with purposeful marching steps they came singing *'Weit ist der Weg zurück ins Heimatland, so weit, so weit ....'* (The way back home is distant, so far, so far...) an old favourite song that the troops loved to sing as they marched along.

It took Franz back. He remembered the tune well from over twenty years ago when he had to join up for the Great War. It was an English war-time song which had a good marching beat. Someone had fitted German words to the tune and it had become very popular. It didn't matter whether you were packing up you troubles in your old kit-bag or thinking of your distant homeland the tune marched to the same beat.

The German spectators had cheered wildly. They were once again part of Germany. There were others along the way whose Lithuanian messages were anything but welcoming. Vastly outnumbered, it is true, but they were there shouting their disapproval at what was happening. Fortunately, they were being ignored.

Five years later and those voices of disapproval had become louder and more frequent. Many had also been translated into personal action and minor skirmishes. There was still the Lithuanian disapproval at what had happened but more and more this had escalated into personal attacks. Longstanding friendships were being broken by spiteful remarks.

Life for the village people of Rucken was becoming less and less pleasant. There were these local petty disputes and scuffles between the Germans and the Lithuanians but Franz and many of his German friends were convinced that much more dangerous clouds were gathering on the horizon.

It had become more and more evident that the German inhabitants would have to move out of the area, not specifically because of local pressure but to avoid the oncoming Russian army. For most, the time of talking about future possibilities was over. Preparations to leave were under way. Helena Natalier, convinced by her husband that they needed to act, had been systematically preparing for the inevitable, piling in one area those items she saw as most necessary to be taken when they had to flee and laying aside in another those which should be taken if space permitted. The piles were growing; food, clothing, bedding, kitchen utensils and personal items. This was her responsibility. Franz would attend to the wagon and horses and all that would be necessary to keep them going.

'Hmm,' she thought, going through the food items once again, 'we really need to take more flour and salt.' Then going to the foot of the stairs which led up to the girls' room she called out, 'Ruth! Edith! Are you there?'

'Yes, Mama,' came back Edith's faint reply from inside the bedroom. 'What do you want?'

'Could you and Ruth come down for a minute?'

'Sure. We've just finished going through our books. We'll pile them up and be right down.'

A short while later both girls walked into the large kitchen where their mother was still looking over her food piles. 'What else have you two been up to up there?'

'The books were easy and we were deciding which clothes to take with us but couldn't make up our minds.'

'Can you leave that for a while? I want you to go into the shop and see if they have any flour and salt. We don't have very much and really need to take more. The trouble is everybody's been stocking up with these things and they may have run out at the shop.'

'No problem. How much do you want? 'asked Ruth, who was always careful that she had everything just right.

'A bag of salt. That's one kilo. And a ten-kilo bag of flour.'

'Ten Kilos!' interjected Edith, 'How on earth can we carry ten kilos all that way?'

'I'm sure you can manage that between you,' said her mother. 'If you feel that it would be too much, why don't you take the hand trolley? Oh! and see your father before you go. He might want something from the village as well.'

The two girls walked out discussing whether to take the trolley or not. Although they were farm girls who enjoyed working in the fields, they were also young ladies who would feel uncomfortable if some of their village friends were to see them pulling a trolley.

'I don't want to take the trolley,' said Edith. 'What if Anton and Yuri were to see me? I'd never live it down. Why can't Papa go in with the wagon if Mama needs so much?'

'He's working on the wagon. Greasing the wheels and whatever else. And you don't need a whole wagon and horses to bring back ten kilos of flour. He doesn't have the time either. Come on Edith, it's more important to get the flour than worry about what your boy-friends might think.' Ruth never did like those two boys whom Edith regarded as her friends. Always looked at her in a funny way, they did.

In the meantime, they had made their way to the shed where their father was still working on the wagon. No, he couldn't think of anything he needed at the moment, so they grabbed the trolley and made off along the road, taking it in turns to pull the two-wheeled trolley.

They were half way to the village when they noticed two boys riding towards them.

'It looks like your two friends,' suggested Ruth. Edith waved to them.

Even though it was evident that the boys had seen them, Edith waved again. The boys kept coming towards them. The road was wide enough to take cars and trucks but they kept riding directly at the girls.

'They're always up to silly tricks,' remarked Edith as they keep coming towards them.

'Hey! What....' But before Ruth could say any more both girls had to jump quickly to the side to avoid being run into. They landed in the boggy water-table to the side of the road. The boys had swung away at the last moment to avoid running into the trolley and perhaps hurting themselves. Their intent on frightening the girls was obvious. They came back as Ruth and Edith were standing up and brushing mud off their dresses.

'Have an accident girls?'

Edith was quick to tell them what she thought. 'You silly galoots. What on earth were you trying to do? Kill us? Anton, I thought you had more sense!'

'Where are you two farm girls going with that little German trolley?' sneered Yuri.

'What's got into you two?' asked Ruth, who was very taken aback with what was happening and she continued, 'What has brought all this on?'

It was becoming clear that this was not just a boyish prank. Inwardly she had a fair idea of what was happening for she knew that the relationship between the Lithuanian-speaking folk in the village and those who spoke German was becoming more and more hostile. There was an increasingly aggressive attitude being shown towards the Germans. The Lithuanians were giving the impression that they felt that it couldn't be soon enough for the Russians to come and drive the Germans out.

Edith had overcome her initial shock and was wanting to overlook the incident. She felt that her previous open friendship with the two boys must surely mean something to them as well.

'Surely you don't mean any of this,' she said. 'We've been friends since our school days. And Anton, you always said how you loved dancing with me.'

'Did I? We really wanted jobs with old Artur Schröder. Say anything against you lot and we would have been told where to go,' replied Anton without showing any embarrassment. Edith continued to look blankly at him, speechless at what he was now saying. And he continued, 'And at school I could never get over how you two ladies would always refuse to learn our language. A whole lot of others thought that too. "We speak in German, so why should we learn Lithuanian?" you would say. Well most of us Lith kids learnt German. Now we have no trouble telling you where to go.' And at that they both laughed.

After they had worn out their laughter, Yuri continued with the verbal bombardment, 'From what I hear the Russians will be here soon and you lot are busy packing up ready to clear out. A good thing too. My dad says he can't wait to see the back of old Schröder. We will probably move into his house when he goes. It's much nicer than the dump we are living in now.'

Ruth put her arm around her younger sister in an attempt to console her. She had always felt that older-sisterly love towards her. Being less excitable benefitted her as well in this regard. Ruth had spent many a night comforting her younger sister after they had received word that their brother Gert had been killed in action near Warsaw. Now this horrible episode was unleashing further disappointment and sadness, and Ruth was standing ready to help her younger sister. Goodness knew what else lay ahead.

'Come, Edith. We must keep going. There's no point arguing with the likes of them. They will only upset you further. They've made up their mind about what is going to happen and nothing we say is likely to change it.'

They collected the trolley and continued their journey to the village store. Here they were able to buy the salt but no flour. They weren't to know whether the store-keeper had any or not. He said not.

'All that for just a kilo of salt!' rued Edith as they walked out the door. 'We could have left the damned trolley at home!'

Chapter 7

Wer Fuhrwerk hatte mußte damit fahren, die andern wurden mit der Bahn verfrachtet.

(Whoever had their own vehicle had to travel in it; the others would be transported by train.)

It was now the beginning of August 1944, and the word was spreading rapidly.

Franz, Helena and the girls rose at their usual time and set about the routine tasks as on any normal day in their farming life. The situation was such, however, that their normal days in the present unsettled times were anything but normal. The worry, the tension, the uncertainty of the future bore heavily on them as on all the German inhabitants of the region. The preparation for departure had continued in spite of reassurances from Gauleiter Keller that the German army was holding firm against the Russian attacks, and indeed in some areas pushing them back.

Wishful thinking was the verdict of the locals who could see the signs of defeat moving south along the main road running through Rucken.

Neighbour Walter Kreise was the first to arrive with the news.

'Greetings, my old friend,' Walter began, and then continued, leaving no one in doubt as to the reason for his visit. 'The notices have been put up. Keller has finally seen sense and issued the order for the Germans to leave.'

All German citizens are advised to leave their homes in the threat of the advancing Russian army. There can be no guarantee of safety to any German-speaking citizen who chooses to remain in this area. All are advised to move south to safer regions. Those with their own transport should make ready and move as soon as possible. Trains will be available at Tilsit to convey those who do not have their own means of transport.

'So it has come to this, Walter. For sixty-five years this has been my home and now I must leave. I am not young anymore and my arthritis is not improving with age. You know as well as I that the good Lord is counting down the years I have left in this world wherever it might be. If it were not for the women I would probably stay here. But for them I must go. We will leave. But once we leave, I wonder if we will ever get the chance to see our homeland again.' Franz looked intently at his neighbour, sadness dulling the sparkle which was usually to be seen in his blue-grey eyes.

'That I don't know, Franz. Pray God that we can return when all this stupidity is ended. But we can't sit around now bemoaning the fate that has befallen us. I must go. I will not hold you up from your packing. We also want to leave tomorrow if possible. Come by and see us before you go.' With that he took Franz' hand, 'Keep well. My greetings to Helena and the girls. May the good Lord be with us all.'

With that the old friends parted. Walter walked briskly back towards his house and Franz made his way inside to the kitchen where the women were working.

'Greetings from Walter who was just here,' he began as he walked through the front door. 'The notices are up. We should leave as soon as possible. See if we can get everything onto the wagon today, have a good night's sleep and be off at sunrise in the morning.'

The women looked up from what they were doing. Surprise did not register on their faces but resignation did. And perhaps relief. Finally, there was the relief of being freed from the clutches of uncertainty.

They all knew that this day was coming. They all knew that one day they would have to accept the reality of it being with them. All the while they were secretly wishing that it would never come. But wishing won't halt the inevitable. Nor was now the time to stop their preparations to discuss the stupidity of politicians, the megalomania of Hitler. The Fatherland could provide no help in the present situation. Most people, like Franz, would say that the Fatherland had caused their present predicament. Now it was individual steel and determination which might take them from a certain death in their homeland to an unsure location somewhere in the west.

Organized activity was now needed in the household to make sure of an early departure in the morning. The sadness of having to leave behind loved personal items had been addressed in the previous week. Sentiment must now give way to practicality. Each family member would now set about making ready for departure.

'What about Aunty Therese and Katie? What are they going to do?' asked Edith for Therese was her favourite aunt and the girls had grown up together with Katie.

'There is supposed to be train transport waiting in Tilsit for those who don't have their own. It will probably be only grain wagons and cattle trucks, but that's better than nothing. The way things are, one can only hope that there will be something there. From what I hear there are a lot of army vehicles going that way and they are quite happy to pick up people if they have the room. They, better than most, know what will happen to the people if they are not able to get well away.' Franz wanted to appear positive although it was hard in the circumstances.

Naturally, he also was worried about his sister, Therese, and Katie. It had been a struggle for her after her husband had died. No one could ever pinpoint the cause of the illness which had taken his life so suddenly. Should he take both of them with himself and family in his wagon? No question about it. He would if there were no other options. But it would add even more weight to an already overloaded vehicle. And horses can be expected to pull only so much over long distances. Even as it was he envisaged himself and his family walking beside the wagon for most of the way. He would go over to her place later in the day once he had everything under control and make sure she had made her arrangements. He explained all of this to Edith to reassure her.

'But where are we going, Papa?' Ruth wanted to know.

'I am not quite sure. The first important thing, as I see it, is to get over the river at Tilsit. If the Luise bridge should be bombed there's no other way we could get the horses and wagon across.'

'And then what?' Edith wanted to know.

'Your cousin Otto still lives in Tilsit, doesn't he? Could we go and stay at his place?' Ruth offered this suggestion.

'I don't think that would be possible. He would be getting ready to move just as we are. I can't imagine what will happen to Tilsit once the Russians start bombing and shelling it. It certainly wouldn't be safe there. And if they get so far there would be nothing to stop them from moving right through Prussia till they met the Yanks coming the other way.'

'But where can we go then? We don't really know anyone else in East Prussia.' Edith's concern went to the core of their problem. Not only their problem but that of most of the people in these eastern regions who would be fleeing from the Russians.

They would be at the mercy of the goodwill and generosity of the local people wherever they might arrive.

'I think it will be a matter of going where the army tells us to go. Don't forget there will be a lot of army movements going on as we try to flee. I suppose they would have plans to stop the enemy and that means that there would be areas more dangerous than others. There will be places where we definitely would not be allowed to go. And I wouldn't like to be caught in the middle of a battle.' Franz was trying to be confident that things would work out well for them all; but he was uncertain.

How would thousands and thousands of fleeing citizens and retreating military forces move in an orderly way through the countryside? Germans, they all were, that is true, but mostly unknown to one another, all caught up in a terrible experience. Franz was sure that it would be a matter of looking after himself and his family, even at the expense of others.

'We will just have to be strong, help one another and do the best we can,' he concluded. Then as an afterthought, 'Are you sure you have organized everything you want to take?'

'Papa,' replied Edith very quickly and cheekily, 'there is no way you would allow me to take everything I wanted to.' With that she went skipping back to the house.

Franz was left working out how best everything could be fitted on the wagon. Most difficult was to organise the packing so it would be possible to make room for sleeping without having to shift everything around. He had thought of building a platform with bedding above and other items packed below. That idea was abandoned for it would add too much weight to an already overloaded vehicle.

The entire process was so difficult for him because there were so many unknowns and very few definite factors.

The weather would pose problems but that was one factor

which could be quite accurately anticipated. It would be wet and cold, becoming more and more so as the year moved on. Then snow and ice would be a factor. The stream of refugees could not rely on finding undercover shelter for themselves and their animals. They would spend most nights relying solely on what they had brought with them for warmth and protection. Sleeping on the ground was no option. They would need to be able to sleep in the wagon.

All of a sudden, there they were — Winnetou and Old Shatterhand. Could they help in this situation? From out of nowhere he pictured these two heroes of Karl May's wild west novels. As a child he, like millions of other German boys, had enjoyed reading of the adventures of the proud Indian Chief, Winnetou, and his blood brother, Old Shatterhand. A covered wagon like those described in Karl May's stories; a covered wagon like those that helped in opening up the wild west of America for European settlement. Yes, that's what he really needed — a covered wagon.

He remembered how he and his younger brother, Emil, would sit on their father's old farm wagon and pretend they were travelling across the prairies of Oklahoma, or Dakota, or wherever.

'Look, Emil. What's that over that rise there?'

'What? Where? It looks like dust, Franz.'

'Scheiße! That's an Indian war party. What are we to do? We can't outrun them in our covered wagon.'

'Leave the wagon. Let's hop on our horses and go after them before they get to us. That will surprise them.'

And so the brothers would become the good, brave Indian Chief Winnetou, and his friend Old Shatterhand spurring their steeds onward.

The two neighbour's boys who were coming over to play with

Franz and Emil were at first surprised. They heard the whooping and a-hollering of the oncoming pair and immediately realised what was happening. They had been branded the Indians before they had any chance of disagreeing. So, they mounted their ponies, drew their pistols and raced off shooting over their shoulders as they went. There were many bullets but seldom real causalities.

Then on other occasions the action would be reversed. The Indians would be chasing Winnetou and Old Shatterhand out of pure spite. So go the rules of battle.

And Franz stood gazing at his wagon, which would never live up to the standard of those westward-ho covered wagons in the stories of his youth. They were the result of imaginative fiction. No, his covered wagon would remain the old farm wagon and those bearing down on him would not be as forgiving as the neighbouring boys of his childhood. This was the present reality.

The day had begun as a normal day in these uncertain times. Walter Kreise's visit and the news he brought with him changed all that. It had become alive with hectic activity. Preparations had proceeded. Much had been achieved. Now, however, as evening of the eve of their forced departure approached, many problems remained unsolved. These would have to wait, either to be proved irrelevant or solved by trial and error.

Supper was quiet. Each of the four members of the family ate quietly, alone with personal thoughts. They finished, rose and all held hands while Franz spoke, 'Lord, tomorrow we leave our home to face the unknown. Give each of us the strength to keep moving towards safety. Stay with us and our friends.' Going to his local church had always been a part of Franz and Helena's life, but he was never one for long drawn-out prayers. 'Say what you have to say and let God get on with his business,' was always his motto.

His family was probably surprised by this petition for God's help and guidance, but they recognised the depth of feeling that lay behind his simple words. He then continued, 'We have a big day tomorrow and so I will need my sleep. Good night my dear daughters. Good night my dearest wife.'

Chapter 8

Wir mussten am 2.8.44 flüchten.

(We had to flee on 2nd of August, 1944.)

Wednesday, 2nd August, dawned foggy but fine. The warmth of the late summer sun would soon dissipate the wispy pockets of lingering fog, and Rucken would be revealed lolling sleepily in full sunlight. Temperatures at this time of year never become excessively hot during the day and at night are pleasantly cool. Not all days however are sunny, warm and pleasant — days in which one can revel. There would always be rainy days in August — this was not one of them — for it is one of the wetter months of the year. For those wanting to enjoy the pleasures of warmth and sunshine, August can be dampening, hindering and horrid. For the farmers on the other hand, rain is necessary and good.

Franz always maintained that August was the farmer's best month. Long days of summer labour could be seen coming to fruition. The rain would give the crops that final boost before they ripened for harvest. During the day, the temperature was pleasant for working. It was a month designed to bring smiles to the dourest face.

This Wednesday, however, although inviting the farmer to a day's work out in the fields, had other tasks in mind for Franz and his family. They were packing their wagon to flee their farm. They were not at all concerned about the state of the weather at this moment. That weather conditions would play such an important factor in their lives in the months that lay ahead was something different and lay menacing in the backs of their minds as they packed. They knew that winter would bring misery to travellers. Now however, what might have been a lazy summer day was alive with hectic activity and concern about approaching winter conditions.

Even though they were soon to depart, some farm work could not be left unattended. It was mooing, snorting and cackling for attention. The six cows had to be milked, for they expected no less. They had moved from the far end of their paddock closer to the farmhouse to have their udders eased. The most placid, luckily also one of the strongest, was selected to be taken with the family on the flight. Leaving the other five was heart-breaking but there was no alternative. They would have to fend for themselves. Hopefully some kindly person from the village would see to their needs. Franz tried not to think about their final fate.

The pigs received extra rations. Their sty was left open so that they were free to seek food for themselves. At night, they would be able to return to the security of their pen. What else could be done? On these small farms in the Memelland, farmers would form close bonds with their animals for they were part of their livelihood. Having to leave them unattended for any length of time was heart wrenching.

Edith as usual gave the poultry run her final attention. The geese remained aloof as usual. The rest of the farmyard flock also appeared to be unaware of the change of circumstance which was ahead of them. Eggs were collected to be taken. Three hens were also selected to be taken along with the family. Lucky not to be left behind? Not really. Eventually they would be eaten. Finally, Old Hermie the drake, received a final tickle on the top of his head. 'Now you look after your girlfriends,' said Edith and she left with tears appearing in her eyes.

Wagon packed, horses harnessed, teary-eyed, they set off

down the road. And what a strange procession they made. Franz was walking in front leading the two horses which were pulling the wagon. Helena sat in the wagon. Franz's prize mare which he would not leave was tied on behind the wagon. Her foal trotted beside her. Taking up the rear, the girls were taking it in turns to lead the cow.

But Franz had turned right on leaving their home and not to the left which would have taken them into Rucken where they would meet the main road running from Heydekrug to Tilsit. Helena called out to him, 'Where are we going? Aren't we going out to the main road?'

'I want to drop in and say good-bye to Walter and Lotte. And I always thought it would be better to take the back road down to Pogegen. There would be less traffic that way and we would have a better chance to see how everything is travelling.'

'Yes, that's you all over.'

Regardless of the state of the war, whether the Russian front was advancing or retreating there would always be time to say a last farewell to his neighbour and life-long friend. He had seen Walter only the day before when he called in to tell them that the evacuation notices were posted around the village but it had been a very quick parting. Friends should do better than that.

Activity around the Kreise home clearly showed that they had not yet left and so Franz lead his caravan in off the road. Walter and Lotte's heads popped around from the other side of the wagon. Franz said nothing, waiting for Walter to come up with some appropriate comment. He did not have to wait long.

'It looks like the travelling circus has come to town.'

'Well, it's leaving actually. So, what have you been doing?' Franz replied as he looked around at the piles of sundry goods scattered around Walter's wagon. 'When are you likely to moving out? Sometime soon?'

'No,' came in Lotte, 'it hasn't gone as well as we had hoped. It doesn't look like it but everything is under control now.'

'And we don't have two healthy young beauties to help us like you have,' Walter added. 'We won't be going today, so why don't you stop for a while and we can have a quick drink or two.'

Helena appeared a little impatient. 'There's no doubt about it. Danger could be rumbling down the road towards us but there would always be time for a quick drink for you two!'

Franz looked at his wife but ignored her comment. He then began tying the horses' halter to a post meant for that purpose. 'I was hoping you would have the time. I've got just the thing here.'

The women in the meantime had all moved inside to prepare a cup of coffee. Walter poked his hand into a box and came out with two small glasses. He placed them on the wagon pole and waited while Franz arrived from behind his wagon with a bottle half full of red liquid. He generously filled both glasses.

'Prost!'

'Prost!' as Walter emptied his, but then he coughed and spluttered. '*Gott im Himmel!* What is this red stuff?'

'It's some Polish slivovitz Fritz brought back with him last time he was home on leave.'

'Well, I'll tell you something,' replied Walter. 'You should give it to the Panzer Brigade in case they run out of fuel. Here! Let's have another one. A man can't stand around here on one leg.'

Walter's oesophagus was ready for the next assault by the slivovitz and reacted less violently. 'Hmm, might get to like this after a while, but I suppose that will have to wait. Let's go and see what Lotte still has in the house.'

Around the kitchen table the conversation became more serious. Their main concern was where best to head.

'There have been various ideas from people I've talked to over the last few weeks,' said Franz, 'but no one seems to have any idea which might be the safest and best.'

'It will probably depend on where the army and local officers direct us,' suggested Lotte.

'And on how many people are on the move,' Ruth joined in the conversation.

'It would be impossible for everyone to keep to the main roads. It would be impossible to move. It would be dangerous too. Imagine the targets that would give the Russian fighter pilots,' said Edith.

Ruth took Edith up on this. 'Edith, you don't really think that they would shoot at simple people who are fleeing for their lives.'

'From what Katie told me, that's exactly what they do. We are German and they don't care if we are in the army or not.'

And so everyone had their own idea of what might or might not happen. The future remained unknown and no one could be sure exactly where the road might lead.

Franz explained his sketchy plan. 'First we must get over the river to Tilsit. There will be a problem there for everyone will be wanting to go over the bridge. There will be hold-ups there, I have no doubt. Then I want to call in on a cousin of mine living in Tilsit. I'll see whether Otto has heard where best we might go. He would have a better idea of that area as well. He was always travelling around, visiting places. As you know, Helena's second boy, Kurt, works on the railway in Königsberg. I think our best plan would be to make for there. He should be able to help us and suggest how to move on from there. A lot, I know, is in the lap of the gods.'

'And you are going the back way down to Tilsit?' asked Walter.

'Yes. That will give us a better chance of settling down and seeing how best we should move and set up camp for the night. We will be out of everybody's way. Well, I hope that will be the case.'

'A good idea,' agreed Walter. 'We'll be going that way too. But after we cross the river at Tilsit I don't like the idea of everyone heading for Königsberg. There will be just too many people and everything will become clogged up. The port and industrial areas there are coming under more and more attack. I'd hate to walk all that way just to be killed by a bomb. The two of us will probably be able to move more quickly that the four of you, so I will probably try to stay further inland. But as you say, it will all depend.'

A little more discussion followed until Franz got up from the table. 'Walter, Lotte, we must go. I want to get a few kilometres under my belt before we stop for the night. Farewell. Thank you for everything you have done for us over the years. God speed, and I hope we all come out of this safe and alive and get back to normal lives when it's over.'

The friends departed and Franz and his family continued down the road.

One last look back and Franz said, 'That's it then. We are leaving our home with its memories. I hope it fares well. We must now look after ourselves. It will probably be very difficult for a while but one day we will be able to return and continue our lives here.'

Helena was sobbing.

Chapter 9

. . . .

The Wedding

For many, Pastor Koehler seemed to be going on and on in his address. Some were becoming restless. They seemed to be finding their seats uncomfortable for they were wriggling this way and that. Reg and Pearl, however, were looking intently at the pastor apparently absorbing everything he was saying. Whether their minds were fully on the message he was delivering could not accurately be determined. Perhaps their minds were far away.

'Yes, Reg and Pearl,' the pastor was saying, 'you are about to start on a new journey. You are leaving the homes which have nurtured and sheltered you since childhood and heading towards a new life. Ask your parents, ask any married couple here and they will tell you that the road will not always be easy. You will meet with many obstacles along the way. Your dreams will not always be realised. Often your joy will turn to sadness. Friends of your childhood could drift away and be lost. But knowing your families as I do, I can assure you that they will always be there to lend a helping hand. And not only your immediate family, but,' here he swept his arm over the people in the pews in front of him, 'also our congregation gathered here to witness you take your wedding vows.'

A few heads in the congregation were nodding in agreement. Some of the older heads were also nodding in the sultry spring afternoon but for other reasons. Many were still finding their seats a little uncomfortable.

And Pastor Koehler continued. 'And you are here to make those vows in front of our Lord as well. This I can assure you most definitely: he will go with you in your journey. He will always be with you in times of need....'

And so the church and its congregation heard once again the central message of Pastor Koehler's wedding address. It had been heard many times before, for wedding ceremonies in this church were a frequent occurrence. In this community with many of the families related by blood, and all united by friendships and acquaintanceships, most of the district would be in attendance at most of the weddings. Even if not invited, people would turn up at the church to see what the bridal party looked like. It was always of interest to see what sort of gown the bride had selected and what colour was chosen for her attendants' dresses.

To the relief of some, the final blessing was pronounced, the final hymn sung and the bridal party was ready to leave the church. The congregation rose as one. All eight in the bridal party turned towards the congregation, faced the future and waited. Then the old pedal organ, trumpet stops fully extended, volume controls at a maximum and bellows extended, obedient to organist Maria's firm touch, sounded out Purcell's *Trumpet Voluntary*. Pearl took her husband's arm and they moved off down the aisle. She was beaming. He seemed uncomfortable. They had to stop at every row of pews, she to be hugged, kissed and congratulated and he to be slapped on the back with a 'well done, mate'. Friends, relatives and onlookers were overflowing with joy and excitement.

Once outside the church it rained confetti, bringing colour and future happiness into the lives of the newlyweds.

With the church ceremony now competed and the box Brownies having recorded a host of black and white images to be eventually placed in family albums for posterity, minds turned to the reception. For members of this farming area the availability of money for the reception would never reach that required for fine dining at some wedding reception centre in a nearby town. Here, guests looked forward to a do-it-yourself function held at either the church hall or at the residence of the bride's parents.

Today it was off to Fred and Martha's place where an hour after the completion of the official ceremony the farmstead was abuzz with activity. Actually, the main activity was in the kitchen area. Here the women were busy making sandwiches, cutting cakes and filling plates with biscuits and lollies. Others were decorating the trestle-tables, borrowed from the church hall, which had been arranged in a large marquee set up beside the house.

The men, regarded on these occasions as more of a hindrance than a help, were seated yarning on the verandas or under nearby trees. Some were showing more than a casual interest in what was happening in the laundry. Here, draped in wet corn bags to keep them cool, stood the kegs of beer, a necessary adjunct for any wedding reception. When the designated barmen for the occasion had successfully tapped the first keg and filled a number of jugs, frothing at the top, word soon spread that the beer was ready.

The afternoon moved pleasantly on, the men enjoying their yarning kept lubricated with cool drinks, the kids away somewhere playing and the women adding the final touches to the festive tables. All was in order for the return of the bridal party from the photographer's where the formal photographs were taken. A pleasant quietness reigned.

Suddenly a young boy ran into the kitchen.

'What on earth has happened to you?' gasped a horrified Mrs Manteuffel as she looked at her eight-year-old son with blood streaming down the right-hand side of his face.

'I was shot,' replied young Percy.

'Shot? What do you mean you were shot?' asked the now very worried mother.

'It was just with an air rifle, and we weren't using real slugs.' Percy seemed quite contented and resigned to his mishap.

By this time someone had arrived with a bowl of warm water reeking of Dettol, clean cloths and a roll of sticking plaster. After cleaning the blood from her boy's face, and assessing that the wound was only minor, Mrs Manteuffel had settled down to some extent. 'Now start from the beginning. How did all this come about?'

A group of young boys had now arrived. They were looking on with interest and making a variety of comments, some appropriate and some less so.

'We decided to play wars. So we picked sides. Each team had two shanghais and then Clem said he would get the two air rifles they had in the shed. So each team had one.'

Then another boy took up the story as Percy's wound was being plastered up. 'We didn't use the real lead slugs for they would be dangerous and hurt too much. We used the berries off the pepperina trees. They fitted in the rifle perfectly. And we were only to shoot at the enemy's backsides. The berries sting, but they don't really hurt under your pants or shirt.'

'Oh great,' put in one of the mothers, 'and we can see what happens when someone doesn't shoot straight! What about the shanghais? Did you shoot stones with those?'

'No. We're not so stupid. We used the wild figs. They squash and splatter when they hit you but they don't really hurt.'

'What you kids get up to when we are not watching. Seems as if we can't leave you alone for a minute. What would have happened if Percy had been hit in the eye? And where did this war of yours take place?' asked Mrs Manteuffel.

'Down along the creek bank. There's lots of long grass and bushes there for camouflage.'

'What? Don't you realise there are snakes about at this time of year. And they are full of venom?'

'Yes, we saw one too. Des chased it with a stick but couldn't get a real good whack at it. It disappeared under a lantana bush and we lost it.'

'You boys! Now listen. I'm declaring the war definitely over. And I suggest you go and find a cricket bat and ball and find somewhere to play cricket. Hopefully that will be less dangerous. Off you go now. It won't be long before the bridal party is back and we can start with the meal.'

Across the paddock in the neighbour's front yard, a different group of young lads, and older too, was assembling. Their Sunday-best suits were still hanging in the wardrobes back home. These boys were more casually dressed. Some of the outfits would have been rejected by the most down and out swaggie. Added to their scraggy clothes their faces had all been blackened by charcoal.

'Are we all here yet?' a question from a blackened face.

'I don't know. Who's supposed to be coming?' came an anonymous reply.

'Let's have a head count,' suggested another. 'Put your hand up if you are not here.' Everyone looked around to see who had their hand up.

'Bert, where did you get that dress from? Have you been rooting around in your Granny's cupboard?'

'No, it's my sister's. She threw it out some time ago and we have been using it in the shed to clean our hands. I thought it would be just the thing for tonight.'

'Oh, you're so cute Bertie, dear. But you didn't have to wash your face. It's seems cleaner than it usually is.'

'Ah, pipe down, Noel. You're not so eye-catching yourself.'

'If you fellows could put a plug in it for a while and make sure you have everything, we can make our way over. But no yahooing and don't start banging your tins and stuff before we are all there and ready. You all know your way around the place. We'll gather under the fig tree beside the dairy.'

This was the self-organised group of tin rattlers who would turn up at the reception and rattle good fortune into the life of the newly-weds. It was the usual custom around these parts. Sometimes they would wait until the couple had come back from their honeymoon and were in their own house. Then they would turn up in the middle of the night and create a memorable racket.

'Hey, wait for me you fellows!' An extra kerosene tin and rattling stick came galloping up as the others were moving off.

'Well, hurry up. Where have you been all this time?'

'Someone let my horse out and she was in the big hill paddock and I had a devil of a job trying to catch her.'

'Well tie her up somewhere, but not in Sarah's garden or she'll be eating the gerberas, and crapping everywhere.'

Finally, the group set off across the paddock making a beeline for the reception. Half way there and everything had been going very quietly when there was a shout, a rattling and some coarse language.

'Terry, be quiet. What has happened to you?'

'I tripped over a confounded log here. I think I've broken my leg. Why can't old Augie keep his paddocks clean instead of having logs lying all over the place? Here, come and give us a hand.'

'You can't have broken your leg. Here, stand up and put some weight on it. See, you'll be OK. A few beers and you won't know anything is wrong.'

So with Terry limping and complaining under his breath, they reached the fig tree without attracting any attention from the wedding guests. Their leader went to have a quick reccy and soon returned. 'The beer's on, the bridal party is back and they are getting ready to go in to the reception, so we needn't sit here waiting around. On three. One...two... three!'

Then followed ear-deafening shouting, yodelling and hefty banging of four-gallon kerosene tins. The chooks in the hen-house awakened and joined in the noise with their cackling. The horses in the home paddock neighed in terror and started a mini-stampede. Inside the marquee and kitchen everyone stopped what they were doing and looked up knowingly.

'Sounds as though the tin-rattlers are here.'

'Yes, I'd say so. Better get a few plates of sandwiches and cakes ready for them. They won't stop until we feed them and I don't want to put up with that racket for longer than necessary.'

Ten minutes later the noise had stopped and the uninvited, but expected, guests were devouring their cakes and sandwiches washed down with a few glasses of beer.

'Goor, that was good!' determined one of the blackened musicians. 'Hey, see if Arnie has brought his squeeze-box.'

'Hey Arnie! Arnie!'

A middle-aged man came down from the veranda. 'Yes, what's the problem?'

'Did you bring the old squeeze-box? Let's give them a few songs.'

Soon an impromptu version of *Roll out the Barrel* could be heard floating across the valley. Then followed *She'll be coming round the Mountain when she comes* and *In the Quartermaster's Store* and many other rousing songs, well-known by all. By now, a number of guests had gathered around listening to the unexpected concert. They agreed that the quality of the singing far outweighed the look of the singers. These same loud, clear voices, trained by calling the cows and shouting at the dogs, could also be heard on Sunday mornings singing in the church choir.

Duty done, hunger and thirst satisfied, the tin-rattlers moved off allowing the reception to continue as planned.

It was nearing the end of the celebrations and the time had

arrived for the speeches. The MC for the occasion rose to his feet and banged solidly on a beer jug with his pudding spoon. 'And now to propose the toast to the bride and groom I call upon a long-time friend of both families, Emil Hoger.'

There was a shout of 'Let's hear it, Emil' audible between the spasmodic clapping, as Emil manoeuvred out from behind a crowded trestle-table. Unfortunately, he bumped the table rather solidly, for he himself was rather solidly built, and upset a number of glasses of beer. With a 'Sorry about that', he made his way to the music stand which was doubling for a lectern for the evening. Once there, he ran his thumbs down behind his bracer straps to the top of his trousers, hitched them up and began.

'Mr Chairman, the brand-new Mr and Mrs Natalier (as he smiled towards the bride and groom with shouts of approval coming from a number of seated guests who by this time were in a merry mood), in-laws and outlaws (more laughs), friends and foes (ohs and aahs).

Let me begin by saying that I feel very privileged to be asked to say a few words about Reg and his lovely bride, Pearl ('You would have got up and talked anyway,' came from some way back, and this was greeted with murmurs of agreement).

'As all of you know, I have known these two young people ever since they were born, and as older folk here will remember, I was one of Pearl's sponsors at her baptism. I am so happy that the wedding has gone off so smoothly and that they both seem so happy, although Reg still seems a little bewildered by it all (A smattering of laughs came from the groom's brothers). While talking to Pearl a little while ago I asked her what she will remember about the church ceremony. One thing to be remembered she said, was when she was walking down the aisle on her Dad's arm. There were the flowers on all the pews, all the faces turned to look at her, especially Reg's. She will never forget the aisle. Then standing with Reg in front of our church altar. A simple alter but she saw the beauty in it. And a third thing she mentioned was the final hymn ('Emil, you told this one last year,' came from somewhere among the guests, as also 'Shh! Let him finish!'). Yes, she said that has always been my favourite hymn and the choir sang it so beautifully. It's probably those three things that I will remember into my married life, she said — aisle, altar, hymn (then loud laughter and applause from the gathering).

Encouraged, Emil continued, 'Yes, I'll alter him. I think that's what my Bertha remembered when she married me, for I am not the man I used to be ('You can say that again', came from some wit, and 'You're twice the man' from another).

For the next ten minutes, Emil in front of his captured audience, related incidents from the life of the bride and groom, some amusing, others less so. This was the nature of wedding speech making in the country community, friendly, entertaining, well suited to the occasion.

'And to conclude,' continued Emil ('Hear, hear,' from a guest probably speaking for many others), a simple word of advice to Reg. Laugh and the world laughs with you, argue with your wife and you sleep alone. And now without any further ado, I would ask you to charge your glasses, be upstanding and drink to the health and happy future of Reg and Pearl ('To Reg and Pearl' could be heard throughout the gathering as glasses clinked).

And the speech list progressed. The bridegroom had to reply to Emil's effort and also propose a toast to the lovely bridesmaids. The best man replied to this. Then followed speeches about, and toasts to, the bride's parents, the bridegroom's parents, both sets of grandparents (if they were still alive) and finally to the caterers (most of the mothers present). After each toast, there was a rousing rendition of *For they are jolly good Fellows.*

It came time for the bride, accompanied by her attendants, to go off to change into her going-away outfit. While this was happening, Arnie entertained the gathering with his squeeze box. Most of the tunes he played were accompanied by an undisciplined chorus of merry guests. Then the bride returned to the oohs and aahs of many of the mothers.

Finally, with a backing of cheering and clapping, the two newly-weds moved off to Reg's car which was decorated with a large 'Just married' on the back window. To the sound of many tins bouncing and banging behind the vehicle they drove off into their married life.

Chapter 10

Und überschwingend weit den Strom und weiter ins Land ausgreifend steigt die Brücke da in Bögen auf ins Sonnenhelle, ja aufleuchtend höher, eine Himmelsleiter.

From Die Vaterstadt by Johannes Bobrowski
(And there swinging wide over the river and further into the
countryside is the bridge. Its arches reach into the bright sunshine,
yes, and shining even higher, a Jacob's ladder).

'See, way up there ahead, girls, that's the steeple of the German Church. It's over 60 metres tall and it's the first thing you see when you're travelling to Tilsit. So, it won't be long now and we will be at the bridge.' Franz liked to keep up a steady flow of information as they travelled along, even though it was not always met with enthusiasm from the girls. This time Edith was ready with a reply.

'Great. I'm looking forward to getting there. I suppose it has not been so bad so far but I'd still prefer travelling down by train like last time. Walking can make it seem a long way.'

'What's wrong with you Edith?' said Ruth. 'Walking has never yet hurt anyone.'

'Everyone says that, but it's not really true,' said Edith as she took up the challenge. She and Ruth would often engage in sisterly differences of opinion. 'You remember young Michel walking home from school last year? He put his foot in a hole on the side of the road and broke it. And even worse. Old Oma Lemke was walking home from church a few years ago and fell down dead. Didn't she Papa?'

'Hey? What? What are you talking about?'

'Oma Lemke. She dropped dead walking home from church, didn't she?' replied Edith.

'That's right,' agreed Franz. 'It was on Trinity Sunday in 1942.'

'Papa, how do you know that? I think that sometimes you just make things up and say that you remember.'

'I might pull your leg sometimes, but usually I remember things quite well. I don't read a lot like you and Ruth and so I use my brains to remember things. I'll tell you something else. I remember what the pastor spoke about in his sermon that day.'

'Well, tell us,' said Ruth.

'He spoke about how the Lord is my strength.'

'How can you remember that? Usually I've forgotten what he has talked about before I get home,' was Ruth's honest comment.

'Well,' began Franz, 'I probably really remember what Walter Kreise and I were talking about at her funeral. He said how funny it was that she died on Trinity Sunday, for that was her third stroke. The Lord was her strength for the first two times, Walter reckoned, but he must have run out of strength by the third time.'

Ruth was quick to defend her understanding of God. 'I think it was probably Oma Lemke who ran out of strength, rather than God.'

'You're probably right,' agreed her father. 'Anyway, what got you talking about Oma Lemke?'

'Edith said that she was walking home from church when she died and so walking is dangerous.'

'Frau Lemke did die walking home from church. That is a fact. You can't say that it follows that walking will kill you, or that God is somehow involved or not. So, let's keep that walking going a little longer and see if we can find some place to stop for the night.'

Edith looked at her feet and shrugged her shoulders. 'Well,' she sighed in a very mocked-resigned fashion, 'I suppose I can go a little further. It wasn't too bad until the rain started and then it became a little tiresome. I hope this rain stops before we have to stop for the night or else we will have to look for someone's empty shed like we did last night.'

Her father expressed his doubt whether that would be possible. 'With all these people moving towards Tilsit I doubt if there will be any empty sheds to use. What I'm thinking is that we might be able to find shelter under this end of the Queen Luise bridge. On this side, it starts a long way back from the actual water in the river. There would have to be a hundred metres or more of space there. There would be plenty of green picking for the animals there too. They would enjoy that. But then I suppose everyone is thinking the same as I am. We will just have to wait and see.'

And they moved slowly forward making for their goal for the day. The three great arches on the bridge became more and more imposing the closer they got. The church tower was more clearly defined also. Instead of an indistinct, thin, tapering triangle rising above one end of the building, the intricate nature of its construction became more apparent.

Something else was becoming apparent as well; the crowds of people. The bridge was covered with a slow-moving mass of humanity with their wagons, carts and trolleys, their horses and cattle. Then there were sundry army vehicles attempting to force their way through the congestion.

'Oh, my God,' exclaimed Helena, 'all of Memelland must be trying to get across the bridge.'

'Just as I thought,' replied Franz. 'Not many would have hesitated when they heard the word that they should move. They would have all been half packed, as we were, ready to move. Now here we all are wanting to get across the bridge while it is still here.'

'What are we going to do?' his wife wanted to know.

'I was telling the girls before, that we would try to shelter under the bridge for the night. We could get going early in the morning and get in the line to move across.'

'Is it going to be any better in the morning?'

'Probably not, but we've had a long day and I don't think any of us would like to spend another couple of hours slowly moving with a crowd of people across the bridge. Edith is complaining about her sore feet already, not that that is surprising.'

Instead of staying on the road which would have taken them to the main road which was amass with people, they moved off to the lower ground. Following this, where there was no defined road but simply grassland, they would end up under the north approaches of the bridge. Hopefully they would then be in the shelter with the crowds above them.

After becoming bogged down in the wet soil a number of times which caused considerable strain on the horses pulling the wagon and meant that all members of the family had to help push the vehicle out of the soft ground, they arrived under the bridge. But they were not alone. Hundreds like them had the same idea. They were all Germans fleeing a common enemy. Fleeing for their lives. This however was early in their flight and desperation had not yet affected the mood of the people. Space was made for the new arrivals.

First the animals had to be attended to. Franz loved his horses as his family well knew. His insistence that they be attended to first was not because he put them above his family but stemmed from more practical considerations: if we want them to pull us and our wagon to safety then we have to care for them.

Then it was time for the family to have supper, relax and meet the neighbours; neighbours newly created who were thrown together by a similar overall situation where the individual details varied slightly. Now was time to find some mutual bond, time to sit and talk. It was time to tell stories and to discuss their predicament. A small group had gathered around Franz and his family as he was reminiscing.

'Isn't it strange,' he was saying, 'I am about to sleep under this bridge here. It is almost thirty-seven years to the day that I slept here under this very same bridge, almost in this very same spot.'

'You slept under this the bridge thirty-seven years ago?' someone asked. 'You must have a very good memory.'

Edith couldn't help herself. 'Papa does have a very good memory even if we don't always believe everything he remembers.'

The quiet chuckles could not stop Franz as he continued his story. 'Yes, thirty-seven years ago. I remember it clearly. It was in October 1907. That is when this Königin Luise bridge was officially opened. It was a very special occasion for the people of this area.'

'Special? Why was it so very special?' put in someone as Franz was taking a sip from his bottle of beer.

'It was something they really needed here. Before that we had a pontoon bridge connecting us to Tilsit. Or as the Tilsit people would say, connecting them to the other side of the river. The pontoon bridge worked OK but it had a number of problems. If boats wanted to pass through — and there has always been a lot of traffic on the river — they had to pull a section aside and then replace it after the boats had gone through. Then in winter when the river would freeze solid, the whole bridge was pulled up on the bank of the river. They really wanted this new high-level bridge.'

'How come you were involved, Papa?'Ruth wanted to know. 'And Mama, did you know he used to sleep under the bridge?'

Helena answered to keep the record straight. 'That was well before I knew your father, Ruth!'

'If I can continue,' Franz was warming to his story. 'I wasn't involved in building the bridge, but it did create a lot of interest at the time. It was a big project. I was in my early twenties and a number of us young fellows would come down from our places up at Rucken and watch the project from time to time. We made it our business to be at the official opening.'

'So you and your mates were at the official opening?'

'Yes, a day to remember. It was a big day for Tilsit and for us Memellanders as well. Prince Friedrich Wilhelm of Prussia, he was the Kaiser's cousin or something, did the opening. It was our chance to see royalty.'

Another old Memellander who had just joined the group interrupted. 'It's a pity we still didn't have someone like the old Kaiser running the country. Then we wouldn't be in the mess we are now. We would be still back on our farms. Hitler and his Scheiss war. It will be the death of all of us.'

Many, including Franz, would have probably agreed with this sentiment but Franz continued with his story. 'He and the officials were on the bridge and the square in front of the church was packed with thousands of spectators. There were decorations everywhere. There was a band and choir to the side of the officials. The official proceedings started at midday. The choir sang praise to the Lord and then the speeches began. Don't remember much about them. After the opening, there was a big sort of street party. The band was playing and the people were dancing. Thousands walked across the bridge. Others went in boats looking at it from underneath. We joined in everything. Had a great time. But then it was late. We decided to stay the night under the bridge rather than go home. Yes. That was thirty-seven years ago. Now here I am again. There were thousands of people streaming across the bridge then too. But in a completely different mood. They were having a party, having the time of their lives. Now we, and the people up above us, are running for our lives. Ah, the stories this bridge could tell!'

'Probably in thirty-seven years' time some of us will be sitting around remembering how we spent the night under the Tilsit Bridge on the banks of the Memel,' someone suggested.

'That's if we are still alive then!'

This comment changed the mood of the small group.

'And if the bridge is still here,' an old veteran from the Great War said. 'I remember when they were building this bridge too. I wasn't at the opening like Comrade Franz here. But I do know what happens to bridges in wartime. They usually get bombed or blown up by one side or the other. As I see the present situation that will probably happen to this bridge too. I would be surprised if it lived to be fifty years old. What do you reckon Franz?'

All eyes turned back on Franz as they had been while he was relating his story. Sitting there they all felt that they were now part of the history of the bridge. They were waiting for Franz's opinion.

He gave it. 'I would have to agree with you, but you never know.'

The old veteran added, 'Perhaps it will be lucky like last time.'

'Last time?' came from the back of the group. Obviously, everyone was keen to learn a little bit more of the history of their shelter for the night. 'What do you mean it was lucky last time?'

'It was at the beginning of the Great War and the Russians were advancing towards Tilsit. We were retreating and the officers wanted to blow up the bridge to stop the Russian advance. The Lord Mayor of the city pleaded that the bridge should be saved. He must have been a very good negotiator for he finally got his way. The bridge remained intact. The Russians came and they did occupy the city for a few months. Then they had to withdraw. Before they withdrew they had set the explosives to blow up the bridge. Captain Fletcher from a German artillery division risked his life to disarm the explosives before they went off. So the bridge was saved again. Tomorrow when we get to the other side of the river we will go through *Fletcher Platz* (Fletcher Square) in front of the German Church. It was renamed in honour of what he did for the city. It used to be called the grain market but they had stopped selling grain there years ago.'

'We really are sitting under a lot of history,' said Ruth. 'Tomorrow we will walk over this bridge with our horses and wagon and become part of history ourselves. In future, the history books of the Memelland will say that in August 1944 thousands of German citizens from the Memelland had to flee to safety across the Königin Luise Bridge. We will be part of that.'

'Not a nice way to get into the history books,' said Franz. 'Yes. That will probably happen, and then... after we leave Tilsit what will then happen? I don't think we will be able to write much more history before it really happens. Right now, let's take tomorrow as it comes.'

Chapter 11

'In Tilsit ist ein Kirchturm,' sagt er, der ruht auf acht Kugeln, und darum hat ihn der Napoleon immer nach Frankreich mitnehmen wollen. Er ist ihm aber zu schwer gewesen. Eine so merkwürdige Sache muß man doch sehen.'

From Eine Reise nach Tilsit by Hermann Sudermann
('In Tilsit there is a church tower,' he said, 'which rests on eight spheres and for this reason Napoleon always wanted to take it with him to France. But it was too heavy for him. You really have to see such a remarkable thing'.)

Knowing that one is not alone can be of great comfort to someone who finds problems and difficulties crowding in and who sees little but a dim and unsure future. So it was with the small group of refugees who sat with Franz and his family under the bridge of Tilsit on that rainy August evening. Relating their stories, often with a smile, was a fine way to shield off present realities, if only for a short while. However, it did help to counter that ever-present thought: 'Why is this happening to us?'

Even though they all had the same major problem — protecting their lives — the oft-quoted maxim still applied: 'a problem shared is a problem halved.' The thousands on the bridge, and the many sheltering under it, were visual evidence that they were not alone in their flight. A friendly chat with fellow refugees showed that they were not alone in their fears and anxieties, their hesitancy in facing the unknowns of the future.

Early next morning there was further evidence that Franz and his family were not alone.

'What on earth is happening?' was Edith's greeting to her family whom she saw moving around in the lamp-light. She had woken to the rumble and grinding, the roar and clattering of vehicles moving over the bridge a few metres above her.

'It's the army. It sounds like a division of Panzers is crossing the bridge. But they are moving north. They are moving towards the front,' said her father to satisfy her curiosity.

'What are we going to do? Do we keep going or should we head back home?'

'Who knows,' said Franz. 'No one around here seems to know what is happening. While you see to the animals and pack up I will try to get closer to the main road and see what is happening.'

With that, Franz moved out from under the bridge and walked along the side road which led up to the road on the bridge. Here he met a crowd of people who also wanted to know how this would affect their wanting to move into East Prussia and further.

'Don't know what is happening,' was the message which filtered back through the anxious refugees crowding along the road. 'Military police are keeping everyone well back.'

'They probably don't know what is happening either,' suggested one bystander.

'Does anyone?' offered another.

'How long will we have to wait?' called Franz to no one in particular.

'Someone has heard that it will be two or three hours,' came an anonymous answer.

'Probably waiting for the officers to finish their breakfast.'

'Good for them. But I'd rather be going in the direction we're heading!'

There was no lack of comments coming from the growing number of refugees.

'Maybe we should turn around and head back home after the army goes through. The people of Tilsit and the Ragnit and Labiau shires haven't been told to move yet.'

'Not before someone who knows what's happening tells us to.'

'Who would know? Gauleiter Keller?' This with a sarcastic laugh.

'No, the best way to go is away from the front, believe me!'

Noddings with 'yes' and 'I agree' dominated. There was general agreement that all should keep fleeing from the front and not get their hopes up. Nothing could be done but wait. There was no other way over the river. The army had priority. Be ready and waiting to get onto the bridge as soon as the military police allow it. Franz made his way back to his family with the news.

'No one really knows what is happening other than that tanks and heavy trucks are moving north across the bridge. The military police there would say nothing. They probably don't know themselves.'

Helena asked, 'What are we going to do? Stay here under the bridge? It's still raining and at least we have shelter here.'

'We would be out of the rain, sure; but how long would we end up staying here? I think we must keep moving, rain or no rain. We should get ready and go up and be in line ready to move over to Tilsit when the army has moved through.'

Helena could see the sense in that. Getting over the Memel river was important. The bridge was the only way of getting across the two hundred and fifty-metre-wide river. There was a rail bridge a little way downstream but no way could the horses and wagon be able to move over that bridge.

Belongings were packed, the covers tied down and the horses harnessed. Soon the family was ready to move up to the road and join the end of the queue of anxious people. All could see the importance of getting over the river.

The waiting began. The quietness of the crowd was remarkable. Thousands of refugees were waiting with a steely determination to flee a deadly enemy. There was the occasional shout of encouragement to a soldier sitting atop the moving panzers who waved back in thanks. He, as well as most of his fellow conscripts, probably realised that theirs was a very difficult task. Their lives would be put at risk even more so than those civilians fleeing the advancing forces.

Once the last of the military vehicles had crossed, the military police departed, leaving the pushing crowd to organise itself. It would have been amazing to the bystander to see how the refugees showed discipline and neighbourly consideration to ensure a trouble-free continuation of their flight. In spite of the two-and-a-half hour wait the impatience did not overflow into altercation. The columns from the side roads blended effortlessly in with the stream of humanity which once again had the main road to itself.

By midday Franz was able to point out the southern portals of the bridge to his daughters as they slowly moved through them.

'Look up there. You can see a bronze plaque of Königin Luise.' And the girls looked up dutifully.

'Papa, do you really think that we are going on a holiday. You will be wanting to stop for a picnic soon,' said Edith a little sarcastically.

'Well, it's something a little more pleasant to think about,' replied her father. 'Being completely absorbed in gloomy thoughts wouldn't help much. Oh! and this section of the bridge we are walking on now is a draw-bridge.'

'A what?'

'A draw-bridge. This section between the main portals and those pillars there can be swung up to allow ships with tall masts to sail through. Didn't I tell you about that before? It's a great thing on the bridge.'

'You probably did, Papa, but maybe we were not listening,' said Edith.

'And this is *Fletcher Platz* beside the German Church. See I was listening,' joined in Ruth.

The square was a mass of people not knowing which way to go. Even in normal times *Fletcher Platz* was a busy hub in the city. Tilsit grew up where a small stream, the Tilze, flowed into the larger Memel River. The city was first established when the German Order of Knights erected a fort on the acute-angled piece of land at the confluence. Later the smaller stream was dammed, creating a small artificial lake, large enough however to hinder the growth of the town to the east. The city's growth pattern resembled a piece of cheese, or a V-shape, with the apex of the V at the confluence of the streams, and the streams themselves forming the sides of the V.

The streets in the centre of Tilsit all ran towards this point which funnelled onto the bridge. The two main streets, *Die Deutsche Straße* (German Street), running parallel to the river, and *Die Hohe Straße* (The High Street), which ran from another major hub which could have been called the five ways, met in the square. A smaller road crossed the Tilze river and ran upstream and a street running downstream along the bank of the river lead to the port and industrial area.

City police were slowly unravelling the mass of refugees and their various vehicles of transport. Patience was required.

Rather than complain about the slowness of progress, Franz continued the stream of information to his female, family audience. 'And down there towards the train station is a big army barracks, the Cavalry Barracks.'

'I don't think that it would be a good idea to head in that direction,' said Edith. 'What with the army barracks and the train station, I'm sure that area would be on the air-raid bombers' list.'

'Don't worry, I have no doubt we would not be allowed down there even if we did want to go that way. But I clearly remember going there as a young boy with my father to watch a big parade.'

'You seem to have been everywhere, Papa. Why on earth would you and your dad want to see an army parade?'

'It was a cavalry parade and we both liked horses. But the main reason was that one of my father's brothers, Uncle Fritz, was in the dragoon regiment which was stationed there.'

'Grandad's brother was a Dragoon in the army? I don't remember anyone ever talking about that,' said Ruth.

'Yes, he was a Blue Dragoon, and his regiment had its headquarters in the Cavalry Barracks down there in the *Bahnhof Straße* (Station Street). It was the most famous dragoon regiment in all of Germany. He liked horses like me and I think that's why he joined up. As a young boy, I was fascinated by the parade. All those shiny, black horses with their riders in their blue uniforms. I can still see it clearly as they trotted around the parade ground with the band playing. I was disappointed that I never had the opportunity to go there again.'

'Why couldn't you?' Edith wanted to know.

'Uncle Fritz left the Regiment and migrated to Australia.'

'Migrated to Australia! I didn't know that you had an uncle in Australia. Why did he go to Australia?' asked Edith who was becoming very interested in this lost uncle of her father.

Franz continued telling the girls what he knew about his uncle. 'As I said, I was just a young boy then so I don't really know what happened. I believe that although he loved horses and liked being with them, he was not so keen about army life, and the soldering part of being in the regiment. He had joined up as a volunteer and so he was allowed to leave. But there was not enough land on the family farm for him to become a farmer like my father and so he decided to migrate. I remember being very sad when he left for he was my favourite uncle. He was always ready to play with us young kids and tease us. He wasn't married then either.'

'Do you know what happened to him there in Australia?' Ruth wanted to know.

'Not a lot really. He did keep in contact with his parents and then with my father. He got married to a girl from Coadjüthen who went out on the same boat as he did. I know that he had two sons and some girls. One of the sons was named after me — his favourite nephew he would always call me. The other he called Heinrich — in Australia they called him Henry — after his younger brother here in Rucken. Then when the Great War came Australia was on the other side and we seemed to have lost contact with our relatives in Australia. So I don't really know about the family there.'

Ruth seemed disappointed. 'Isn't it a pity that families can lose contact so quickly?'

'That's true; but don't forget that Australia is a long distance away and the Germans there weren't liked very much during the war. But how did we start talking about Australia and the Great War?'

'Because we have been sitting here for the last hour waiting for someone to tell us where we can go. We don't want to go down to the station or the army barracks. Are they still there or have they been bombed?' Edith wanted to know.

'I don't know what has been bombed in Tilsit. There have

been a number of raids, so I don't like the idea of staying in the city longer than we have to,' her father replied. 'I still think we should try to get to Otto's place and see what he can advise us to do. He lives a little further out from the city centre and we should be safe there even if there is a raid. They live down near Jakobsruhe Park. And it's sort of on our way out of the city as well.'

During all this time Helena had been listening to her husband and the girls talking about things which dated back to before they were married. Franz was nearly forty when they were married and so most of his life was spent before then. There was a lot she did not really know about him. She did realize that before 1919 when the Memelland was taken from Germany by the Treaty of Versailles Franz had had a lot more to do with Tilsit. It was no surprise that he could tell the girls a lot about the city. As a family, they seldom had gone to the city although it was not so very far away. Now as they were slowly moving down *die Hohe Straße* she did remember one of the visits they did make as a family. That was only a few years ago.

That trip to Tilsit had been to see a film at the *Lichtspielhaus* (movie theatre) here in the *Hohe Straße*. It was a film that caused quite a lot of excitement in and around Tilsit for it was the movie version of a novella by a local author entitled *Die Reise nach Tilsit* (The Journey to Tilsit). It was filmed on site in Tilsit and this gave it even more local interest.

Helena remembered going but being a little disappointed. It was great to see the Memel River and the various locations around the town featured on the screen but the two main characters in the film were Lithuanian and not German. In a way, the film reminded her a little of their present journey to Tilsit. She was making this journey not knowing what was really in store for her, just like the young wife in Sudermann's book on which the movie was based. Here the young wife was being taken by boat up the Memel River to Tilsit by her husband who had plans to drown her on the way. His wife was unaware of what he had in mind. Helena also was unaware of what was about to happen to them. Would things for her and her family turn out differently from what they had planned? Only time would tell.

'Keep that cart moving, Old Man,' one rude, impatient policeman shouted out to Franz.

Franz's reaction was one tempered with understanding. How would anyone feel after battling with anxious crowds all day? he thought to himself. He looked up, smiled and urged his horses forward.

'A little longer,' he spoke to them, 'and you can have your rest for the evening.'

This was the case. There was a square at the end of *die Hohe Straße* where a number of streets converged and the refugees moved in a number of different directions. It was not long before Franz pulled up in front of Otto's residence near the park.

'Franz, Helena, for heaven's sake. You're on the road already? Come in and tell me what's been happening.'

'The animals…' Franz started to speak.

'They'll be right here for a while. I'm sure the neighbour's boys over the road will keep a good eye on them.' And Otto called out to two young boys who had been watching intently. 'Hey, you two scallywags. Keep an eye on the wagon and the animals for a while, will you, please? I'm sure I'll be able to find something for your trouble.'

'Yes. Yes. We'll look after everything, Uncle Otto.'

The four weary travellers were happy to move inside, sit down and relax in the comfort of Otto's lounge chairs.

Chapter 12

Wo man arbeitet, da ist genug; wo man aber mit Worten umgeht, da ist Mangel.

(Proverbs 14:23)
(All hard work brings a profit;
but mere talk leads only to poverty.)

The evening meal was completed and Otto and Franz retreated to a corner seat in the lounge room to enjoy a few medicinal schnapps — that's what they called them — and left the women to talk over the dining table.

'So what do you think?' Franz opened the conversation with a very non-specific question, leaving Otto to choose what they should talk about. Both knew however that they would end up talking about the war.

'You're being here with your family and wagon and gear reinforces what I think,' answered Otto. 'It seems clear that things are going from bad to worse. Clearly you Memellanders were given orders to move out. The whole city has been chocked full of them for the last few days. To tell you the truth, I've been expecting you.'

'Yes, eventually the word came that we should move. What about you? What have they been telling you?' Franz wanted to know.

'Our Gauleiter thinks that he is Hitler himself. He refuses to accept reality and has given strict orders for the people not to leave. I know for sure that our city councillors want the people to start moving out but Gauleiter Schmidt stops them. He alone has the authority to give the orders. I think a lot of people would like to get rid of him. And I mean just that! I also know that a lot of business people are preparing for the worst. Helmut Schroeder from the boot and leather shop is actually giving his stock away.'

'Giving stuff away?' Franz was amazed.

'Well, he says he won't be able to take his stock with him when he has to leave so he may as well give it away rather than have it blown up, bombed and burnt or left for the Russians.'

'I can understand that,' said Franz, thinking of what he had left behind. 'I just hate to think what will happen to my farm, the house and the animals while we are away.'

'How has it come to this?' Otto queried. 'And why are the Russians so barbaric towards us Germans? From what I hear they single out the German speakers and leave the other local people more or less alone. If the reports are true no German is left alive.'

'I really don't know. Maybe they are reacting to what our army did to their country. Leningrad was under siege for many months and you can't tell me the citizens there didn't suffer. No doubt many thousands died. Or maybe it goes back much further.'

'But to rape and kill. I would hope our officers would have more control over the troops than to let them run wild like that,' said Otto.

'That our officers have control over the soldiers, I have no doubt. I still think that ours has been a very disciplined army,' agreed Franz. 'But I really worry about what some of our leaders and officers have ordered our soldiers to do. You hear rumours and have to start putting two and two together.'

'What are you getting at?' Otto wanted to know.

Franz thought for a moment and then explained. 'I have always been uneasy about what has been happening to the Jews up here. You hear stories. Some quite unbelievable. But they make you stop and think. No one seems to really know, and those who should know don't know either, or don't say anything.'

'Now that you mention it,' Otto came in, 'there used to be a couple of groups of Jews who brought rafts of birch down for somewhere near Grodno in Poland, or wherever, but they haven't been coming for a few years now. That didn't seem unusual, for other groups stopped coming as well. It changes around a lot. We get timber from one place and then from another, and the raft crews vary quite a lot.'

'There used to be a number of shops here run by Jews. Do they still operate? Probably not, by the way you look. We used to have a number of travelling hawkers who would move through the district. There was old Yaakov in his bright red wagon, who had all sorts of materials to sell. Helena used to buy her dress materials and other items from him. Then Moishe would come with all sorts of brushes and brooms, pots and pans. Then they stopped coming. Completely disappeared. The rumours are that Nazi police took them away. To where? No one seems to know.'

'You are right. The places run by Jews have been closed for a number of years now. No one seems to know what happened to them either. No one seemed to care either. Makes you wonder.'

'Maybe Otto,' suggested Franz, ' it is now our turn to suffer. Hopefully we will have a chance to get away with our lives.'

The women had finished chatting and clearing the dining table. They came over to the two men, the girls to say good night and go to sleep in a real bed, and the two wives to join in the conversation.

'So how many schnapps did you two need, in order to stop

your indigestion? Or haven't you got rid of it yet?' Helena wanted to know. 'And what has all this serious conversation been about?'

'The war, of course. What's been happening. How we would have done things differently. You know us. But now I think we should be looking at what we should be doing in the next few days, or weeks,' replied Franz.

'Well yes, I do think that is rather important,' agreed Helena.

At that point loud, piercing sirens made any further conversation impossible. When they stopped Otto was the first to speak. 'It appears we are in for another bombing raid tonight and....'

'What are we to do? Just sit here?' Helena wanted to know.

'Some people run down to the cellars in their building where it is probably a little safer. I feel that if a bomb hits your building, being in the cellar would not help much. Yes, we just stay in our apartment. We are in the safer part of the city here. Just wait a.....'

He was interrupted by Ruth and Edith who came running into the room. 'What on earth is happening?' Edith cried out. 'Are we being bombed. Shouldn't we be going somewhere safe?'

Her father tried to calm her. 'Otto was just explaining that we are probably as safe here as anywhere else.'

Then Otto continued. 'As I was saying. If we wait a moment or two... Listen. Can you hear that? They are bombing the industrial area and the port again. That's where most damage has been done. A few times they hit the city centre but that was probably a mistake. There have been no attacks out here as yet. After all there is just that big parkland area and houses nearby. They are not interested in bombing that. A problem might arise if they decide to bomb the railway line running out of the city. It runs right beside Jakobsruhe Park.'

'I hope you are right. I don't like the idea of being bombed,' Edith confessed.

A few minutes and quiet ruled once again. The attack seemed to be over.

'That didn't last long,' was Franz's comment.

Otto had to agree. 'That has usually been the case. But I bet Königsberg copped a lot more. We and Königsberg always seem to be bombed on the same night. It appears that most of the aircraft concentrate on the larger, more important city, and a smaller number come over to us. I wonder will I still have a timber yard to go to tomorrow?'

With that he walked to the window, pulled up the blind and looked out. 'Something has been hit. There's that awful red glow coming from the port.'

'It is the port?' his wife wanted to know.

'Yes, it is certainly in the direction of the train bridge and not the Luise bridge.'

Tilsit, with its 60,000 inhabitants was more a regional centre for Government and agriculture than an industrial city. The forests which were so abundant and widespread in the area provided the raw material for a number of mills and other industries related to timber. At the end of the nineteenth century it boasted of being the most important timber town in all of Germany. Large rafts of timber coming down the Memel River from further afield were a common sight. Factories produced carriages and wagons, chemicals, iron products, soap and alcohol. Tilsit cheese was noted throughout Europe. A lack of heavy industry producing armaments and war equipment had kept the city free of air-raids, but now with the enemy closing in, this was no longer the case.

'I think we will soon be experiencing a lot more air-raids,' was Otto's considered opinion. 'If this is the case I don't see how they can expect us to stay here much longer.'

'I see your point,' agreed Franz.' We want to move on in the morning. We certainly didn't plan to stay here in Tilsit for long. We called in to see how you were faring and to ask for some advice. What do you suggest? Where should we head for in the morning?'

'That's a good question. You are relatively lucky in having horses and a wagon to travel in. So food and clothing is not such a big worry for you now. The horses are still relatively fresh. But for how long will those horses be able to keep you going? The weather is okay at the moment and there is no desperate hurry. You can go along at your own pace. If you make sure that they are always well fed, they should be able to keep that up for quite a while. But what if the weather comes in cold? Or if we have rain and early snow? What if the Russians break through and you have to travel more quickly? There are so many unknowns. You will have to take all these things into consideration.'

Franz and his family could see the sense in what Otto was saying. Many of those possibilities had already come up in their own considerations. To date it had been going fairly well, uncomfortable at times, frustrating at others, but they had been under no real pressure or danger. It would be unrealistic to expect this to continue.

Otto continued with his assessment. 'It's a hell of a long way from here to safer regions. The Germans will have to move out of all of East Prussia and Poland to ensure their safety. I have no idea how many hundreds of kilometres that is. What with all the others who will have to leave their homes that would be very difficult. I don't see that you would be able to do that with your horses and wagon. I think you should head for Labiau and then on to Königsberg. There you might be able to get either a train or boat to safety.'

Helena was listening to the men talking and to Otto's suggestions. At the mention of Königsberg she offered a comment. 'Heading to Königsberg would be good in another way, too. My son, Kurt, works on the railway there. He has done so for years. I'm sure he would be able to help us get on a train if we needed to. Don't you agree, Franz?'

'Yes, I don't think we have a lot of other options.' He suspected all along that that was the most probable route. He was pleased, in a way, that Otto had suggested the same. Nothing would be worse than to make a wrong decision without talking about it with others. In this case the stakes would be high.

Otto's further information eased Franz even more. 'You should find it easy going. It's a bit hilly in places but generally you will be travelling on relatively flat country. That will make it much easier for the horses.'

Making it easier for the horses would always be a high priority for Franz.

Chapter 13

Das Fallen der Blätter, die blaue Ferne, der Glanz der herbstlichen Sonne über den abgeernteten Feldern, das ist vielleicht das eigentliche Leben.

From Namen die keiner mehr nennt
by Marion Gräfin Dönhoff
(Falling leaves, the blue horizon, the light of the autumn
sun on harvested fields; that perhaps represents the real
meaning of life.)

The weather had cleared. The bright, sparkling morning sun gave promise of comfortable travelling. Franz now had a definite idea of where he should be headed. Freed of that uncertainty, he and Helena went about preparing for their departure from Otto's house with much lighter hearts. The girls in the meantime had gone to the park to milk the cow and bring her back to the wagon ready to continue their journey.

'Papa, Papa! The mare and her foal are not with the other two horses. Where did you put them last night? Weren't they all together?' Edith was quite out of breath after running the fifty metres back from Jakobsruhe Park.

'What? I tied her up near the other two. She and the foal must be there.'

'No, she is not there. The foal neither.'

'She must have taken fright with the sirens and the bombs

exploding last night. I didn't tie the foal up. I never do. But she would have stayed with her mother. They must still be in the park somewhere. We will have to go and look for them. I can't leave them behind.'

The search began. You go this way. I go that way. They move off to the right. The women move off to the left. Get Otto's suggestion. Enlist the help of the boys from across the road who had looked after the wagon on their arrival. They probably know the park better than most. Hurry now. We have to get away too. But we have to find those horses. Don't frighten them. Come back and tell us if you see anything. Hurry now. Back in half an hour whether you have found them or not. No, no one would have taken them. Well I hope not. There's a lollypop for each of you boys if you spot them. Well, OK. Even if you don't find them. Yes, you can bring some of your friends. No, there will not be a lollypop for all of you. Now off you go.

Yes, Franz was worried about his special mare and her foal. Frantic? Well not yet; but he needed to find them as soon as possible.

Half an hour goes slowly if nothing is found. The stillness of the green of the parkland was invaded by the enthusiasm of young boys searching for the lost horses. The sounds of boys running around shouting, 'Horsie. Horsie,' would not have a calming effect of horses already spooked by sirens and bomb blasts. All steps have to be accepted in an emergency. And to Franz, this was an emergency.

Ruth and Edith were first back after scouring the southern section of the park. 'Plenty of trees, but no horses,' reported Ruth. 'But we did see this beautiful, white marble statue of Königin Luise. The Tilsit people must have really liked her. She seems to be mentioned everywhere.'

'Uncle Otto, Uncle Otto,' sounded from the distant tree-line.

'We've found them. We've found them. Uncle Otto. Uncle Otto, where are you?'

Otto gave a shout, 'Over here.'

Soon half a dozen boys came running. 'Fritz and Freddie saw them over near the oval.'

'I hope you didn't scare them off with all of your noise.'

'No. Fritz and Freddie are still there watching that they don't run away.'

Search over. Relief all round. Catastrophe — well from Franz's point of view — avoided. Lollypop payments distributed, the whole team of boys being rewarded, and now the preparations for departure could continue. The family, complete with all animals, soon joined the long line of refugees heading south onto the plains of northeast East Prussia.

The extensive plains of Northern Europe extend from the west coast of France through many countries to the Ural Mountains of Russia, the full length of the continent. Throughout history this area of flat land has been regarded as a highway along which armies could march without having to change into second gear. It had recently seen the movement of the German military machine both eastward and westward from the heartland of Germany. More recently it was seeing this same army, significantly depleted, being forced back by the invigorated opposing forces which were now moving south and westward (the Russians) and eastward and north (the allied forces).

This flat terrain has not only been used by advancing and retreating armies but also by migrations of non-military populations. Franz and his family were now part of one more great migration of peoples. More than 12,000,000 German citizens were forced to flee their homes in the eastern areas of the German Empire in this migration and be resettled in the historical heartland of the nation.

This is the sad scene which is moving slowly along the roads radiating from Tilsit.

Six hundred years prior to this historical event the land was covered with forests and low marshy swamplands with very little evidence of human presence. It had been evolving this way since the retreat of the ice sheets at the end of the most recent ice age.

During this time, ice which had built up on the Scandinavian Peninsula flowed slowly, but relentlessly over these regions. This large sheet glacier bulldozed hills of rubble and rocks and soil in front, and within, its advancing face. When the icesheet melted, some 12,000 years ago, the piles of material left behind formed hilly country with numerous lakes. A wide stretch of lowland developed between this line of low hills and the emerging Baltic Sea. Rivers flowing from these loosely consolidated hills, created more flat, marshy land, pushing further and further into the sea. Pine forests soon colonised the area awaiting the arrival of groups of people to utilise the area for their needs.

Franz, his family and thousands of other refugees were now moving across this plain land, not in its immediate post-glacial form but as thousands of years of natural evolution and five hundred years of agricultural husbandry had transformed it. Large areas still remained forested. Much of the swampy land had been drained to become fertile arable land. The fertility of the remainder had been constantly improved over the centuries to become very productive. Agricultural villages and towns were scattered throughout the region surrounded by fields of grain, pasture and vegetables. The region was a peaceful food bowl criss-crossed by a network of roads and railway lines ready to deliver the produce to hungry markets.

Franz almost felt at home. In less dire circumstances he would have felt very much at home. He was travelling through a landscape not dissimilar from that which he had left behind. He could appreciate the fields of green pasture with cows grazing contentedly. He could admire the fields of barley, wheat and rye now starting to ripen. He could appreciate the sun setting over dark green forests. The villages, small clusters of farmers whose fields fanned out from the buildings, reminded him of similar settlements in the Memelland. All of this was very understandable for these neighbouring districts had developed under the same cultural influences.

The time came for him to move off the main road running south from Tilsit, move out of the main stream of refugees, and find quieter, more peaceful paths. A side-road was taken heading for a small forested area. They were approaching a village so Franz decided to follow a narrow, farmer's track leading directly towards the forest.

'Should we be doing this?' Helena was a little apprehensive.

'No one will worry. It's not far to the trees. There will be a nice sheltered spot there and good grass here for the animals. 'Careful here old friends,' he was talking to the two horses pulling the wagon, 'the ground is a bit soft.'

He hardly had said this when the horses began to snort, and strain, trample up and down, snort once again and eventually stop pulling.

'Come on, Boys. What's the problem?'

'Papa, Papa, come and look here. The wagon has bogged down.'

'Scheiße!'

Hearing this come from Franz caused the women to stop and stare in utter amazement. He was one never to utter even the mildest of expletives. This surely indicated the strain under which he was living. Leaving behind his farm with the grain ready to harvest was a deep disappointment. Leaving his animals to fend for themselves on the abandoned farm was a heartbreaking decision. Having to leave his homeland was a catastrophe. Now having to take on the burden of seeing to the safety of his family, indeed keeping them from certain death if left to the hands of the advancing Russians, was an enormous responsibility. Throughout the journey so far, his continual reminiscing was merely a mechanism to keep his mind off the serious experiences they were undertaking. Now this relatively small matter of bogging the wagon was the last straw.

'Scheiße!' came out a second time. 'Why haven't I been paying more attention to the track instead of looking to the trees ahead? Now what?'

'We could all get behind the wagon and push. That might help,' suggested Edith.

'I think that would only push us further into the mud, even if we were able to help much,' replied Franz after looking carefully at the situation. 'No, I think the only solution is to pull the wagon backwards out of the soft ground.'

'And how are we going to do that?'

'I will have to undo the horses from the front and yoke them up to the back of the wagon somehow. The trouble is I don't think the chains will be long enough. And I don't have any others. All we can do is try.'

'And if we can't get out?' Edith wanted to know. 'We can't sit here till the mud dries.'

All attempts proved unsuccessful. With evening closing in the family was still immobile.

'I will have to go into that village over there and see if I can get some help,' Franz finally admitted.

He went back along the track and turned onto the road leading to the village. A little while later he returned. But not alone. With him came two burly men leading two draft horses harnessed up with collars and chains.'

'Hello, ladies,' they greeted Helena and her two daughters who were sitting looking quite depressed. 'Let's see if these two can pull you out of your mess. With the amount they eat they should be strong enough to do it without raising a sweat.'

The local farmers had their horses chained to the back of the wagon in no time and without any fuss. With a few whistles and a 'come on you lazy brutes!' they soon had the wagon clear of the boggy ground.

'Bad idea to come along this track with that heavy wagon,' they stated the obvious. 'But you weren't to know how boggy it is underneath. It's the nature of a lot of the country around here. They say it has something to do with how it was formed. We suggest you come on into the village. You will be able to park in a shed Friedrich here has. That right, Freddy?'

'Yes, sure. You are welcome to stay there in my shed. It's open on a few sides but at least you will have a roof over your heads.'

'How can we ever thank you enough for all this?' Helena was so relieved.

'Yes,' said Franz. 'I feel such a fool getting us into a mess like this. How will I be able to keep ahead of the Russians if I keep bogging the wagon down?'

It was fully dark by the time Franz and his family were parked under the farmer's shed. With a 'I'll see you all in the morning', Farmer Friedrich headed into his house, leaving the travellers preparing for the evening.

Helena was organising something to eat by the light of the lantern. 'Don't feel badly, Franz,' she consoled her husband who was still feel uncomfortable with what had happened. 'It has probably all turned out for the best. I'm sure we are better of here than out in the open beside that forest.'

Chapter 14

Und Schweine wurden auch fett gemarkt.

(...and pigs were also fattened for market.)

Franz would have loved to lend a hand with the early morning chores but on this first day of their being in a stranger's farmstead it would have been overly nosey and not the right thing to do. So he tended to his own animals and stayed with his family. Now, later in the morning, the farmer who appeared to have no pressing farm duties to attend to, came around to see how his visitors were getting on. He seemed rather keen to sit down and have a chat. Franz and farmer Friedrich ended up sitting at the entrance of the harness room having a pipe together.

After the initial tentative get-to-know-you topics — Where are you from? What do you do? How long have you been travelling? and similar — Friedrich made a very generous, but to Franz also a rather unexpected and hard to understand offer, 'You're welcome to camp here until we all know for sure what is happening.'

'What do you mean? Will we ever know for sure what is happening?'

'Not if we rely on the authorities,' agreed Friedrich. 'But it does seem strange that all you Memellanders have been told to leave and we here have been told definitely to stay. More than that! People here have been getting into trouble for making preparations and suggesting that we should flee. Defeatist

117

attitude they call it, and it's completely against the orders of the Führer. The officials say that the front has been secured and that there is no immediate danger.'

'I can't see how they can be saying things like that,' replied Franz. 'From what I've seen and what we know for a fact from people we know north of Memel, everything is falling apart. And then we don't really know what is happening east of here around Minsk. It does seem that our boys are on their last legs there.'

'Yes Franz, that's been the case all along. What are we to believe? The trouble is we have to obey the official orders or suffer the consequences. They can be dire. I know of people who have been put into gaol for getting their wagons set up to move their families. Between you and me I don't have much confidence in most of those Nazis who have been appointed to positions here. But what can we do?'

'I know how you feel. The same applied to ours back in the Memelland. They like to throw their weight around, but they often refuse to face reality. They don't seem to know what is happing around them.'

Friedrich continued, 'It's a pity that attempt to blow up Hitler back in July failed. If it had come off, the war would have been over by now, and you would be back on your farm carrying on as before.'

'What really happened then? Do you know? All that was reported was that some traitors had been shot for making an attempt on Hitler's life.'

'There has been a lot of talk about that in the district here, and a lot of folk around here think like I do. One of those involved was a local count.'

'Oh!' exclaimed Franz.

'Yes. Graf Lehndorff — everyone called him Heini — owned a couple of large estates in the district and was very well liked by everyone who knew him. He was always ready to help people in need. His main estate, Steinort, down beside Mauer Lake, was even used by the Government and the army as an eastern headquarters. The attempt on the Führer's life happened not far from the estate.'

'You mean Hitler was over here when they tried to assassinate him?'

'Yes, he would quite often be over here in East Prussia. He had a fortified bunker built in the forests near where Heini Lehndorff lived. It was known around here as the Wolf's Lair. Everyone in the district knew about it. Well, we had all heard about it, but we didn't really know much about it. It was all very secret and heavily fortified. It was from here that he sent out orders to his Generals on the eastern front. It was one of his advisors who would meet with him in the bunker that took along a briefcase full of explosives to blow Hitler up. It didn't work out as planned and the Führer survived.'

'Bad luck for the poor beggars who were involved in the plot.'

'Yes, they were soon rounded up. Lehndorff had gone to Königsberg and was ready to take over the army administration as soon as he received notification that Hitler had been killed. He had to flee when he heard what really happened. Then he gave himself up, for the Gestapo had taken his wife and young children and would have killed them if he didn't turn himself in. The word is that they are now in a concentration camp somewhere. Graf Lehndorff was hanged.'

'And now we are still in this mess, which is worse than ever,' concluded Franz by way of an amen.

Men talk of war and their farms; women of households and their families. This was the case here. Gertrude (Friedrich's wife of many years), Helena and the girls stood in front of the farmhouse and looked across at the two men deep in conversation.

There was the occasional puff of smoke rising from one or other of their pipes.

'I wonder what they are talking about?' queried Helena looking towards them.

'The war.' Gertrude seemed quite definite in her suggestion. 'And then perhaps pigs and horses.'

Ruth was the first to agree. 'You are most certainly right. Papa was always talking to Franz Habedanck from the big house next door back home about the war and his horses. The Habedancks have a big stable of pure Trakehnen horses. He loved going over there to look at them and dreaming of owning one himself. That will never happen. He will have to be happy with our mare here and her foal.'

'And who isn't talking about the war, these days?' said Edith. 'That's all the men talked about at church. They all wished that it had never started and now that it would be over as soon as possible.'

'Yes, the men never stop talking about the politics of war. When it's all over I suppose they will have more time to talk about their horses and pigs. We women think mainly about the loss and sorrow,' said Gertrude, and she continued. 'Has the war been kind to you?'

'Kind?' replied Helena, 'Can a war ever be kind to anyone? Or is kindness when sadness does not come calling?'

'I probably haven't put it very well. What I mean to ask if any of your immediate family has been involved in the fighting?'

'Yes,' replied Helena. 'Whose family has not been involved? Our son, Gert, was killed outside Warsaw and my oldest boy, Fritz, from my first marriage, is a captain somewhere on the eastern front.'

'I am sorry to hear of your loss, but I know how you must feel. We had two sons, but at the moment, I don't really know if they are still alive or not. Ever since the enemy, the British and Americans I mean, landed in France, things have been going from bad to worse. And we can't believe anything we are told. The last we heard, was that Kurt was with the eastern army somewhere near Minsk. What's happening there now I've no idea.'

'That's the trouble,' consoled Helena. 'Not knowing what is happening. They were always ready a few years ago to tell us about all the victories the German army was having, but now the reports seem to be mixed. What about your other son? Do you know where he is?'

'Young Willi was still in school when they came and took him away. Well they didn't actually take him away, but they might as well have. And he wasn't yet seventeen. He was in school in Kreuzingen when these naval officials walked into the classroom. "These boys," they said, "will not be finishing school, but will report to the naval base in Gotenhafen in two days time for training for the navy." They then read out a list of names and our son was one of them. What could we do? We knew no one to go to for help. All we could do was pack a few things in his bag, take him to the railway station and see him off. The war can't be going too well if they are forcing young boys like our Willi to become fighting men.'

'Have you heard what's happened to him?' Helena wanted to know.

'We did receive a few letters from him and as far as we know he is still in Gotenhafen. It's been four weeks since we've heard from him last and we are starting to be worried.'

These two families, brought together by the results of random wartime experiences could well represent any two families comparing their involvement, voluntary or otherwise, in a war which was drawing to its conclusion. There was suspicion and animosity towards the Nazi appointed officials who still had control. There was confusion brought about by the conflicting reports which were reaching the common people by various routes. There was the ever-increasing evidence of family sadness brought about by the news of a son or father, brother or husband, missing or killed in action.

Here in the small East Prussian farming village of Parwen, two families were caught in the confusion, but united in their loss and sorrow. Two families, far from the seat of political power, who worked the land, not only to provide a livelihood for themselves and food for others, but because it provided satisfaction for the hours of toil required. This simple life had been taken away from them by the inhumane ambitions of their political leaders.

The common attitude towards their work and the war, initiated very quickly a bond between Franz and Friedrich. This was what allowed, even encouraged, the open frank discussion which was taking place. At this time in Germany such expressions of opinion could have resulted in dire consequences if heard by someone with Nazi sympathies. Here both men felt they could express their frustrations without any possibility of repercussions.

Franz had accepted the offer to remain in Parwen at least for a few days or until the evacuation situation became a little clearer. It was hard to see how the people here in East Prussia were required to stay while those over the Memel river, a short distance away, were told to leave. Now for a while he felt he could relax. He could do nothing about the wider picture of the war. What was happening in the western theatres of the war had no immediate effect on his wellbeing. He and most of his friends and acquaintances acknowledged the inevitability of victory for Germany's enemies there. Since the beginning of June when the German forces had been unable to halt the landing of a revitalised and strengthened force the fate of an over-extended German military force was sealed.

And he could do nothing about the confusion which surrounded everyone in the east. Much more satisfying at the moment would be to accompany Friedrich and check the condition of the pigs. The pig shed held surprises.

'What the... good heavens! I had no idea that you would have so many,' was Franz' response to the shed-full of squealing and grunting that faced him.

'Yes, that's my main source of income. It's the case with many of the farmers around here. Haven't you heard of the Kreuzingen pig sales?'

'No, I must admit that I haven't. No, wait a minute. I think I may have heard about it, but I know nothing about it.'

'That's strange,' was Friedrich's comment. 'It's one of the biggest in Germany and you know nothing about it?'

'That's one of the problems about living in the Memelland for the last twenty-five years. We all thought of ourselves as being German, but we didn't have a lot to do with Germany. It was different before the Great War. Then we were part of the German Empire and all our dealings were with Germany. But when we became part of Lithuania a lot of our contact with Germany was cut off. When I was young, Tilsit was our main city and our produce went that way. But after we were cut out of Germany our farm produce went to Heydekrug and Memel to the north.'

'I suppose you were happy then when Hitler took it back again?'

'Sure, a lot of people were happy then and were looking forward to better times. Others of us were less convinced.'

'Anyway,' said Friedrich steering the conversation back to their immediate interest, 'see that pen of fat porkers there? They're off to the market tomorrow. And why don't you come with me? I take them into Kreuzingen in my old truck. It's your chance to take your mind off unpleasant things. You will probably be really surprised when you see what happens there.'

'What do you mean by surprised? Do you do things differently here?'

'No,' explained Friedrich. 'I mean you will be surprised by the number of pigs there for sale. Especially now when we don't really know about the future. A lot of farmers are trying to get rid of as many as possible. The buyers are still coming from all over Germany and the trains are still taking them across the land.'

'The markets are held every week?'

'Yes. Every week thousands of pigs are loaded onto rail wagons and sent all over Germany.'

'Makes my two sows and their litters seem quite insignificant. Poor old things! I wonder how they are getting on? I left their pens open when we left so that they could get out and look after themselves. There's plenty of water in the pond and no doubt they would have found the rye paddock by now.'

'I'm sure they would have been looking after themselves quite well,' said Friedrich. 'If the truth be known, they are probably eating more now than when you were feeding them.'

The day passed. If it were not for the circumstances over which neither family had any control it would have been regarded as a most enjoyable visit, but all feelings were dampened by the reality of the situation. Whatever topic was touched upon in conversation, whatever aspect of the farm the men were inspecting, whatever household or family matter the women were discussing the reality was that this was happening under the cloud of mortal danger closing in from the north and east.

Franz knew, his family knew that this was but a brief, friendly interlude in a journey towards a dimly determined destination, into an unknown future.

Chapter 15

Da jedoch der Russe noch nicht so weit vordrung, sind wir nach 14 Tage wieder nach unser Zuhause zurückgekehrt.

(Because the Russians had not yet advanced so far we returned home again after 14 days.)

It was early on Thursday morning; very early, for the sun would not be up for another hour. As arranged on the previous evening, Franz and his farmer-host, Friedrich, were travelling on the road to Kreuzingen in Friedrich's old Büssing truck. Loaded on the back were eight prime fat pigs that were being taken to the weekly pig sale there.

But they were not alone on the pre-dawn road. No, they had joined a steady stream of sundry vehicles moving in the same direction, heading for the same destination — the pig sales.

Franz voiced his surprise. 'Is this a special sale today that all these people are headed there?'

'No. It's quite normal. People from all over the shire, as well as neighbouring ones, head for the markets here on a Thursday.'

'It's more than just a pig sale, then?' Franz wanted to know.

'Yes, indeed. Pigs are probably the most important, but there are all manners of goods for sale. Fishermen come from the Curonian Lagoon with their catch. There are farmers with every imaginable vegetable for sale. It's also the place to buy poultry. I will show you the largest egg market in this part of the country. And there are other animals beside pigs — cattle and horses in particular. Kreuzingen is the most important market town in all of East Prussia.'

Franz was travelling towards a town with a population of a little over 2,000 but which doubled in size on market Thursdays. Kreuzingen was a wealthy, progressive town. It owed its wealth and importance to the hard work of the farmers in the surrounding area. It didn't grow up over night but the seeds of its present-day success had been sown more than three centuries previously.

In 1576, a Lutheran Pastor, Caspar Hennenberger, with the help of a number of Prussian mathematicians published the first detailed map of Prussia. This was after Hennenberger had spent a number of years travelling throughout the area. It was produced to a scale of 1:400,000 — 1 centimetre representing 4 kilometres — so he was able to show quite fine detail. It is noticeable that on his map the north-eastern area of Prussia, i.e. the area around Kreuzingen, is significantly lacking in detail.

It does contain streams and marshes, low land and forested areas. Hennenberger wrote later, in a book meant to be an accompaniment to the map, that this area was basically unpopulated, supporting only hunters, fishermen and bee-keepers. On his map a thin line, representing a track, ran through the area, joining the two fortress settlements of Ragnit on the Memel river to Labiau on the Curonian Lagoon. These two settlements had been established in the late thirteenth century by the Teutonic Order of Knights who had set out to bring Christianity to the Baltic regions of Europe.

Agricultural development occurred around these two settlements but did not reach far afield. For two centuries, the trail between the two remained the domain of those wishing to move from one to the other. Only at the end of the sixteenth and beginning of the seventeenth centuries was this area gradually settled. It is recorded that in 1583 a man with the name of Domasch lived in Skeisgirn (Kreuzingen). This makes it the second oldest town in the region.

Once started, settlement branched out and soon farming villages dotted the countryside. Settlers arrived, some from German-speaking areas in the west and many from Lithuania to the north. This resulted in many of the villages being given names ending in 'girren', 'ischken', and 'ingken'. In the 1930s, the Nazi Party in Berlin deemed many of these names to be too un-German and decreed that they should be changed to more German-sounding names. Towns which for centuries had been known as, for example, Groß Skaisgirren, Parwischken, Lankeningken and Makohnen now were officially called Kreuzingen, Parwen, Altmühle and Mühlenkreuz.

Whereas most of the official signage was changed, the settlements all had reminders of their previous names which had not been properly painted over. The residents also felt uncomfortable in changing age-old names of places, where they had lived all their lives, to new politically correct ones and so they continued referring to their own village by its previous name. Friedrich maintained that, on principle, he would continue calling his home village Parwischken although the sign coming into the village read Parwen.

As the land was developed moving out from Kreuzingen (which was formerly called Groß Skaisgirren) the newly established roads all lead back to the main town. It became the focus of the district.

By the end of the seventeenth century the district was settled with small towns and villages with the farmers living in these, rather than in farmsteads dotted individually over the landscape.

Some were very small consisting of five to six farmsteads. Many, like Parwen where Franz and his family were staying at the moment remained a small village of barely two hundred people. In villages of this size, only a few inhabitants, if any, were not dependent on farming activities to earn a living. Others grew a little larger with non-farming inhabitants like bakers, butchers, shop-keepers, teachers, pastors providing basic needs.

Kreuzingen, because of its focal position in the region grew into a thriving town. It had hotels, numerous shops, a courthouse, medical facilities and a whole range of urban services. It grew whereas the others did not.

Franz and Friedrich were now on one of the roads leading into the market centre. There were six main roads leading to the town as well as rail links to neighbouring towns and beyond to Germany's heartland. All these roads were now bringing people and produce into the markets. Town officials claimed that every week 1000 — 1500 vehicles of various types, from push carts to motor trucks, crowded the streets of the town.

It was not yet daylight and our two farmers, new friends, were approaching the street-lights of the main street. 'All that light!' remarked Franz. 'Do you even light up the streets here?'

'They have had electricity in the town since the beginning of the century,' explained Friedrich. 'And it's not only on market days that the street lights are on. That happens every night. But we do not need to stop in the main street. We can go straight to the pig market which will be well lit as well, and be waiting there for when the buyers arrive.'

After joining in the steadily moving convoy of miscellaneous vehicles, they arrived at the less than brightly lit market space. The area was full of ghostly shapes moving under the direction of a number of traffic organisers who appeared to know what they were doing.

'No, you have to get up really early to be the first here,' remarked Friedrich, noticing that Franz seem surprised that they were not the first to arrive at the sale. 'Once here there is always time to sit around having some breakfast and discussing what's been happening in the district.'

'I suppose I can easily guess the topics talked about lately,' suggested Franz.

'Yes, indeed!' replied Friedrich. 'And it's not only about the price we are getting for our pigs. We are really worried about how long we will be able to continue holding the markets here. The buyers too are complaining. They are having trouble arranging transport for the produce they buy. I have no idea how we will be able to sell our goods when that happens.'

'Yes, no doubt that time will come,' replied Franz looking in amazement at the numerous vehicles arriving with their loads of squealing porkers. 'It will probably happen sooner than later.'

It was hours later and the frantic activity at the pig and cattle sale had lessened. Many of the farmers were heading back into the town centre. They had sold their pigs for the week and were now looking at the other market stalls, buying what they required. This was where they obtained their food requirements for the following days. Others were relaxing over a meal and glasses of beer at one of the cafes in the town.

Franz and Friedrich had risen early and they also were now enjoying lunch. There was a loud buzz of conversation as the farmers sat enjoying these leisure moments in what was really a very hard-working life. Then a man, clearly not a farmer, came into the dining hall and said in a loud voice: 'Quiet please! Listen up!' He continued in spite of the fact that most of the diners continued with their loud talking. They generally had little time for official looking interlopers. 'Notices have been put up at the Post Office and the Court House. These are telling the Memellanders who have evacuated to here to start moving back home.' At the mention of "Memellanders" Franz looked up, paying full attention.

'After lunch,' he said to Friedrich, 'we need to go to the courthouse and read the notice and see what it is all about.'

'Yes, we must do that. It seems as though you will be going home sooner than expected.'

A visit to the courthouse confirmed the report. The two set off back to Parwen with the news for the women.

'I think that they will be happy to be going back home,' was Franz's assessment of the situation.

Chapter 16

Yanks and Hogs

'Howdy, son. That's some mighty fine hogs you got yourself there,' commented a couple of American soldiers to young Ron Natalier who was chopping up pumpkins to feed them.

'Yes, Father says they are coming along very nicely,' replied young Ron, putting down his tomahawk.

'So what do you call them?' asked one of the soldiers who seemed interested in farm work.

'We call them pigs.'

The soldiers looked at one another, apparently a little confused, and then one of them said, 'I know you call them pigs, Kid. We wanted to know if you have special pet names for them like Clara or Rosie.'

'No, that's what we call our aunties. We also have an Aunty Olga,' replied Ron who seemed quite happy to have stopped work and was now standing and talking happily to the strangers. 'They are not really pets and we don't give them any special names. We do name some of our cows but.'

'That's fine; but if you are standing somewhere talking about the pigs how do you know which one you are talking about?' asked one soldier.

Ron could see the soldiers smiling to one another when they asked the question so he replied, 'Father calls them 'this pig' and 'that pig'. But you couldn't do that.'

'Why couldn't we call them that too? Is our accent so hard to understand?' one of the Americans wanted to know.

'Because if you called that sow over near you 'this pig' she

131

would get all mixed up, what with father calling her 'that pig' and you calling her 'this pig' it would be very confusing for her.'

'Say, kid, do you ever get a clip round the ears at school for being so cheeky?'

The soldiers were clearly enjoying talking to this Australian farm kid. They obviously had nothing better to do and wanted to stay talking.

'Anyway, tell us, why are you chopping up those blue marrows?'

'They are not marrows, they're the pumpkins we grow on the farm. Father sells the good ones, but if they are too big and knobbly or have mouse holes in them, we chop them up and boil them in this drum with sweet spuds and wormy potatoes. We feed this to our pigs.'

'Say, that sounds more appetising than some of the chow they often serve up to us. No wonder they look so fat and juicy.'

Ron continued with the conversation, 'We do have a special pig as well as these.'

'Oh, tell us more. What is this special hog of yours? Or should I say special pig? Do you have him here or are you hiding him somewhere else?'

'No,' replied Ron. 'We have him here in the pigsty. That's him down there under the gum tree in that pen. He has a special name.'

'Really? And what is his name? Is it 'this special pig' or 'that special pig'?'

'No,' answered Ron, 'he's called the Christmas pig.'

'The Christmas pig?'

'Yes, Father keeps one and fattens him up. A bit before Christmas he takes him up to Toowoomba to the bacon factory. They kill him for us and make him into different things — bacon, pork chops, roasts, a ham and pork sausages. They even send the feet and head back. Mum makes brawn out of the head.'

'The Christmas pig, hey. That fellow down there under the gum tree must sure feel lucky to be the Christmas pig.'

'Yes, and then when he has gone Father keeps the wurst pig in the same pen,' Ron kept the conversation going and the soldiers were happy to stay.

'Worst pig? What do you mean by worst? Is he the naughty one and doesn't get on with the others and has to be locked up by himself?'

'Not worst! Wurst. We make wurst out of him.'

'What on earth is wurst?'

'Wurst is sausage we make. Don't you have that where you come from?'

'No,' they agreed, 'we've never heard of it. So what sort of sausage is this wurst of yours?'

'Well,' began Ron, 'Uncle Harry fattens up a steer — you know what that is don't you? — and Father fattens a pig. Then when they are big enough we kill them up at Uncle Harry's place. They are minced up into sausage meat and squeezed out into the cleaned pig's guts. Then we hang them up in the garage and smoke them in the fire Father lights there. He puts plenty of sawdust on it so that it smokes well. That's wurst.'

'So it's a sort of smoked sausage,' remarked the American.

'Yes, that's what I said.'

'I'll tell you something,' said the one American to the other, 'I sure bet the litters of pigs here sit around hoping that they don't get put in that pen with the gum tree. Say, kid, you'd better get back to that chopping of yours or your dad will put you in the stew.'

'Bye for now,' said the other soldier. 'Been nice talking to you. Now we know all about Christmas pigs and wurst pigs. Wurst? That's how you say it isn't it?'

'Be seein' ya, Yanks,' said the cheeky farm boy.

Soldiers had come to this farm but not war. Planes were flying overhead but their guns were silent. For these Nataliers on their farm in Australia, the death and destruction of war remained on the pages of the newspapers. The soldiers that had invaded their farmlands had come in peace.

For months now a company of American soldiers had been camping in one of Henry Natalier's paddocks. This was one of the many sites throughout the south-eastern region of the State of Queensland in Australia where US servicemen were stationed awaiting further orders.

There had been concern about the southern advance of the Japanese war machine which seemed unstoppable as it moved south through the Malay peninsula, the islands of the Dutch East Indies and into New Guinea. But the advance had been stopped and the Japanese were being pushed back to their own island nation. Danger of invasion was now far from the minds of the citizens of Australia. The papers were reporting battles in which the US and Australian forces were victorious and casualties decreasing. They were all looking forward to the end of it all when they could get back to their normal lives.

For the soldiers camped on the farm the prospect of being sent to face a strong, victorious force had diminished. If sent into battle it was more likely to be in what was termed mopping up operations. Danger still existed in these situations for many Japanese soldiers regarded defeat and capture as a disgrace and would rather die fighting than submit to the enemy. The soldiers in this rural camp understood that their armed service future was becoming brighter and less frightening.

Fear, although mostly dormant, still existed, and the boredom and homesickness in all the camps would often bring it to the fore. It was important for camp morale that this be kept in check. The camp officers were aware that the minds of the soldiers should be kept away from negativity. Practice-shooting every day could not do this. Nor could drilling on the grassy slope.

Young Glen, Henry's youngest son, was trying to shoot sparrows with his shanghai and not having much success. They stayed high in the tree which made it difficult to get a good, clean shot at them. He was now in a drain looking for small stones to be used as ammunition when he was approached by a couple of officers from the army camp.

They smiled down at him. 'What ya doing, Son?'

Glen replied, 'I'm finding some nice smooth stones for my shanghai.'

'That's a formidable weapon you have there. Do you plan to come with us when we go off to fight the Japs?'

'No, Sir, I'm trying to get a few sparrows, but haven't hit any yet. Anyway, my father says that you will probably be going home soon and not going to fight. We've already beaten the Japs.'

'I hope your dad is right. But we would like to talk to him. Do you know where he is?'

'I think he's down in the hay shed sharpening the chaff-cutter blades. Do you want me to show you?'

'No, Son,' said the captain, 'you stay here and frighten the sparrows.'

With that they made their way down to the hay shed to speak to Henry. They found him, as his son suggested, busily filing the blades of the chaff-cutter.

'Hi, there,' they called out from the doorway to the shed.

Henry stopped work and looked around to be surprised by the two uniformed officers. 'Come on in,' he said as he waved them in with his file.

'Can we interrupt you and talk to you about a few things?' asked the Major.

'Sure,' replied Henry. 'You won't find a farmer around here who is not willing to stop work for a while and have a yarn. Have a seat on that bag of chaff there.'

'Thanks,' and they chose not to sit on the bag of dusty chaff. 'We really want to ask a favour of you.'

'Don't know how I could help the American army. But what's the problem?'

'As you have probably seen, most of the soldiers here are still only boys, nineteen or twenty years old. They've been away from home for months now, some even longer, and they miss their home. Don't we all! Some of them are country lads and they miss their farm life back home.'

'I can understand that,' agreed Henry.

Then the Captain took up the request. 'We've heard how some have said that they would like to...' But here he had to stop talking for no way could he be heard. The noise from the five P-39 fighter planes screaming up the valley made conversation impossible. Most of the families in the district had gradually become used to the noise of war planes on training runs. The planes usually came from the air-force base at Mt Tarampa, a mere twenty miles away from Henry's farm.

'I doubt I'll ever get used to that noise,' commented Henry when it was possible to be heard once again. 'And it still disturbs the horses. But as you were saying?'

'Yes,' continued the Captain. 'Some of the fellows have said how they would like to help you with some of your farm work. They mentioned milking and feeding the pigs. Apparently, some do know how to milk a cow. They are generally good kids, wouldn't get in your road and it might help with their homesickness.'

'I can't see any problem with that,' replied Henry. 'Those extra hands could be a great help. Let my wife off milking now and then. But I would need to know how many and when they were coming. I don't want your soldiers running around my farm doing goodness knows what.'

'No problem there, Sir,' reassured the Major. 'We run a pretty tight ship and the men here must keep within the designated area unless allowed out with special permission. I will organise one of my corporal to liaise with you. If it is not working out for you, all you have to do is to tell him and we will discontinue the whole idea.'

'That sounds good,' agreed Henry. 'So I'll wait till I hear from a corporal of yours?'

'Yes, and thank you for your understanding and you consent,' replied the Major. Then with a half salute they left Henry to continue sharpening the chaff-cutter blades.

A week later, neighbour Otto Krenske wandered down at milking time to borrow a crow bar. He was very surprised at what he saw in Henry's milking bails. Half a dozen singing and laughing Americans seemed to be having the time of their lives. And the cows were being expertly milked as well.

'What on earth is happening here?' Otto wanted to know.

Henry explained the arrangement and how so far it had been working out so well. 'They have proven to be a great help,' Henry explained. 'You know, last night Aggie and I were talking about that article in yesterday's QT. The one on how the armies in Europe are causing so much damage. Here it is the exact opposite. For us anyway there are being a great help.'

'But how long will it last?' asked Otto.

'That's the problem. One day we'll wake up and see the whole lot packing up and pulling out. And when you think about it, that won't be so bad either. It will be good to get back to ordinary times again.'

'That's what I think too,' agreed Otto. 'But enjoy the help

while you got it. Don't suppose you could send a few up to my place as well?'

Four weeks later, events turned out just as Henry had supposed. The soldiers moved out. Within three days, what had been a camp for a company of soldiers was once again an open paddock. With the rain from a few summer storms the grass quickly returned, the cows had their grazing land back and only pleasant memories remained.

Chapter 17

Aber wie sah es da schon aus!

(But oh! What it looked like there!)

The foal was standing in front of the horse stables greeting them as they turned through the gate of their property. 'Welcome back home,' it seemed to be saying.

'Yes indeed,' agreed Franz. 'There is nothing like being at home. Coming home to where you belong is a very satisfying feeling.'

Already three hundred metres from home the foal had run from its mother and trotted ahead of the family. It knew where it was. At that point Franz had also commented, 'It's remarkable what horses seem to know. Here's this young fellow who knows exactly where he is and wants to be back home in his stable. But you know something, when we left Parwen and started back you could tell that the horses knew that they were heading back home. The tension of walking away from what was familiar had left them. There was a spring in their step and more purpose in their pulling.'

'I agree with you, Papa,' said Ruth. 'Way back there the mare seemed different as well. There was no need to lead her. She walked happily along as if she knew exactly where she was headed.'

'I always knew that on the farm the horses would know when their work was finished for the day and they were headed back to their stalls. I didn't know that this would happen from so far away. But now they are home. Now we are home again, thank the Good Lord! Let's unyoke the horses and see what's been happening here while we've been away. I hope it's not as bad as I feel It might be.'

This had been occupying Franz's mind ever since they left Parwen to head back to Rucken. How could his farm run itself for two weeks? He knew that it couldn't. The pastures would keep growing, yes. The grain crops would keep ripening. These were the least of his worries.

But the animals? How would they fare for being left without attention for two weeks? He was soon to find out.

How truthfully the English romantic poet, John Keates, wrote concerning autumn: *'Season of mists and mellow fruitfulness.'* Whereas he drew his inspiration from the English countryside, a poet wrapped in the bounty of a Memelland September would be impelled to express similar sentiments. Here in Franz's homeland the ripening, shimmery heat of summer makes way for the softer, oft clouded light of autumn. This light signals that the time of waiting for the harvest is over. The time of reaping is upon the land.

The fields are waiting for the sharp scythes. Small stacks of drying fodder are dotted over the green pasture fields. They are drying out completely and awaiting that time when they would be collected and carted to the haylofts to provide winter sustenance for animals. The yellow-brown paddocks of ripening grain contrast markedly with these green pastures creating a chequerboard pattern across the plains. Farmers are now able to reap the rewards of their long, hot, sweating days of labour and the generative warmth of the summer sun. Then comes the joy of the harvest time, often celebrated in harvest festivals and services of thanksgiving.

Even without its religious symbolism the old American gospel hymn illustrates the joy and satisfaction of concluding a job well done:

'*Bringing in the sheaves, bringing in the sheaves,*
We shall come rejoicing, bringing in the sheaves.'

Harvest joy did not await Franz and his family on their return to their farm in Rucken. Without their protection and guiding hands, the orderliness and routine which were features of the farm, and which maintained and encouraged its productiveness, decline, collapse and eventual ruin was inevitable. This road to ruination had begun when they first left the property and continued during the two weeks of their absence. The joy of returning was soon dampened by the reality of the farm's predicament.

The mournful lowing from the cattle stalls indicated that all was not well with the milking cows which had been left behind to fend for themselves. Lack of food and water was not a problem, for they had been left to roam free in the pasture. But as Franz was well aware, by leaving the cows unattended, the udders would become overfull and infected with mastitis when not being eased by daily milking. This had happened to three of the six milking cows left behind. The three which had calved earlier in the season were already producing less milk and so were less affected.

Franz had three sick cows, obviously suffering and running a high temperature. They would need urgent attention.

The three young heifers were showing no ill effects of being left to fend for themselves for two weeks. They did show their emotions at seeing the girls again. Being hand-raised, as they were on this small farm, they developed an affinity with the girls, a bond which would always remain.

The feathered fraternity fared less well than the heifers during the family's absence. No geese had been there to honk a welcome as was always their habit. Nor had they appeared since. One could only assume that they had been stolen. Of the flock of ten hens only two remained scratching under the elm trees. Old Hermie the drake came waddling up from the ditch where he apparently had spent most of his time. His charges were nowhere to be seen.

The fate of the poultry flock soon became obvious. There was a pile of decaying, severed heads amidst a scattering of bloody feathers beside a chopping block. Some of the local non-German people who had remained in the village, knowing that the family had fled had come and helped themselves to the defenceless poultry.

'Why would anyone do this? Why?' Edith was distressed.

'There are quite a number of Lithuanians here in the village who resent the German farmers being here,' explained Franz. 'This is their way of getting back at us. They have simply stolen the food that we were growing for ourselves. And they don't need to fear the Russian soldiers. The Germans are the Russians' enemy, not the local Lithuanians.'

'Maybe it was the army.'

'What, soldiers?' We know that the Russians haven't been here. And yes, that's what they would have done. I'm quite sure. They have left a trail of destruction wherever they have been. And our forces? I hope they would have more discipline than that. Surely our officers are still in control to stop that sort of behaviour,' replied her father.

'But we've seen small groups of German soldiers and even single ones in the last two weeks while we've been away. They didn't seem to have anyone in charge of them. They could probably do as they pleased,' Edith continued.

'That's true; but what's been done is done. We can do nothing about it.'

The pigsty had an even more gruesome tale to tell. The

two sows were down beside the ditch from where Hermie had emerged. But the six porkers which were ready for market? No sign of them. But in the sty, they soon found blood-stained straw and piles of pigs' entrails, rotting, stinking.

'Oh, what have we come back to?' began Helena, as they family was sitting at the supper table that evening. 'It's hard to believe the state of the farm outside. At least things are not so bad here in the house. Some items are missing — bedding, kitchen pans and the two good lounge chairs. But they haven't smashed everything up.'

'It's good we left the house unlocked, or else they would have forced their way in. Those who took what you say is missing probably planned to come back and keep taking what they could.' Franz was convinced that the people from the local village had been raiding the property. 'But we are back. That is the main thing. Tomorrow we will have to get to work and get the place back into order. The cows need attending to. The sheds will need to be cleaned out. And the grain will soon be ready to be harvested. I hope that the cattle have not trampled it down too much.'

Next morning revealed that Franz' hopes of undamaged grain fields were dashed. The field had suffered. So much of the upright rye stalks had been trampled down. Trodden by the random ramblings of cattle satisfying their hunger, free from the constraints of a farmer wanting to keep his crop intact. The pigs also had had free rein enjoying rooting in the fresh earth. The damage was not restricted to one particular area. No, the damage was distributed throughout the paddock as the cattle and pigs moved, as though restlessly, from one place to another.

'And it was such a good crop,' bemoaned Franz. 'The heads are really full. We will have to try to save as much as possible. I will scythe down as much as I can and bind up the sheaves. You girls can go up and down the rows where the stalks have been broken and snip off the heads of grain. In that way, we can still save a lot of the crop.'

And that was how the next few days were spent. From daylight to dark, Franz and his two daughters, as well as Helena for a considerable time after she had attended to the household work, were bent in the grain field. The crop had to be saved. This was a big part of their livelihood.

The sheaves were then taken into the barn to the thresher. After two weeks of solid toil, many bags of precious grain were ready to be taken to the railway station, from where they would be hauled to Heydekrug and sold to the grain merchants there.

Two weeks of very tiring work. Many bags of golden grain. All for nought.

Not one single bag of grain was taken to the station. No freight wagons were available to haul the grain to Heydekrug. There was no indication that any would arrive. Nothing could be done. It remained stacked in the barn.

The elation of returning home was dampened by these days of disappointment. Tired and dispirited the family contemplated their present situation and the future. Most of their neighbours also had returned from their abbreviated flight. They found themselves in similar situations. A few must have avoided the Nazi officials in East Prussia or chose to ignore their orders to return to their homes. Perhaps they were able to move quickly through East Prussia and were now somewhere in the heartland of Germany. Their farms remained abandoned and in disrepair.

Those who did return slowly dropped back into the routine of the pre-flight life. The first few weeks after the return had presented few opportunities to socialise and report on their movements into East Prussia. After the necessary urgent work was completed there was time to relax. Time to walk over to the neighbour and share a relaxing moment over a pipe. Experiences were generally the same. There were the hold-ups and frustrations. All experienced a general reluctance by the Nazi-appointed officials to give assistance. They shared the lessons learnt on how to travel and live in a wagon. All praised the friendliness of the common local people who were always ready to help where possible.

In all conversations, there were guarded statements of frustration on not really knowing the situation of the war, but a clear hope that it would soon be over and they would be left to get on with their lives. Guarded such statements must be, for there were still Nazi sympathisers around and often one didn't know who they were. A statement deemed to be contrary to the aims of the Government or not giving one's full support to the war effort could be seen as treason and land the unwary citizen in deep trouble.

But what would happen in the long run? Or indeed in the immediate future? Life must go on, but the people's whole existence was played out with the sword of Damocles refusing to disappear. The front north of Memel had been secured, and the advance of the Russians halted. But for how long? Then there were alarming reports filtering through from the east near Minsk. Sure this was five hundred kilometres away but should the German army be routed there, nothing would stop the Russians moving quickly towards Königsberg. East Prussia and the Memelland would be encircled by enemy forces intent on revenge and wreaking havoc on the German civilian population.

So the question remained. The question many had been asking for years. What can the citizens do when the powers that be have taken control and sent the country down the path of war? For Franz, his family and their friends and neighbours living in this far-flung corner of the German nation options were few. Now they could do little but continue working their farms, hoping for a peaceful future, but at the same time planning for the worst and preparing for a speedy evacuation.

Uncertainty lasted a mere three weeks. Then on Saturday, 7th October, 1944, came the orders: Flee. The Russians are coming.

Chapter 18

Am 7.10.44 kam wieder Befehl zu flüchten

(On 7.10.44 orders to flee came again.)

Oh, the frustration of it all. Oh, the uncertainty of it all. Two months ago, the Memellanders were told to leave for the Russians were advancing and they were in danger. The majority of the German nationals living there took this advice, packed what belongings they could, and fled over the Memel River to East Prussia. Most of these spent two uncomfortable, uncertain weeks struggling along crowded roads, not really knowing what they should be doing or where they should be going. Then they were told to return to their homes for the front had been secured. And according to the orders, they did return.

Franz and his family arrived back at their home to be confronted with a very heart-breaking scene. Seven weeks' of hard labour followed, trying to rescue their farm from further deterioration and to earn some much needed income. Their work had gone unrewarded.

Now to flee again was a heart-breaking prospect. Throughout the district it was met with a very down-hearted, and often critical, response. After having been misinformed and misled so many times before, their first reaction was to query whether there was any substance in this order to leave. Should they? Shouldn't they?

Helena put it bluntly. 'Can we believe the Gauleiter this time? Need we do what he says?'

'I can understand you concern here, I really can. Believe him? Obey him? I know both can be hard to do,' consoled Franz. 'This time, I believe, there is really no sensible alternative but to leave.'

'And if we do decide to stay?'

'Well, we probably wouldn't get into much trouble from Gauleiter Keller and his offsiders. I'm sure they would be well on their way by now. But I don't think we should really be thinking about staying. If the Russians have broken through our lines they will move down here very quickly and if they catch us here, the outcome would be too horrible to imagine.'

'Wouldn't they just take what they wanted from the farm and keep moving?'

'I hardly think so. You've heard, as well as I, the stories that have reached us from up north. I'm too old to be sent back to their labour camps so they would simply shoot me. And you women? I'd rather not think what would probably happen to you.'

'So we really have to pack and get ready to leave again? And now with winter soon here, I don't know how I will manage.'

'None of us want to leave again, I'm sure of that, but this time I think it's deadly serious; a matter of life or death. Knowing you, I'm sure you will soon be urging us to get a move on. Yes, I've no doubt we should go and not waste time about it. The sooner we leave the better. We'll start getting ready today. After the church service tomorrow, we will finish packing and be ready to leave early on Monday morning.'

And so began the heart-breaking task of preparing to leave once again the place which was dearly loved, which had always been home. There was the added sadness on this occasion for the rehearsal of two months prior had shown what would happen to their farm. Last time during their absence there was no invading force to do as they pleased but the remaining villagers seemed to have lost no time in raiding the abandoned farm.

Reports this time seemed to indicate that the advancing Russian forces were unlikely to be stopped before the Memel river. This would mean that all of Memelland, including their home village of Rucken, would be in the hands of the enemy to do with as they deemed fit.

It would be heart-wrenching to leave the animals as before; but what could be done? They could not all be taken. All the farmers were in a similar position. This was the result of war. Not only people suffered, but also the natural and cultural environment as well as the helpless members of the animal kingdom.

These were the topics to be heard in each group of worshippers before the church service began on Sunday morning. From where does one get the strength to leave one's past life with all its achievements, to face the uncertain future which would include possible destruction? To the people gathered in front of the red-brick church in Rucken their Christian faith was their answer.

In spite of imminent danger, further reports confirming the hopeless military situation to the north and the rapid advance of the Russian forces, the majority of the local residents postponed their flight until after the Sunday church service. Franz, Helena and the two girls left their loaded wagon in the shed and joined their friends and acquaintances at their local church. Beneath the sadness of the situation there was also the hope that sometime in the future they would once again be able to return to their homes and their friends.

Now they were all inside the church quietly sitting, meditating, praying and then listening to what would probably be Pastor Joneleit's last sermon to them. He did not mount the pulpit as was his normal practice when delivering an address, but stood in front of the altar, Bible in hand. He was united with his congregation in their perilous position. He began his address:

'It is not easy to know what to say to you on an occasion such as this. I think we all agree that the situation is very dire and to have a chance of saving our lives we must flee this area. The Gauleiter has stated that we are to leave and so we need to heed what he says.

'Also, we cannot ignore the reports that have been filtering through from the north and the east. German citizens who have been caught by the advancing Russian armies have been barbarically dealt with. It makes sense to flee even though last time it proved to be unnecessary. I have prayerfully considered my situation and have come to the conclusion that my staying here would serve no useful purpose. My flock, i.e. you my dear friends, will have hopefully all moved out towards safer areas, and I also have my wife and children to consider.

'My family and I will be moving early tomorrow. I pray that our dear God will stay very near to us in the troubled times ahead. We will flee putting our trust in God that he will watch over us and protect us. We trust that he will guide us to safe pastures. Trust in God. I believe that I am lead to leave you with that message, and the assurance which that message gives.

'Let's turn to the Psalms many of which, including this one, have been attributed to the great Israelite hero King David.
When I am afraid, I will trust in you.
In God, whose word I praise, In God I trust; I will not be afraid.
What can mortal man do to me? Ps. 56: 3-4.

'Our biblical scholars assure us that this Psalm refers to a situation in David's life before he was the powerful leader of

Israel. Indeed it was a situation similar to that in which we find ourselves in recent times. David was caught up in war. And savage, unforgiving war it was in those days too, if biblical records are to be fully believed.

'I shall not try to detail the political situation concerning Israel and her warring neighbours at this time other than to say that David found himself between a rock and a very hard place. There was bad blood between King Saul, Israel's king at this time, and David, who as you know was himself a proud Israelite. With his life in danger from King Saul, David and 600 of his followers and their families fled, and went to live in the land of the Philistines in a town called Ziklag. While they were living there they sided with and even fought with the Philistines. When, however, the Philistines were about to go into battle against Saul and the Israelites, David and his men were sent back home to Ziklag. They were told that they could not be trusted.

'Arriving back home they discovered that their village had been attacked and burnt and their families, including David's two wives had been carried off by the attacking Amelekites. Then his own men turned against him saying he should have stayed home in Ziklag rather than wanting to fight with the Philistines against King Saul and the Israelites.

'Yes, I agree; a confusing situation. Clear however that David was in danger from a number of sides. What was his reaction? What was he to do? The biblical record in 1st Samuel 30: 6 tells us that "David found strength in the Lord, his God". My sincere prayer is that you also will seek to find strength in our Lord and God. Various Psalms suggest how David achieved this. Our text for today says that he put his trust in God.

'We can do that by remembering the many blessings we have experienced in our lives. We readily accept that God must have been with us through those many happy times. At these times it is easy to see God's presence and acknowledge him for the care he has given us. We have also experienced sadder moments in the past. These have passed and we have seen God's hand in how they worked out. He did not forsake us in those testing moments. Nor will he abandon us now. We must trust him. We must be positive in our beliefs.

'In hurting times it is not always easy to accept the lot that has fallen to us. Perhaps we should think of Job's reply when his wife said to him, "Are you still holding on to your integrity? Curse God and die!" His reply was: "You are talking like a foolish woman. Shall we accept good from God and not trouble?" (Job 2: 9-10). Now I don't suggest that you should ever say that your wife is talking like a foolish woman but Job's response to his hardships bears remembering. Shall we accept good from God and not trouble?

'Good has come to us in the past and will come again. Bad has come to us in the past and now evil in upon us. We need to accept both. But through all — good times and bad — we believe that God will stay with us.

'Jesus says that we should call on him when in trouble and he will hear us and help us. Don't forget this. David's approach is recorded in another Psalm.

Because your love is better than life, my lips will glorify you.

I will praise you as long as I live, and in your name I will lift up my hands.

My soul will be satisfied as with the richest of foods;

with singing lips my mouth will praise you.   Psalm 63: 3-5

'Stay close to him with your prayers and your reading of his word. We have an ordeal ahead of us. Do not leave God out when facing this. Trust that in some way he will help you. And sure, this can cause a worry. It may not always be in the way that we envisage. But our faith tells us that he will help.

'It is this unshakeable trust in our Lord and God that we must take with us on our perilous journeys. We must pack our wagons or our bags with what we need. We must decide which road or pathway to take to lead us to safety. Throughout the journey there will be so much each of us will have to do to remain safe. Yes, there will be so much WE have to do. My encouragement is that whatever you do, wherever the fugitive's path may lead you take the Lord, our Saviour, with you.

'I shall let David, that Israelite hero who trusted firmly in God, have the last word:

My soul clings to you:
Your right hand upholds me. (Psalm 63: 8)

'Let us all stand and pray. Dear Lord, throughout our lives you have granted us many blessings. We thank you sincerely for all that you have done for us. Let us not be tempted to blame you for all the difficulties and dangers that have now come our way. We know that you will be with us and not allow more to come to us than we can bear with your help. Whatever the days ahead may bring, may we never stop praising your name and putting our trust in you. Amen.'

The whole congregation stood and echoed a loud amen. They remained standing to sing:

Lead thou me on, lead me my journey through, In weal and woe;
No other light, no guide but thee I know; With thee I'll go.
Cheer thou my heart; my faith and hope increase;
'Midst storm and strife, let all within be peace.

After the celebration of the Lord's Supper and the benediction the people filed solemnly from the church. There was a noticeable lack of the cheery conversation which usually would have been heard in the church yard. In its place were stern, set faces and teary goodbyes. The yard quickly emptied and the groups could be seen making their way to their homes.

Travelling slowly, walking slowly, reluctantly they were making their way towards the beginning of the inevitable.

Chapter 19

Unter vielen Strapatzen sind wir wieder bis zum Kreis Labiau gefahren.

(After a lot of effort we got to the Labiau shire again.)

It was mid-morning on Monday, and Franz and his family were ready to take leave of their home once again. The parting was much more difficult than that first time over two months before. This time they were leaving with a good idea of what would happen to the place in their absence.

How long would they have to be away? This was a question worrying all those who had to flee, but no one could really give an answer. Most assumed that when the war had passed through the region, when the danger from fighting forces had abated, it would be possible to return to their farms, to their village, to their homeland.

Most also realised that the war would not go on for much longer. News of German defeats, of enemy advances, the breakdown of transport infrastructure and the confusing information being given out by officials who appeared to be under severe stress were sure signs that Germany was losing the war. How much longer would Hitler and his advisers allow the country to struggle on? How long could this situation continue? This, no one could tell. All of the confusion translated into an inability for anyone to indicate how long the refugees would have to stay away from their homes.

Being Memellanders they were in an even worse predicament.

Prior to March, 1939, their homeland had been part of Lithuania for twenty years. For only the past five and a half years, they had been part of the German nation. If Germany were to lose the war — or as many were now beginning to say, 'When we lose the war' — their Memelland would certainly be given back to Lithuania. The tensions between the German nationals and the Lithuanians which were evident in the 1920s and 1930s would certainly return. That would be a price the people would have to pay to return to their homes.

They were living with many uncertainties that only time would resolve. All of these were adding to the stress which pressed heavily on the refugees.

Convinced that they had no option but to flee, this family of four worried people, three horses and a foal, a cow, a crate of three hens and a heavily loaded wagon slowly moved away from the small piece of the world that they had called home. When they were out of the house gate and the family caravan turned to the left.

'Why are we going this way, Papa? Wouldn't there be fewer people and much less traffic if we went on the back roads like last time?' Ruth wanted to know.

By turning left in front of their home they were heading the three kilometres towards the *Memeler Chaussee* (Memel Highway). This was the main artery that ran the length of the Memelland from Tilsit in the south to the main city and port of Memel in the north. It passed through the centre of the village of Rucken, past the church, the school and the few general shops located there. Many of the farmers lived along this road, but others like Franz were not clustered near it but lived on their farms a kilometre or two away. It was a village whose residents were more scattered than was typical in the area. Franz had decided to head to the centre of the village and travel down the *Memeler Chaussee* to Tilsit.

'I hope I'm doing the right thing,' he replied. 'I was, well, really still am, in two minds. It's mainly because I don't want to become bogged down on those back roads. They go through low, swampy areas in parts and they could be very wet. We've had quite a lot of rain in the past few weeks and at this time of year the water just stays put and doesn't evaporate. Get bogged there somewhere and there would be no one to pull us out. Remember what happened down at Parwen?'

'Yes,' joined in Helena, 'Papa and I spoke about it last night and decided that it would be safer going this way. The last thing we want this time is to be held up somewhere and not being able to move.'

They soon reached the train line and were stopped by an army vehicle parked across the road. There were German soldiers milling around it.

'You will have to wait,' explained an officious-sounding sergeant. 'We have to keep this crossing open for two trains which are coming through soon.'

'We certainly will keep back out of the way, but can't we get across first? That train is more than half a kilometre away,' noted Franz as he stood looking down the rail line.

'Sorry, but we have closed the crossing until the two trains have gone through.'

'Please,' pleaded Franz, 'our family has to keep moving. Surely you know how important it is for us to get away from here.'

All to no avail. The sergeant was unmoved. No one moved the army truck. They all sat and waited for a slow-moving train to approach.

And an alarming sight it made as it moved past them. The freight wagons contained a variety of heavy armaments — guns, tracked vehicles, covered trucks and light tanks. Crowded in among the vehicles were troops. These were not proud German fighting men. These were not soldiers singing heartily one of the many German military songs which they would have known, and indeed have sung before on many occasions.

Travelling south through the rail-crossing was a defeated army. Haggard, tired, unsmiling faces looked out over the countryside as the train chugged forward. No suggestive shouts to the two young girls standing beside the loaded farm wagon. No cheery waves to Franz or their comrades manning the crossing. Most were simply sitting with their heads in their hands, not looking up, depressed.

'What is happening? What do these trains really mean?' Franz asked the sergeant.

He became less stern and officious. 'Things are in a mess up around Memel. The main Russian force is moving on the port. Somehow this group became cut off and are now moving to Tilsit to set up another defence line there. That's what I imaging. But I really don't know.'

'God help us,' managed Franz before the sergeant continued. 'I was ordered to come here and ensure that two trains were able to move through without any delays. I should think the other one will be following close behind this one.'

'You're right, thank goodness. I can see it coming now. So it won't be long and we can be on our way.'

'Sure,' replied the soldier. 'As soon as it has passed through we will be out of here and you will be free to keep moving. And the best of luck, because, by God, you will need it when you get out onto the main highway. Even in our army vehicle we had a devil of a time getting here.'

The second train, almost identical to the previous one carrying similar-looking equipment and pensive, defeated soldiers slowly made its way south towards Tilsit. Once passed, the rail crossing detachment quickly jumped into their vehicle and headed back towards the village.

'This had not been a very good start to our journey,' remarked Helena as they were moving off again. 'But I suppose almost everything is out of our control. We can only do our best in whatever problem we run into.'

'Yes,' said Franz, 'but isn't it so very typical of our German army. Not allowing us to cross. It was obvious that we had plenty of time to get over the line before that slow-moving train came through. So often they put orders before common sense.'

'But it seems that the danger to us and everyone here is very real this time,' said Helena, obviously realising the significance of what they had just witnessed.

'Yes, it is very worrying. Losing Memel would be a severe blow. But it appears as thought that is what is happening. Then the Russians will be able to move down to here without very much resistance.'

The port of Memel had been developed over the last four years as an important naval base. It was the far north-eastern outpost of the German Empire. It had become the centre for German naval operations in the Gulf of Finland. Throughout its history it had experienced the destruction of war. It had been sacked and burnt by invading armies on a number of occasions. It appeared that another such episode was about to be enacted. Franz and his family could now only imagine the terror, suffering and death of the inhabitants there as they tried to escape the clutches of the Russians. They would be fleeing as bombs and artillery shells systematically destroyed their city. And all this would be happening in the face of the brave but hopeless efforts of the German forces caught there and ordered to defend the city.

Ruth brought the thinking nearer to home and family when she asked, 'Will we stop to see whether Aunt Therese and Katie are still there?'

'Of course,' answered her father, 'although I understand that they were going to leave immediately after church yesterday.'

They stopped on the road and Franz and Ruth walked into Therese's farmstead. Like their own place, it was abandoned as they expected. Cattle stalls, horse stables and pig pens were all left wide open. No one was in the home. They could only assume that they had left and were on the road somewhere ahead of them. Carefully closing the road-gate behind them, they soon were moving again towards the *Memeler Chaussee*, hoping that their worst fears of an overcrowded highway would not be realised.

But they were. At the intersection to this main road they were met with a solid wall of fleeing refugees. It now appeared probable that after travelling for the whole day they would barely be out of their own village.

The *Memeler Chaussee* was the only direct road running through the Memelland from north to south. In normal times, it was very adequate to cater for traffic moving between the two large towns of Memel and Tilsit or the number of intermediate towns. In this time of crisis, it was totally inadequate. Indeed, what road wouldn't be? Tens of thousands of Memellanders were now fleeing to cross the Memel river at Tilsit. This was the road leading to that crossing point. With their bicycles, cars and trucks, wagons and handcarts, on horseback or on foot they were all squeezing along the road.

Added to this immobile confusion were the sundry military vehicles which were also endeavouring the cross the Memel river at Tilsit. They should have right of way but that was often physically impossible.

Franz with his wagon, horses, cow and family joined this crush. Progress was frustratingly slow. Impatience, as many soon found out, did not help.

The day moved on. Mid-October and the evening was

beginning to close in earlier than in the long summer days which are experienced in these latitudes. At four o'clock the sun was already disappearing below the fir forests. There was a noticeable coolness settling over the land. Will winter arrive earlier this year?

'Are we going to stop somewhere for the night?' Edith wanted to know.

'Stop. Where? How? No, Edith I don't think it would be wise to break off from this slow-moving mass. We must keep going,' her father replied. 'If we make it to Pogegen during the night we might see if we can find a place somewhere to rest for a while, but here we must just keep going. The horses haven't had a hard day as yet, so they can keep going.'

'But how will we be able to see where we are going? Full moon was a week ago.' Ruth had entered the conversation from the back of the wagon. Sitting beside her, Edith started singing quietly, remembering the final hymn that the congregation had sung the day before: *'Lead Thou me on, Thou kindly heavenly light...'*

'Shush!' said Ruth looking at her sister. 'Papa had better not hear you singing that. He would be very upset.'

'OK. OK,' returned Edith leaving off singing and then speaking more loudly to her father. 'Papa, can't your horses see in the dark? You are always saying how clever they are.'

'Well, yes. You are right,' replied her father not reacting to Edith's mild sarcasm. 'I'll just let them have their own way. They will keep walking behind the wagon in front of them. When that stops they will stop. They won't get us into any trouble.'

And the column crawled forward. At times people pulling hand carts passed the slow-moving wagons and cars. But the slow wheels of fleeing did keep turning.

Darkness had descended over the countryside by the time they reached the town of Pogegen. No one chose to stop there.

The compact column kept creeping forward. The Memel river and the Königin Louise bridge over to Tilsit were only a few kilometres away and they all considered it important to get across that bridge. The retreating German army would have in mind to blow the bridge to halt the advancing Russians. When that happened the escape route for the refugees would be cut as well.

Press on. Keep moving. Don't stop. Get over that bridge.

After finally crossing the bridge Franz and his family arrived in a city which already seemed to be under siege. In the early hours of the morning, when darkness and cold still held sway, army vehicles and personnel were everywhere. Clearly the refugees would find no resting place here.

'Keep it moving! Move along there! No entry! Stay on the main road!' Orders and directions without ceasing kept the weary wanderers moving away from the river and out of the centre of the city.

'It's probably for our own safety,' suggested Franz. 'You never know when the city might be attacked and it would be tragic for a crowding mass of people to be shelled.'

'Will we be able to get to Otto's place and rest up there for a while?' asked Helena of her husband.

'It would be good if we could; but we will just have to wait and see if we are allowed off the main road near his place.'

When they finally arrived at his turn-off there was no sign of soldiers giving directions. Although in two minds — would it perhaps be better to keep moving rather than losing time here — Franz turned his horses out of the creeping column. They soon arrived at Otto's apartment building which was in total darkness as were all the others.

'We will ring his buzzer and see if we can rouse him,' said Franz making his way to the front of the house.

He rang. No answer. He rang a second and a third time. Still no response.

Suddenly from across the road: 'What the hell's going on there. It's hard enough getting any sleep at the best of times. Who on earth are you?'

'We are trying to contact Otto, but he doesn't seem to be answering.'

'Oh, it's you from the Memelland. Seems ages since you and your caravan were here last time. My boy still remembers how he found your prize horses.'

'So have you seen Otto around?' Franz wanted to know.

'No. They left a few days ago. Said he wasn't waiting around to be shot up by some Russian peasant. We haven't been told to evacuate yet, but that didn't seem to worry Otto. I'll leave you to it and try to get back to sleep.'

With that the voice disappeared into the dark apartment. Franz and his family prepared to have a short rest now that they were away from the pressing crowds. Come daylight and their trek would have to continue.

The icy north-east wind which blew down Otto's street into their faces next morning signalled the onset of a severe winter. October in these regions is normally cold heralding the coming of winter, but this wind, thought Franz, was colder than one would have expected. Under normal circumstances, living in their own homes, the people are prepared for the weather experienced at this time of year. The cold comes, the snow falls, the landscape freezes, vegetation becomes dormant and outside farming activities virtually cease.

Farm animals are herded into their indoor stalls. Here within these enclosed barns they are tended throughout the cold months. Food which has been grown and stored in the growing months is now readily available to satisfy the needs of all the farm animals.

There they stay till the warmth of spring beckons them to the freshly emerging pastures.

Farmers and their families likewise spend most of their time indoors, doing all those jobs which could be postponed until this time. This was the standard routine on a Memelland farm. All was geared to the seasonal cycle.

But now Franz and his family were not at home in the warmth and familiarity of their Memelland farmstead. They were out in the open with little protection from the harshness of the weather. They were on a refugee-clogged road living in a wagon with their few animals. An encroaching war and inclement weather now dictated their lives.

The distance from the enemy must be extended. The wheels must be kept rolling.

The horses — they alone provided the necessary power — had to be well fed and kept healthy. Already Franz could imagine the difficulties which lay ahead. When roads froze, when vegetation lay buried beneath layers of snow, when no stalls were available to shelter his horses and cow from freezing night time temperatures, how could they keep moving?

Now however as they moved out of Tilsit these extreme conditions were a future hurdle to be negotiated. How soon would they become a reality? Only time would tell, but the early signs were ominous. The east wind was very cold, but the light dusting of snow which had fallen in the early hours of the morning soon evaporated on the above zero road surface.

They moved slowly south-west on the main road out of Tilsit, on the road twice travelled only a few months previously. Slowly keep moving. Now however they could afford to stop occasionally. Stop where it was possible to cut some grass for the animals. The horses need to be kept healthy and strong. Franz knew that the heavily loaded wagon would soon extract its toll.

He realised that the horses had to be kept in good condition for his family's sake. As a man who loved his horses, he would suffer as well if the horses were allowed to.

And so his reaping hook was ready to attack any stand of available grass. But so had the many other reaping hooks and hungry horses that had already passed this way. This meant that Franz's horses' not Lilliputian appetites were seldom fully satisfied. Finding food for his hungry horses was fast becoming a major problem.

'You would think the local people would be happy to give us some fodder for our animals,' commented Ruth one day when passing another *No Fodder* sign in front of a farmstead.

Her father could see the farmer's point of view. 'I'm sure if there was just one refugee and his horses there would be no problem. But think about it. There are thousands of us. If they started, when would they stop? No, they have to look after their own stock first. I can understand why they have to put up those signs.'

'But what will happen to our horses? Will they be able to keep going?'

A worried Franz replied: 'We will just have to wait and see. We can only do the best we can.'

'Should we call in to that farmer in Parwen, where we had stopped last time? They were wonderful, friendly people,' Helena suggested as they were approaching Kreuzingen.

'I've been thinking about that,' replied Franz. 'It would probably be the right thing to do. As long as he understands that we are not there begging for food for the animals. And it would be an advantage to be off this main road.'

'Yes, and he might be able to give us a better idea of what is happening,' added Helena. 'The local people don't seem to be moving out yet. All the refugees we have met on the road have been from north of the Memel River.'

'That's true. From what I remember, he said that the local Gauleiter is a real Hitler man and doesn't believe we are being defeated. He is insisting that the local people stay put.'

Helena continued, 'Let's see what... What's his name? Friedrich, wasn't it? Yes, that was it. Let's see what Friedrich has to say.'

So at Kreuzingen they took the familiar road back to Parwen where they were staying on their first flight before the orders came to return home. Farmer Friedrich welcomed them in a cheerful manner. 'I was wondering if you would be coming this way again. We heard that the Memellanders had been told to move out. Been expecting you for the last few days. I had almost given up hope.'

'It's been slow going,' explained Franz. 'It was good to get off the main road and come over here.'

'Well, stay a while now that you are here. You look as though you should relax a little.' Farmer Friedrich was his cheerful self.

'Thank you kindly. We would certainly love to stay the night here but tomorrow we should keep moving.'

'I see your point,' agreed Friedrich. 'I think it is very wise to be as far west as possible. I hear that we have blown the bridge at Tilsit, but that won't hold the enemy up for very long. As you will see we are getting organised too, so that when the order is given we will move as soon as possible.'

'I can't imagine the crush on the roads when you East Prussians start moving. It will become impossible to move.'

'We will just have to face that problem when it comes. Anyway, your horses look hungry to me. Bring them in here so that we can give them a good feed. And have you been finding shelter for them at night? It's starting to be cold earlier this year.'

'No,' answered Franz, 'the locals haven't been so helpful.'

'Lousy buggers!' commented Friedrich. 'What are they saving

their fodder for? Another month at the most and we will all have to flee. And you won't be able to take a barn-full of fodder with you.'

That evening Franz's animals enjoyed a little bit of home comfort in Friedrich's barn. His family also spent a relaxing evening with these newly-acquired friends.

Come morning, loaded with more provisions and food for the animals they set off once again. Franz was reminded of the boot-maker in Tilsit that his cousin Otto was telling him about. He had been giving away his stock to all who came into the shop. 'Rather give it away to fellow Germans than leave it for the Russians'. This was the same attitude adopted by Friedrich as he said, 'My pork would taste all the sweeter in my mouth knowing it would not be taken by the enemy.'

'Friedrich, my dear friend,' said Franz on departing next morning, 'I trust the good Lord will go with you when the time comes for you to leave here and flee. When this calamity is finally over it would be my earnest desire to meet up with you again. Aufwiedersehen.'

Chapter 20

Es war als ob der jüngste Tag angebrochen wäre.

(It was as though judgement day had arrived.)

'I've been thinking a lot about it and I find the whole situation difficult to understand,' Franz startled the others out of their individual anxieties. For the last half hour, they had been making their way towards the town of Labiau and during this time no one had spoken.

'What situation? What are you talking about?' Helena wanted to know. 'Friedrich's situation? Our situation? What?'

'No, this whole problem of the civilian population fleeing from the Russians. A few weeks ago, we were told we had to leave in a hurry. Now here we have the East Prussians not being given permission to go. Why hold these people back? Surely no one expects our army to hold the Russians on the other side of the Memel. And what about the main Russian force coming from the east near Minsk?'

'So what should be happening?' Ruth wanted to know.

'Well, it's about time people were left to make up their own minds and do what they think best rather than be ordered around by the authorities. We've had enough of that. Those who want to leave should be allowed to.'

'You can think what you like, but nothing is going to change. More importantly, what are we going to do now?' replied Helena. 'Should we just keep moving or should we go to some place where we can stay and then wait until we know for sure what is happening in the war?'

'Friedrich and I talked about this when we were there. He suggested we head for Wehlau on the Pregel river and wait there for a while. Then when things become a little clearer, we can either go to Königsberg and escape by boat or keep moving south if that is possible.'

'But what about the horses? How will they survive living in the open in this very cold weather without proper food?' Helena brought this up knowing that Franz would take his horses into account.

'I really don't know. We will soon have to find a place where they can get shelter and I will have to find food for them. It's becoming vital.'

And the winds swept over the flat countryside. Forested areas offered some protection from the biting winds but not from the cold. The cold seeped in everywhere. To make matters worse they were basically living on the road. Indoor shelter was seldom available and to date the only protection was that found in the lee-side shelter of the wagon. It was clear that they could not continue like this. They had to find some sheltered area where they could stay for a period.

They drove on, looking in vain for a solution. They had turned south and were now heading towards Wehlau as planned. The road took them into the small village of Gertlauken — a long strung out settlement still some kilometres north of Wehlau. The snow and sleet were blowing into the faces of the two horses wearily pulling the laden wagon. Franz was sitting on the front of the wagon fully exposed to the elements with the sodden reins in his hands and his head bowed low. The three women were huddled within the bowels of the cart combining their warmth for comfort. The cow and the mare were lead by ropes tied to the back of the wagon and the foal did not leave the side of its mother.

Franz stopped the horses whose heads immediately dropped lower in an attempt to ward off the cutting wind. He turned and spoke to the women.

'This can't go on. We must stop and find shelter.'

'Where are we Papa?' asked Ruth.

'A place called Gertlauken.'

'Gertlauken? A name with Gert in it must surely be a good sign.' The girls had doted on their brother.

'Whether it's a good sign or not, I don't know; but I'll go into the house here and ask if... wait a minute... That looks like a store at the cross roads up there ahead. We'll go there and I'll ask the shopkeeper. He'll know where I might be able to go to find some help.'

A short while later, Franz was brushing the snow off his clothing before entering the shop. The warmth struck him as he opened the door. A couple of local villagers were talking to the proprietor. They stopped talking and turned when they heard the shop door open. Three sets of eyes looked questioningly at Franz as he stood there.

'Good afternoon,' Franz meant his greeting to include all three.

'And good afternoon to you too,' the shopkeeper's reply included the greeting nodded by the other two men. He then continued, 'This is not a day to be outside.'

'You are right, my friend,' Franz replied, 'but there are many things we mere mortals cannot determine. Unfortunately, my wife and family are caught up in a number of them.'

'So where have you come from?' one of the local men joined in the conversation. Village locals could easily recognise refugees coming to their area.

'We left Rucken in the Memelland a month ago, but are just

about all in. We need to find shelter somewhere close by. I came in hoping you might know someone here who might be able to help us. My wife and two daughters have everything we need but the horses need shelter and food.'

'No, you can't keep moving in this weather,' agreed the shopkeeper as the two other men nodded in agreement. 'It would be suicide, and it's not going to get any better for a long time. But finding a place here to stay could be difficult. Many of the folk here work in the forest and only have small plots with a few animals. They just have enough stall space for their own and storing enough fodder is always a problem. I know that a few have taken in northern refugees already, but for others... I'm not sure. Fred, do you have any suggestions?' He directed this question to one of the local men.

'That's difficult,' the man replied. 'I know we want to help you unlucky ones who have had to leave everything but we have to make sure we get through the winter too.'

Franz was taken aback by this. Surely, he thought, they don't think they will not have to flee like the rest of us. But he did not risk saying anything which might create bad feelings. He was a visitor here and he wanted aid not an argument.

'Can we find a sheltered spot close by, where we would be a bit protected from this weather?' he ended up saying.

'Wait a minute,' spoke up the other local man who until now had not entered the conversation. 'What about old Anton Struppat? His place is over near the forest. It's fairly sheltered there. And I think he even had an open shed there that he doesn't use any more.'

'Yes, old Struppat would be a good bet,' the others agreed.

'Struppat?' said Franz, 'With a name like that I'd think I was still back with the Lithuanians in the Memelland. How can I reach him?'

The shopkeeper replied, 'Yes, there are a few Lithuanian people around here. Have been here for ages. The Pastor up at Laukischken still conducts a service in their language as well as the usual German one. Anton was in here earlier today. He might still be in the hotel across the road. He's always very partial to a good drop that would help warm him up.'

And the three locals laughed. What, thought Franz, was he getting himself and his family into. But he was desperate. He decided to search out Anton Struppat. He thanked the men very much, indicating that he would go across to the hotel and see if he could locate this man they mentioned. He opened the door to a blast of icy wind and left the others in the warmth of the shop.

He was there. He said he would be pleased to help Franz and his family, that he was about to head home and that he would show them the way.

He turned off the main road along which the village had developed and for a full kilometre and more lead them down a lane towards the forest. Here was his farmstead consisting of an old wooden farmhouse and a couple of other buildings. He directed them to one of these — not a large structure — which had a small interior and a lean-to fixture built in on two sides.

'It's not the Crown Prince's castle, but it will give you some shelter. The lean-to will give some protection for your wagon and horses. If you push the rubbish and wood to one side in the shed you should make enough room for yourselves.'

Franz and his family looked thankfully at the rather inadequate building which would prove to be their home for the next seven weeks.

Evening was closing in and Herr Struppat, a man of few words, bade them good evening and made his way over to his house.

'Tomorrow,' said Helena after he had gone, 'we shall try to make a home out of this abandoned shed.'

'Yes,' agreed Franz,' we must be thankful that we have found a place where we can rest for a while and perhaps find some shelter from this freezing wind.'

The family had sufficient provisions, there was wood available from the nearby forest and so under the circumstances they could exist reasonably comfortably. But for the horses the situation became desperate. Franz had great difficulty finding food for them. This lack of nourishment combined with the fact that they had to bear the cold in the open shed meant that they continually lost weight and became ill.

Shortly before Christmas Franz could stand this situation no longer and he sold his two draft horses and the foal to a local farmer. Only his favourite mare did he keep, not bearing to part with her. The horses now had a home to go to and someone to provide them with adequate feed, but it also meant that Franz and his family were without a means of transport. They and their wagon were isolated, lying off the main road near the forest.

And this posed a problem. Official decisions, recently broadcasted, made their situation even more perilous. Up until then, any refugee who did not have their own means of transport could be taken to safety by rail. Now this service was discontinued.

'Why did they stop taking refugees by train?' Franz asked Anton Struppat, his temporary landlord, one day when they were discussing the Government situation. 'Have they moved everyone already?'

'Who knows,' replied Anton, who proved to be someone sceptical of every official decision. 'Perhaps they think the front is safe and we are winning the war. Otherwise why would they still insist that all the Germans in East Prussia stay put.'

Franz was interested to know how his home area might be

faring so he asked, 'What about Tilsit? Do you know what is happening there?'

'You know that we have blown the bridge?'

Franz nodded.

'Well it seems as though we have been holding the city in spite of it being shelled to pieces. Hardly any buildings are still standing. And no, they haven't crossed the Memel yet. But it only a matter of time. I think the main danger will come from the east of here. That's where the main Russian forces are. Or so I've heard.'

'So what do you plan to do?' Franz asked Anton. 'With your Lithuanian background, it would be safe for you to stay here wouldn't it?'

'Safe! You've got to be kidding! Do you think the Russians would stand around waiting to see my birth certificate? No, me and the missus are getting ready to leave. As soon as the time comes we're out of here.'

As January wore on, with the weather becoming colder and colder, winds roaring, snow being blown around, similar conversations could be heard throughout East Prussia.

Then on Friday, 19th January, 1945, the orders came. East Prussians were to evacuate. Russian forces had broken through on two fronts and could not be contained. What was once a quiet, rural countryside, then more recently a restless, unsure homeland, was soon to become a deadly, blazing inferno.

Flee!

For the third time in the last half year Franz and his family had heard this ominous order. This time, as indeed was the case in Rucken on the previous occasion, it was a call not to be ignored. The importance of the order was soon emphasised by a short column of horse-drawn army wagons which made its way down the lane towards Anton's farmstead and the shelter of the forest. The wagon drivers were in a frantic state.

'Pack up! Move! The place is in turmoil. The Russians seem to be everywhere. They will be here by tomorrow. We are lucky to be alive. Have been shot at from the air and from the ground. You need to get out of here if you hope to survive.'

And so they rambled on. They were desperate. They could see their final fate closing in on them. The horses, too, were in a state of confusion. All were exhausted. Many were bleeding from wounds. Clearly some would not survive. A short while later, from the shelter of the forest, came the sound of gun fire. Some suffering horses were being put out of their pain — more victims of a merciless war. A few soldiers wandered back from the forest to impress on Franz once again the importance of packing and fleeing.

'No time to waste. Pack your wagon!'

'I understand how important it is. I really do. But we have no horses. We sold them a few weeks ago because we couldn't feed them. We thought then we could still be able to move out by train, but that has now stopped. Why couldn't I have waited?' Franz now realised the predicament they were in. 'Can you do something to help us?'

'We certainly won't leave you here if we can avoid it. We will arrange some help for you,' promised the soldiers. 'Be ready to move in the morning.'

And so began a long, cold night of packing; deciding what to take and what to leave behind. This was an agonising task for they knew that what was left behind would be gone forever. Anything useful would be taken by Russian soldiers and the rest probably burnt. Their main consideration now was to keep the wagon as light as possible. Anton Struppat, their host farmer, was also busily making ready to move. He, like hundreds of thousands of other East Prussians, would soon be experiencing the discomfort and danger of fleeing which had been the lot of the Memellanders for months now. It was a taxing night for everyone. Desperation had to ignore the sub-zero temperatures.

Saturday dawned clear and crisp. The long icicles, clinging to the guttering on the roof glittered and sparkled in the morning sunlight. Fresh snow which had fallen during the night covered the dark green branches of the fir trees behind which were sheltering the soldiers and their horses. Quiet and peace surrounded the farmstead.

True to their word the soldiers appeared with a couple of horses. They pulled Franz' wagon out to the main road. Here they gave him a horse with which to continue his journey. However only one was available for them; only one horse to pull them and their wagon along the road to safety. They were depressed by the sight which confronted them when they arrived at the main road. It was similar to that which they had seen when joining the *Memeler Chaussee* in Rucken two months ago. There was a crush of people and vehicles as far as the eye could see.

Then it began. Echoing through the crisp morning air came the sounds of war. The screaming of the fighter planes and the rattle of their guns. The booming of distant artillery and the whining of shells about to land and explode. The reverberating cracks of exploding shells. The shouting of frightened people. The crying of children. War was upon them. They were in the midst of it. Would an exploding shell have their names written on it? Would the bullets coming from above be aimed at them? All was frightening.

They dared not stop. They slowly crept forward, part of the crowded refugee column. They were caught up in a crush of people. They needed to move quickly, but they could not. They needed protection, but they had none. They needed to escape the advancing enemy. Many would not. The brave military horse was straining to keep the wagon moving. The missiles of death kept coming. Where would the bullets strike? Where would the shells land and explode? Fear trembled throughout the entire convoy.

They approached a slight rise in the road. The horse strained. He could not manage. Franz went beside him on the wagon pole and helped him pull. The three women pushed from behind. Then followed a short, sharp downhill slope. The single horse could not hold the wagon. Human help was again needed to stop the wagon careering into those in front. Four pairs of hands held the wagon back. Then came flat land again and the family could rest from their pulling and holding. But not the horse. He had to keep moving.

Two whole days and a night this continued until neither beast nor human could continue. What could now be done? The guns were sounding nearer. Their luck in dodging the aircraft bullets would not last. Should they sit, exhausted, and await that inevitable fate suffered by others overhauled by enemy forces with the taste of blood on their lips?

Their guardian angel appeared in the form of two German Tiger tanks which were crossing the fields to their left. Whether by luck or the keen sight of the tanks' lookout men who recognised that the family was in trouble, the two tanks stopped beside the immobile wagon.

'My friends, you cannot stay there. You will be dead within a few hours.' Then they assessed the situation. 'You need to come with us.'

'What?' called out Helena.

'Come with us, *Tante*. Get as much of your stuff as possible and climb up on the top of the tanks. At least we can keep you moving. Well for the time being.'

Fortuitously rescued from their perilous position the family was now once again heading towards Wehlau, holding fast to the few possessions that they took with them.

They had unyoked the horse from the abandoned wagon and left everything behind. It joined the long row of many other vehicles which had similarly been abandoned. No sentiment. No feeling of loss. This would come later. Now it was a struggle to escape. The shells kept coming but the tanks kept moving. Franz and Helena were sitting on the one and the girls were huddled together on the other grasping their few possessions. In times of peace this would be an adventure. In times of war it was desperation. Survival.

Conversation was difficult above the roar of the tank engine and so Franz and Helena had lapsed into an exhausted silence. They were awakened from their thoughts by a tank crew member who shouted into their ears, 'Hold on tight now, for we are about to go through a deep ditch. We don't want to lose you.'

He had hardly stopped shouting when the nose of the tank tipped precariously forward. Even being forewarned this was very alarming to the two passengers who had never before experienced tank travel. Then the rear end bumped down. This was followed by a clank and a cluttering and the nose of the vehicle swung sharply to the left. It stuttered and stopped. A torrent of abusive language reached their ears. Something had gone wrong.

Desperately wrong as they soon found out. The tank had broken one of its wheel chains which caused the stop. The second tank was close behind. It stopped briefly to check on its companion's damage. Its captain decided he had to keep moving.

'The girls,' cried Helena.

'Let them stay on their tank and go to safety,' said Franz.

'Oh Lord! Oh Lord! Help us. When is all this going to end?' Then Helena shouted as the other tank moved off. 'Contact Hamburg, and please God, be careful.'

Franz's farewell greeting was drowned out by an artillery shell which exploded nearby. Assessing the danger, the tank captain made a decision. 'You can't stay here near the tank. It's too dangerous. We have to stay and see if it can be quickly repaired, but you two must go.'

'But where? How?'

Luck arrived within a few minutes. It was an army truck heading for Königsberg.

'But the girls are heading in the other direction,' pleaded Helena. 'Can't we wait and go that way as well? We can't leave them by themselves.'

'No,' insisted the captain. 'You're lucky that this truck stopped to see if they could help. Grab this opportunity and leave while you can. Now take what you can and get into the truck and be on your way out of here. The truck won't wait forever. And the best of luck to the two of you. Stay safe!'

Chapter 21

Meine Frau hat so viel geweint, dass es nicht mehr zu anhören war.

(My wife cried so much that it became hard to stand it any longer.)

The steel Tiger tank kept rumbling along with the two girls huddled on the top, clutching each other with one arm while the other hand was clinging desperately onto the tank. Shells kept landing in the vicinity exploding in a shower of mud, slush and debris. Every so often there would be a louder explosion and the fire beneath a plume of black smoke would pinpoint the demise of another unlucky vehicle. The mass of people kept moving, leaving behind the death and destruction but aware that these scenes of horror would be continually repeated and accompany them until they escaped the clutches of the enemy. The flames which had reduced the girls' homeland to cinders were still smouldering in places but they had moved on and here in East Prussia flames lit by the same torches were reducing centuries of German endeavour to ashes.

'Ruth,' began Edith after the realisation of being separated from their parents began to sink in, and their parents' disabled tank faded from view, 'what are we going to do? We can't keep going by ourselves.'

'There is nothing we can do now but keep going. That is what they would have wanted. It's impossible to go back and join them now.'

'But we are only young girls. How will we cope in this mess? Oh, Ruth!' and Edith began sobbing.

Ruth put her arm more tightly around her younger sister and drew her close. 'We'll stick together and meet the problems as Papa would want us to.'

The Tiger tank continued edging its way along the crowded road. The girls had to close their eyes to try to detach themselves from the sorrow and hurt through which they were travelling. But even this was to no avail. The cold, hard steel of the tank, the loud explosions, the cries of agony and desperation could not be camouflaged.

'Ruth, I'm scared,' whimpered Edith.

'We all are, Edith. You, me, the soldiers, all those refugees. Everyone is scared,' consoled Ruth as she pulled her sister even closer.

'I don't want to die, Ruth.'

'No, Edith. None of us wants to die. Remember what the Pfarrer said in his last sermon to us? We must trust that God will keep us safe.'

'Yes, I remember, although it seems so long ago. But will he really keep us safe?'

'I can only hope and pray that he does. He has so far, hasn't he?' replied Ruth with an expression that seemed to indicate the end of that topic of conversation.

Suddenly Edith looked up, 'Ruth.'

'Yes? What is it now?' Ruth queried.

'Ruth, I need to pee.'

'I don't see how we can ask them to stop the tank here. You will have to hold on.'

'That's easy for you to say. But for how long?'

'Try not to think about it.'

They kept moving. The whole countryside kept moving,

being driven by terror. This was terror of something very real. The juggernaut from the east was reshaping the country. Twelve thousand years ago the glacial ice moving south from the Scandinavian Peninsular scraped the country in its path pushing great piles of material ahead of its relentless advance. When warmer times caused the ice to melt a changed landscape was revealed which developed into farmlands and forests, rails and roads, towns and villages. Now these were in the midst of upheaval.

A new glacial front, the Russian army, was pushing streams of human moraine ahead of it. Fleeing civilian populations and a retreating, defeated *Wehrmacht* were defenceless against this ice-cold adversary. The ice had previously at first filled the valleys, later overflowed to the hillsides, then covered the hill tops enveloping the entire countryside in its grasp. Now the overcrowded roads and rails spilled out over the farmlands, crowded through the villages and joined the hilly moraines of previous ages. Again, the entire countryside was affected.

When will this stop? When would someone call a halt to this desecration? These present-day streams of humanity are not rocky outcrops that are being ground to glacial flour.

The masses kept moving but the tank stopped and a head appeared from inside. 'We have to get off this road, for the shells are getting closer and closer. It won't be long before one gets us. We will be heading for that forested hill over there to the right to stop and reassess our situation.'

'But where are we?' Ruth wanted to know. 'And what's going to happen to us?'

'That's a good question and we will work that out later. Right now, the ride will become a little rough and bumpy so be sure to hang on tight. We don't want to lose you now.'

'A bit bumpy?' chipped in Edith. 'What do you call the last few hours?'

'Hang on there kid.' Then the head disappeared and the lid closed.

The bumping and lurching eventually brought them to the shelter and relative peacefulness of the wooded hillside. Soon all five crew members were surrounding their outside passengers. The Captain began explaining the situation. 'You have your problems and we also have our own. Let me explain. We were relying on fuel supplies to get us to Braunsberg. The fuel could not get through and so we now must head to this town called Preussish Eylau. We might be able to get there but then again we may not.'

'Can you still take us?' Ruth asked.

'Of course, as far as we can; but then you will have to keep going on your own.'

'What about the other tank which was carrying our parents?' Edith wanted to know. 'Do you know what has happened to it?'

'We have not been able to raise it, so we have no idea what has happened.'

'But Papa and Mama?' Edith sobbed.

'They are probably fine, but we just don't know.'

'Will you be able to find out?' Ruth asked.

'We will keep trying as long as we can, but if they couldn't get the tank moving they would have had to abandon it and make their way towards Königsberg.'

'And the Russian advance? Have our forces been able to stop it?' was Ruth's next question.

'No,' admitted the Captain. 'They are still advancing, quite quickly, and to be honest I don't believe we will be able to stop them. The enemy seems to be everywhere.'

'And you five?' Ruth and Edith were now personally involved in the hard reality of war.

'We are soldiers,' one of them replied. 'It is our duty to stay and fight. It could be hopeless but we have no choice.'

All this was disheartening news but the stop was a welcome break for the girls who had been huddled up on the back of a hard, freezing tank for hours. Here they had a chance to hop down, stretch their legs and see to their personal needs. The tank crew also was pleased to be able to emerge from their iron prison for a brief time. And it was only a very brief time for the Captain was well aware of the need to hasten.

'OK, let's see if we can get this growling Gertie and our two passengers down to Eylau.'

They had travelled a short one hundred metres towards their goal when a spluttering in the engine and a lessening of revs hinted at imminent trouble. Another hundred metres and the Tiger stalled.

Very quickly the Captain and his crew were out looking menacingly at their charge and wondering what to do. Assuming that help would be available some four kilometres away in Eylau the Captain quickly made his decision.

'Schmidt. Zimmermann. Take these two girls, hurry into the town and show them the way to the train station. Then go to the artillery barracks and get help.'

'Yes, Sir,' replied the blond-haired Zimmermann. 'What do you mean by help?'

'Help! For heaven's sake man, can't you see what we need? We're not looking for a pot of pea and ham soup.'

'My Oma would always make pea and ham soup when we visited her. I really like it,' commented Private Schmidt with a slight smile on the side of his face.

The Captain turned swiftly towards him but held back on the comment they were all expecting. Instead he relaxed and said, "Thank you, Schmidt. I'm sure we would all like to sit down with a plate of your Oma's pea and ham soup, but at the moment there are more pressing matters. The help we need now is more fuel and a mechanic.'

'Yes, Sir!'

'And be as quick as you can.'

'Yes, Sir!'

'And be sure to look after these young girls.'

'Yes, Sir!'

'Now don't just stand there repeating "Yes, Sir". Get a move on!'

'Yes, Sir!'

The four moved out with the two soldiers in front carrying the girls' meagre possessions and Ruth and Edith following closely behind. They walked through the trees unaware of the beauty of the snow which had settled on the branches and the occasional squirrel which darted in front of them. The men marched quickly and at times the girls had to jog to keep up. They had soon joined the throng of fleeing people. The soldiers used the authority which their uniforms commanded to move speedily through the crowd. All the time they kept up a flow of suggestions on how the two could continue without their help. One after the other they shot their ideas at them.

'You must push and shove, scratch and scream to make your way forward to the front of the queues. Forget your good manners if you want to see your parents again and not become frozen corpses on the roadside.'

'We are still in East Prussia where most inhabitants are German. After a while you will be travelling through areas where there are more and more Poles. Be careful there. They have no love for Germans — soldier or civilian.'

'Eat whenever and whatever you can. Take what you can. Don't be afraid to ask, to beg for food, if it's a matter of staying healthy. Many shops have been abandoned. If there is anything left that you may need, take it.'

And so they continued, one after the other.

'And here's another suggestion. You are two young girls travelling alone and people will soon realise this. You could become a prime target for the crooks. And they are there, German, Pole, Russian, whatever, it makes no difference. What you should try to do is to join up with someone or some family group whom you would feel safe with. That is, if they want you. There is always safety in numbers.'

Then Edith interrupted them, 'I have an idea. Why don't you two come with us to protect us?'

They stopped, turned around and looked at her. But she was smiling. 'I was only joking. I know you love your Tiger tank too much.'

They were entering the outskirts of the small town when a German officer suddenly appeared from behind a vehicle with a pistol in his hand. 'Halt! You two soldiers, halt. Stay where you are.'

They stopped. Everyone around them stopped and looked at what was happening. One could hear the word "deserters" being whispered. A roadside interrogation began in which the two tank crew members had to explain their being with refugees to a disbelieving officer. Even collaboration from Ruth and Edith did little to convince him of the soldiers' truthfulness. Eventually he said, 'Right. You say you're headed to the Artillery Barracks looking for help, I'll take you there and we will see if you have been telling me the truth.'

'And the girls?' Private Zimmermann bravely brought up. 'What about them? We promised our Captain that we would make sure that they got to the railway station safely.'

'Soldier, count it lucky that I am a father with teen-age

daughters, and I will overlook your subordination.' With that he addressed the girls. 'Some way down this street the station is on your left. You can't miss it.' Then he smiled grimly. 'It's that building surrounded by masses of people.'

As the two young soldiers were handing their belongings to them the officer continued, 'Now you two, into the vehicle. We'll go to the barracks and you two privates can show me just how truthful members of the Panzer Division are.'

Chapter 22

Wir fuhren in Richtung Königsberg weiter.

(We travelled on in the direction of Königsberg.)

Franz and Helena were huddled in the back of a covered German army vehicle slowly picking its way towards Königsberg. Initially, way back or so it seemed, at the beginning of August when they had fled their homeland for the first time, they had thought that they would travel to Königsberg. This was where Helena's son, Kurt, and his wife worked and lived. They had returned to Rucken before they got so far. Their present circumstances now dictated that they travel there. There were no other options available to them.

On this second flight, they dared not have any specific plans in mind. They had moved into the Labiau Shire and for the last two and a half months had been living near the forest beside the village of Gertlauken. They had stayed there knowing deep down that the day would come when they would eventually have to move further west as the Russians made progress.

That day had arrived in a barrage of artillery fire and aircraft bombardment. It was only by good luck that they were not hit by enemy fire and fate had determined their path to safety. They had been caught up in circumstances over which they had no real control. Now they were indeed heading towards East Prussia's major city and port.

Helena's mind was not on the beauty and culture this city had once to offer. She was leaning against Franz's shoulder sobbing.

189

'What will become of the girls? Oh, what on earth will happen to them?' she cried into her husband's comforting shoulder.

'We can only hope and pray that the good Lord will protect them and guide them to safety.'

'Can't we do anything? We shouldn't have left them go off on that other tank when ours broke down!'

'That's easy to say now, but we didn't know that ours would have to stay there. At least they got away from that gully safely. And we are lucky to be alive. If this truck had not stopped and picked us up goodness knows what may have happened to us. And I can't stop thinking about that tank crew. Did they get their tank mobile in time? Did they abandon it or did they wait until the enemy arrived and fought their last battle there? This was one of those little episodes in wartime that are never recorded. For those poor soldiers there, it was probably the end of their lives.'

The truck continued on its way to Königsberg in fits and starts. It passed abandoned vehicles of all descriptions. Standing there on the road and beside the road were loaded wagons, carts and trolleys of the refugees who, like Franz and his family, had left everything to give themselves a better chance of survival. Crates, cases and luggage containers lay strewn beside the road. Burnt-out army vehicles and artillery pieces remained useless. Bloated carcasses of horses and cattle appeared regularly as well as small groups of uncared for animals which were wandering aimlessly around. Every so often human forms, twisted, silent, grotesque, lay unburied, unattended.

The truck lurched past groups of soldiers who stood and gazed vacantly at it as it made its way in the opposite direction to that which they were going.

'Did you see those poor soldiers? Are they really soldiers?' Helena asked the man beside her who was nursing a blood-soaked arm.

'Yes, I think they realise that they probably have only a very short time to live. Against the Russian tanks which are approaching they will stand no chance. And they know that.'

'But Franz! Some look as old as you and others are just school children.'

'You are right, Helena. They don't want to be here, but they have no choice. The young ones are probably members of the Hitler Youth. They are now realizing that it was much more than just a game.'

'What about the old men?'

Her wounded companion replied. 'They look to be members of the *Volkssturm*. A few weeks ago, Nazi officers came through the villages here and forced every able-bodied man to become a member of this local defence force. If they didn't have a gun of their own they were given a weapon of some description and told to report immediately to one place or another. They were to help the army defend the homeland. They knew, their families and friends knew, that they were being sent to their deaths. But they could do nothing about it. Go, or suffer the consequences.'

Franz, an old veteran from the Great War of 1914-18 could imagine the inevitable. 'They're no soldiers. Look at their clothes. Look at their weapons. What chance do they have against tanks and an advancing army out for revenge! You are right Comrade, they are dead men walking.'

A saddening journey through confusion, despair and destruction finally brought Franz and his sobbing wife to the outskirts of the once beautiful city of Königsberg. The truck pulled up at the entrance of what was clearly a military establishment. The driver came around to the back of the truck.

'I'm afraid this is as far as I can take you two. I have to report here to the Haberberg Artillery Barracks. Civilians are not allowed in.'

'Where can we go now?' Helena looked to her husband who asked the truck driver. 'Is this the suburb of Haberberg then?'

'Well, almost. This is a large army area, but the suburb begins on the other side. See that church spire there? Well if you walk down this street, around the army area, you will eventually come to the church. That is the Haberberg Lutheran Church.'

'And the railway station and goods yards? Where are they from here?'

'If you want to go there you are lucky as well. Go to the church and turn left. You will soon come to the railway lines. Best of luck.'

He drove off through the guarded entrance to the barracks, leaving two anxious refugees and their few possessions standing on the side of the road.

Franz began, 'Well we can't keep standing here. I'm frozen through already and it will soon be dark. We'll freeze to death if we can't find some shelter somewhere. Come on, let's start walking. We'll head for the church.'

Slowly they made their way along the road bordering the barracks compound. They were not alone. Many other refugees were also moving along the same path. The temperature was well below zero and Franz's rheumatism in his back and legs was very painful. They must not stop at this time of day and in these temperatures. They had to keep moving. Eventually, darkness having already descended, they arrived at a glow coming from the church. What a welcome sight!

A fire was burning within the bombed-out church and a mass of people were moving about in the ghostly light. Franz and Helena were standing wondering what to do next when a man approached them.

'Hello. I'm Pfarrer Manfred Klein. We have been using our bombed-out church as a shelter for refugees who have been flooding into our city. You look completely exhausted. I hope we can help you in some way.'

'Thank you very much. I'm Franz Natalier and this is my wife Helena. We need somewhere to stay for the night.'

'It's a pleasure to meet you Mr and Mrs Natalier. This is certainly not the Grand Hotel but I hope we will find you something to eat and keep you warm for the night. Where have you walked from?'

'It's a long story. We were caught up in the fighting neat Tapiau and luckily an army truck brought us to the barracks here in Haberberg. The driver pointed out your church and we walked here from the main entrance.'

'What? He left you walk from the barracks? That was a bit cruel. But this is war-time, I suppose. And before that?'

'We had to leave our village in the Memelland at the beginning of October. We made our way down to a village called Gertlauken in the Labiau shire and spent the time there near the forest waiting to see what would happen.'

'From what I hear all hell broke out a few days ago. The Russians seem to be everywhere. This appears to be the beginning of the end. The only way out now seems to be by sea.'

'But if that's the case,' broke in Helena, 'what will happen to Ruth and Edith?'

'Ruth and Edith?' queried the pastor.

'They are our teen-aged daughters who were fleeing with us,' explained Franz. 'We were separated somewhere near Wehlau. We were travelling on a couple of big tanks. Ours broke a chain and we had to get on a truck which brought us up here. The girl's tank headed off towards Braunsberg. So we don't know at all where they might be.'

'Oh, dear! Pray God that they are OK and have reached safety, but at the moment we have no way of finding out. Now, let's look after you two and make you feel a little more comfortable. Some of our parishioners will get you something to eat and see that you are warm for the night.'

Their immediate needs taken care of, Franz and Helena tried to settle down for the night. They were physically tired as the last four days had been very strenuous — packing, loading the wagon, pushing it, pulling it, holding it back, walking from the barracks with their cases. All of this had its effect on these two elderly people.

The mental and psychological pressures had also been great. The uncertainty of whether they would be able to move out of their temporary quarters in Gertlauken was stressful. Travelling in a war zone with enemy aircraft overhead with artillery fire near and far and not knowing when a fatal shot would end their flight was very frightening. Finally, being separated from their daughters was the last straw. This was weighing heavily on their minds. Whereas Franz was able to control any outward expression of emotion, Helena was not. Silent sobbing, interspersed with uncontrollable outbursts made sleep hard to come by. Eventually sheer exhaustion won and they both drifted into an uneasy sleep.

Would Königsberg be their gateway to safety? Hundreds of thousands of other people besides Franz and Helena were hoping that it would be. They were now converging on the beautiful city by their many thousands. For centuries Königsberg had been the focus of many of the activities of East Prussia, and had become the major city with a population of around three-hundred and fifty thousand. It was a cosmopolitan city having the elements of all the various nationalities and religious beliefs which were an integral part of its development.

As was the case with many other cities in the region, Königsberg began as a fort built by the Teutonic Order of

Knights who moved into this area in the thirteenth century to bring Christianity. It was built at the mouth of the Pregel River which flowed into the northern end of the shallow waters of the Vistula Lagoon.

The port which grew up here became even more important when in 1903 an eight-metre-deep shipping canal was constructed from the Königsberg docks on the river to the Baltic coast at Pillau. Thus, large steamers were able to sail directly from Königsberg taking the grain, timber, flax and dairy products to the rest of the world. The wealth created by its economic activities enabled an educational and cultural life to thrive. Imposing public buildings were built, rich merchants and bankers had grand residences constructed and a thriving, beautiful city emerged.

Hundreds of cultural and historical buildings were scattered throughout the urban area, reminder of its past achievements. Prussian kings were crowned here. The Albertina University of Königsberg attracted not only students from the Prussian hinterland but also from Lithuania and Poland. Probably its most famous student, the philosopher Immanuel Kant spent his whole life here, his tomb situated beside the city cathedral.

As was the case with the other cities in the region, it had not remained untouched by conflict throughout its seven hundred years. In its early centuries, the Teutonic Knights established there were constantly being harassed by unfriendly forces. In the Seven Years' War (1756-1763) the city was occupied by Russian forces for four years. In the early nineteenth century Napoleon's French army reigned supreme in the area and during the Great War the city again knew Russian forces in its streets.

Now with World War II nearing its conclusion the city was experiencing enemy attacks as never before. There had been Russian air raids early in the war in 1941,'42 and '43. These raised some alarm but caused little damage and loss of life. In 1944 all of this changed. Under the orders of RAF Air Chief Marshall Harris of England, more than 170 Lancaster bombers attacked the city on the night of 26/27 August. The bombs however caused minor damage as they fell to the east of the city. On the night of 29/30 August almost two hundred Lancasters attacked once again. This time hundreds of tons of high explosive incendiary bombs fell on the heavily populated centre of the city. The city burned for days. Industries were disabled, warehouses burnt to the ground, whole residential suburbs destroyed and thousands of civilians killed. The cruelty of World War II had arrived in the city with a vengeance.

Now at the end of January, 1945, the powerful pincers of the Russian juggernaut were tightening their grip, intent on squeezing the city to annihilation. Franz and Helena had joined the hundreds of thousands of East Prussian German nationals who were seeking escape. This escape would have to be by the sea. No other possibility existed. Land routes were in Russian hands.

The night was cold. It was very cold. It was freezing. Königsberg has a January average low temperature of -4°C. In 1945 exceptionally low temperatures were being experienced throughout Europe, and Franz and Helena had to keep warm in a temperature approaching -30°C. The fire, the crowd of people, the decking of warm doonas made it possible to ward off the deep freeze. Sleep came uneasily, and then only in short bursts.

The night eventually passed and a cold, snowy day greeted the rested, but still weary refugees. Warm food worked magic in revitalising the lethargic bodies.

'Now what, Franz?' Helena wanted to know after they had organised themselves.

'We must first see if we can locate Theresa. They lived in

Haberberg, so someone here should be able to direct us to the street where she and Kurt lived,' replied her husband.

Helena's second son from her first marriage, Kurt, had worked in the railways in Königsberg. In June, he had married Franz's niece, Theresa — the daughter of his younger sister. They lived in Haberberg not far from the railway yards where Kurt worked. Then on the 30th August, barely two months after being married, he was killed during that devastating British air-raid which destroyed much of central Königsberg. His young wife was left devastated. She had contacted her family back in Rucken concerning what had occurred, but since then they had no contact with her.

'Yes, we must,' agreed Helena. 'They lived in an apartment in Moltke Street. Someone here might know where that is. Perhaps the Pastor will know.'

Some of the local helpers put their heads together and soon came up with an answer.

'Moltke Street? Yes, that's one of the streets up there a little way named after German military generals. Let's see, there's Bismark and Blücher. I think they're further along. Hippel. That's just a few streets up from here, and then after Hippel comes Moltke. It about four or five streets up from here.'

'Any idea whether there has been any bomb damage in that area?' Franz wanted to know. 'We had a son and daughter-in-law living there. Kurt, our son, was killed during the second bombing raid but we are unsure whether it was his house that was hit or his workplace. Or he may have been killed even somewhere else. His wife wasn't hurt but we haven't heard from her since she told us about Kurt's death.'

'There has been some damage around here, as you can see by the church, but the main damage was closer in around the centre of the city.'

'Well, we have to walk up there and check. See if we can discover what happened to Theresa. We can't leave without finding out about her, if at all possible.'

'I can see why you must,' said the Pastor. 'After all she is family. But be as quick as you can. There's no knowing when transport for refugees will stop. You will need to get to the port of Pillau as soon as you can. Leave your cases here. We will look after them for you. You will need to catch a train out to Pillau, and to get to the station you will have to come back past here. So you walk up this street and you will come to Moltke street. We will see you back here in a little while, then!'

Franz and Helena made their way along the wide *Ober Haberberg* Street and soon reached Moltke street, where Kurt and Theresa had been living. A couple of the housing blocks had been bombed out but theirs was still intact. Ringing on the bell received no response. Eventually a neighbour, who knew Theresa, could give them some information. Kurt had been killed coming home from working a night shift — burnt to death from the effect of an incendiary which had landed near him. His wife had trouble handling the situation. What could be expected? Being married only a few months and then having to identify the charred remains of your husband. She had remained in her apartment, for months, locked up, without seeing anyone, not wanting to accept any help.

A couple of weeks ago another neighbour saw her leaving with a suit-case. Where she was headed no one knows. That was a good example of what was happening here. The whole city had been torn apart. That's what the English bombing raids set out to achieve. Scare and terrorise the civilian population.

'Oh, the poor dear,' sobbed Helena. 'Kurt burnt to death here. Gert shot to death away in Poland. Our two girls. We don't know what has happened to them. And now poor Theresa, gone off ...to heaven knows where. When is this tragedy going to stop?'

'Thank you for your help,' said Franz to the women who had helped them. And then to his wife, 'Come, my dear, we can do nothing more here. We need to go back to the church, collect our bags and make our way to the railway station and try to get to Pillau.

Chapter 23

Die Töchter waren nach Thüringen hingekommen, während wir in Mecklenburg waren und wussten wir einer von andern nicht.

(The daughters had travelled to Thuringia whereas we were in Mecklenburg and neither knew anything about the others.)

The girls had no trouble locating the train station. During the long period of waiting and not knowing what might happen the comments heard around the station at Preussisch Eylau indicated the tension under which the refugees were fleeing:

'It seems as though they are waiting for the Russians to get here and take us away.' One old lady expressed an opinion probably held by many of those waiting for the next evacuation train.

'I don't think the Russians would bother taking us all away, Oma. Many of us they would bury right here.'

'From what I hear they do not bother burying anyone. They just leave them lie where they shoot them.'

'Does anyone know whether another train might arrive. We are all sitting here waiting but it could be for nothing.'

'It won't be long before one of those shells lands here at the station and blows all our chances away.'

'At least that will put us all out of our misery.'

Ruth and Edith were sitting squashed against the red brick wall of the railway station listening to this airing of despondency.

They had no wish to join in the public conversation. They had nothing to say. Each was isolated in her own thoughts. They had eaten the dry army rations which Schmidt and Zimmermann had given to them. Now there was nothing to do but sit and wait like everyone else, hoping that another train would indeed come. The sun had already set on this bleak January day and the deep cold was intensifying.

'Should we walk around and try to get a little warmer?' suggested Edith.

'Where could we walk?' was Ruth's reply. 'If we leave here we would lose this place and have no hope of pushing our way back here again. At least this mass of people helps to keep us from freezing.'

'We should pretend that we are two bears and hibernate for the winter.'

'You try to go to sleep if you want to.' Ruth was not really in the mood to start a discussion on the habits of bears. 'I will keep awake and make sure no one goes off with our stuff.'

After a few minutes with her eyes shut, Edith realised that going to sleep would be impossible. Shutting out the sight of the crowded railway station only made her think of her parents, where they might be and how she was missing them.

'Ruth.'

'What's wrong, Edith?'

'Who can Mama fuss over now that we are not with them? And who will listen to Papa's jokes?' asked Edith, sobbing.

This reminded Ruth very potently of the reality of their present situation. She also was close to tears. Then a murmuring and movement in the crowd caused them to stand up. Ruth stood up and leant over to help her sister as well. 'They think there's a train coming. Let's see if we can get a little closer to the track. Give me your bag.'

'We should stay behind those two in front of us,' whispered Edith. 'They look as though they could push their way through.'

Edith had just finished whispering when the woman in front, about whom she was talking, turned around and looked at the girls. 'Are you two young girls by yourselves?' she wanted to know.

'Yes,' they answered together.

'Good heavens. Why is that?'

Ruth went on to explain. 'We were travelling on two tanks and the one Papa and Mama were on broke down but ours kept going and brought us here. Our tank captain thinks our parents may be heading towards Königsberg, but we really don't know.'

'You poor dears. Here, you stick close to us and we will make sure you get on this train that's supposed to be coming.'

'Thank you,' managed both girls with a sigh of relief. They were expecting a few harsh words of admonition from the woman who probably heard what Edith said about them.

'Manfred!' the woman directed towards her husband. 'These two kids have lost their parents somewhere and are now by themselves. We are to make sure they get on this train.'

'Yes, my dear.' It was clear that this Manfred was used to being told what to do.

Eventually a train did pull in and despite the efforts of a few railway officials to maintain some order, people were scrambling onto the wagons before the train had stopped. Manfred and his wife Olga did not stand back either.

'Hey, you girls,' he yelled, 'hang on to my bag and don't let go.' With that he barged his way through the more hesitant individuals with the two girls dragging behind. A wagon had stopped in front of him, but it was impossible for the side to be lowered. He, following the lead of others, threw his bag and those of the girls onto the wagon and clambered up over the side. His wife, Ruth and Edith pushed and struggled to follow him.

'I see you must be fit farm girls the way you climbed up there,' commented Olga.

'Thank you so much,' commented Edith. 'Without you two we would never have been able to get on. Papa has always taught us to stand back and wait our turn. It is hard for us not to do that.'

'Standing back and waiting would do you no good in this situation,' said Manfred. 'Here it's everyone for himself. Now that we are on and have a place we can sit down and see what happens.'

To everyone's amazement, within an hour, the train was moving again. This lifted the spirits of those waiting patiently on the overcrowded wagons. At least they were now moving away from high danger, but to where? The passengers had no idea where they were headed. Most could only guess. Those with some knowledge of the geography of the area were making various suggestions but these ideas remained mere possibilities.

Then the official proposed route came drifting down the wagons. This train was headed for the city of Thorn on the Weichsel River, some two hundred kilometres away. All going well this should be reached by next morning., But with this plan came a number of provisos. These included such major issues as whether the Russians had made very quick advances and cut off the line. Or whether the Poles had disrupted the line running through Polish territory. Or whether the rail bridge over the Weichsel at Thorn would still be intact and not blown. Minor issues faded in comparison to these escape-halting probabilities.

For the girls, twelve hours of numbing cold, of aching discomfort and of personal inconvenience followed. All this was lessened to some extent by the hopeful fact that they were distancing themselves from capture and its consequences. Their chance meeting with Manfred and his wife, Olga, provided added comfort and assistance. Their main concern was that the train was distancing then further and further from their parents.

Their friends' help was appreciated especially during the days after arriving in Thorn. The rail bridge there was still operating and they were able to cross to the western side of the river. But they were still in Polish territory and although theoretically under German control, in practice the local non-German population was becoming ever more restless as it anticipated the defeat of their enemies. To the Poles the fleeing civilians from the eastern regions were the face of the enemy.

A week of frustration and disappointment followed. Days of physical and mental exhaustion. Hours of sitting on motionless trains. Kilometres of walking around bombed-out or blown bridges. Hunger, thirst, cold, agony. If it were not for the prodding, encouragement and physical help of a determined Manfred and his indefatigable wife, Olga, the girls would surely have faltered. But these two adopted parents gave them new strength when need, gave them food when they were hungry and gave them consolation when their thoughts turned to their parents. They gave them a purpose to struggle on.

At the end of this week they arrived at the city of Frankfurt on the Oder River. They were now less than one hundred kilometres from Berlin. They were in traditional German territory and surrounded by German people. But they could not consider themselves safe from the enemy still close on their heels.

Manfred brought up the topic of their future movement. 'You can't stay here. The Russian advance will sweep right through this area on their way to Berlin. To be caught up in the fighting would be fatal.'

'But where should we go? asked Ruth. 'Where do you and Olga plan to go?'

'Well, you would be foolish to head for Berlin. That is being bombed to pieces and you would still be on a war front.'

'No,' replied Ruth. ' I don't think we ever thought of going there. We realise the danger.'

'Ruth, should we try to get to Hamburg and find Mama's cousin there. We have his address,' suggested Edith.

'Yes, but Hamburg, like all the other big cities is being bombed and destroyed. It would be foolish to head for a big city. And we don't know whether he is still alive. He could have been killed in the bombing raids,' replied Ruth.

'Where do you and Olga plan to head for?' this time Edith asked the question.

'We had planned to go to Thuringia in the centre of Germany,' replied Olga. 'Manfred knew some people who lived there and we hope to be able to find them.'

'Yes,' came in Manfred. 'It should be safer there. There are no big industrial areas which would be targets for the enemy's bombs. And I think that our enemies coming from the west will reach there before the Russians. I am sure, whoever they might be — English, French or American — they would be treating the locals in a much more civilised manner.'

'Are the trains running that way?' asked Ruth.

'From here? I'm sure we will have no trouble in that regard. If you want to know my opinion, I think you should come with us to Thuringia. When things are over and the country settles down a little you will be able to contact you relation in Hamburg and find out what happened to your parents. Keep yourself safe for the time being.'

'But we've been enough of a burden for you two already,' protested Ruth. 'We can't just cause you more trouble.'

'Don't be ridiculous, child! It's you and Edith who have kept us going,' said Olga.

'Kept you going? How do you mean?' Ruth wanted to know.

'Well,' joined in Manfred, 'we had someone to worry about other then ourselves and that gave us an extra purpose to keep going.'

'That's a funny way of looking at it,' said Edith. 'Ruth, what shall we do?'

'I would certainly like to keep going with Manfred and Olga if it's okay with them. We can find a safe place down there and then contact Hamburg.'

'That's settled then,' concluded Manfred.

Chapter 24

Wir kamen mit einem Güterzug im kalten Viehwagen bei 28° Frost bis nach Pillau.

(We travelled on a goods train to Pillau in a cold cattle wagon, the temperature at -28°.)

It was cold. The evening spent within the sheltered confines of the church, the fire and warm doonas, had left a warmth around Franz and Helena. That warmth would not remain. Already on the walk up to Moltke Street to find out about Theresa the chill was starting to creep in through the outer layers of clothing. Now on returning to the church a cold, biting wind had sprung up. It was not a time when tired, ill-nourished people should be out in the elements.

But the flight must continue. It would be nothing but foolishness to remain in Königsberg longer than absolutely necessary. What escape routes from the city were available? Road transport through Russian-occupied territory was impossible. All rail lines leading west were in enemy hands. The only available way out was by sea. To have a chance of securing a place on a ship one had to get to the port where vessels could enter. Boats could not leave from the centre of the city. The wharves had been bombed and heavily damaged. At this time of year, the shipping canal was frozen and could not be navigated. The only vessels of any consequence which were evacuating refugees were at the outer port of Pillau. The refugees had to travel the 40 kilometres from the city to the port.

There was also an airfield across the shipping canal from Pillau — the Pillau-Neutief Air Field. It was heavily defended and planes were flying in and out from there. They were taking small numbers of refugees to Gdansk, as well as Denmark and Schleswig-Holstein. These were a privileged few.

Whereas the frozen Vistula Lagoon posed a barrier to the Russians for mounting an attack on the German forces which were entrenched on the spit, it also was a problem for those wanting to escape. In desperation, some had attempted to move across the frozen lagoon with their carts, baggage and wagons. Their attempts often met with disaster. The darkly clothed refugees with their belongings contrasted sharply with the white of the frozen water and presented clear targets for the merciless Russian fighter pilots who would strafe the defenceless columns. The slowly moving groups would soon be turned into stationary, blood-stained remains scattered across the ice. Many met their fate in this way.

In other circumstances the overloaded wagons proved too heavy for the ice, broke through and settled to the bottom with their cargo and often their passengers. The German army had marked out safe routes across the ice, but these were often not followed for fear of attack from the Russians.

An added danger was to become lost on the ice. Strangers to the area would attempt to cross the ice by night in an attempt to avoid enemy fire. They could become disorientated and end up far from their desired destination, often wandering back into the enemy's arms.

These were dangerous times with refugees having to battle extreme physical elements as well as the revenge-seeking enemy.

A rail line existed, linking Königsberg with the generally ice-free port of Pillau on the open coast. It travelled north of the Vistula Lagoon, past farming villages, through the coastal town of Fischhausen where it swung south along the northern section of the Vistula spit. This area was still controlled by the German army and the evacuation trains were kept running. This was by far the safest option to get the people closer to safety. In reality, it was the only option open to the older refugees with their cases.

After collecting their meagre belongings from the church, Franz and Helena were making their way to the main railway station and goods yard located to the south of the city centre. So were many others who were desperate to be transported around the coast to Pillau. Confusion awaited them near the imposing main station building. There was a disorganised mass of humanity. A detachment of soldiers was trying to maintain some semblance of order. They were finding it an impossible task.

Staying away from the main mass of people to avoid being trampled, Franz noticed three railway employees, recognisable by their uniform. They were making their way to the 'employees only' entry.

He approached them. 'Excuse me, would any of you have known Kurt Petrowsky who used to work at the rail yards here?'

'Kurt,' replied one of the men, 'yes, I knew him. He used to work in the goods yard but was then training to be a locomotive driver. He was killed in the air raid. Why do you ask?'

'This is his mother,' Franz replied, introducing Helena, 'and I am his step-father.'

'Our sincere sympathies for your loss. A number of our colleagues were killed that night. Kurt was a fine man. He got along well with everyone. He was from the Memelland wasn't he? Have you come down from there?'

'Yes, we have been on the road for over three months and now we are trying to get to the station to get a train out to Pillau. But it's not easy for us, as you can see.'

'Seeing that you are Kurt's folk, I'm sure we will be able to help you a little,' suggested one of the men. 'Come with us and we will be able to get you through this crowd more quickly than the soldiers there. They don't seem to know what they are doing. Here, give us your bags.'

'Thank you very much. You're sure it will be okay?'

'We'll work something out, don't worry. We all work in the goods yard, so we will be able to take you there. God, it's cold today!'

A visibly relieved Franz and Helena dutifully followed the three rail workers through the restricted gate where the guard was happy to let them through. They were taken to the lunch room.

'This will probably be the warmest place to stay until we see which trains will be running out to Pillau today. Hey, Helga,' this directed to one of the women behind the food counter, 'these are Kurt Petrowsky's parents. Look after them, won't you. We want to get them on the first train out to Pillau.'

How wonderful it was, within their nightmare, to be able to sit down in a warm room, on real chairs, at a real table, enjoying a hot drink and something to eat. Shut off from the outside terrors, they realised that there were still friendliness, help and people who had not lost their sense of civility. For two hours Franz and Helena waited in comfort. Then one of their helpers returned with some good news.

'There will be a train leaving here later this afternoon. The workers in the goods yards have been making up a train from the various wagons that have been stored here awaiting repairs. We are waiting for others to return from Pillau but there must be a hold-up somewhere and we haven't been told about it.'

'So we will be able to get on this train?'

'You sure will; but don't expect first class carriages. Some are open wagons and others are enclosed cattle crates. We will get you into one of the cattle crates. At least you will have some sort of protection in there. Better than the open wagons. But it will be cold. Freezing. Make sure you put on all the warm clothing you got.'

'Will you come back for us when it is ready?' an anxious Helena wanted to know.

'Yes, I will. All you have to do is wait here. And I'm sure Helga will find you something more to eat. It might be the last you get for a while.'

A few hours later they were taken to a goods train standing on a siding. They had barely clambered up into the covered cattle wagon when a mass of people flooded across the lines heading for the same train.

'Thank Goodness we are here already and not in that crowd. We would have been trampled to death.'

'Yes,' agreed Franz, 'but I think we are not in for a very comfortable train trip.'

The frantic crowd soon had the train over-crowded. Franz and Helena were pushed to one corner of the crate, but at least they were on the train. Many, many people had to remain standing on the lines. They would have to wait for the next train to arrive. Hopefully it would.

After a brief backwards and forwards stuttering, the train of human desperation and anxiety slowly moved towards the bridge over the Pregel. This was a vital train link between the north and south sides of Königsberg. It had been severely damaged during the August bombing raids but because of its importance had been repaired as a matter of priority. Unlike much of the city centre which had remained as bombed out skeletons the bridge was again operating.

Now as evening was fast approaching the over-laden train slowly moved across the bridge. The sorry remains of the city were in clear view. The passengers had little inducement to mourn the loss of the beautiful city or the lives of those lost on that night of terror. That would certainly remain indelibly imprinted on the memories of the city's inhabitants, but the refugees passing through were living their own nightmare.

The train made its way through the city and was soon travelling in a darkening landscape dusted with snow. Leafless trees stood out as lifeless silhouettes. This reflected the sombre mood of those huddled in the freezing, vile-smelling wagons. The slight relief in knowing that they were moving away from the front was countered by the knowledge that they were also moving away from their homeland. Few words were spoken. Each individual respected the private contemplation of those who had become physically close travelling companions.

Then suddenly the stillness of the winter twilight was broken by the screeching of an approaching plane. There was a loud burst of clattering as the Russian pilot strafed the train. As chance would have it, it was a right-angled attack and the potential for causalities was much less than had it been a longitudinal approach. Even so there was no doubt that a small number of refugees would not live to have a chance of escaping through Pillau. The many souls held their breath waiting for the next attack. They waited. Nothing happened. Winter stillness reigned once more.

The journey continued until it reached the town of Fischhausen at the northern end of the lagoon. Here the train would bend south to move down the spit to their destination. But it stopped. They waited.

'Oh, Franz, what on earth is happening? They can't keep us sitting out here in the freezing cold all night. We will freeze to death.'

'Patience, my dear,' consoled Franz. 'We must not lose heart now. Who knows why we have stopped. It's probably so congested at Pillau and we are waiting here for trains to come back.'

And they sank back into silence. The intense cold had seemingly numbed the brain which then lacked any enthusiasm to hold a conversation. And what was there to speak about?

A train whistle brought them back to reality and it became clear that Franz's suggestion was correct. They watched as a train passed them in the darkness heading back to Königsberg. It passed, but still there was no movement from their train.

Another wait. Another whistle and soon there appeared another train heading towards Königsberg.

Eventually a shudder, a sharp movement which caused the human mass to surge to the back of each wagon. Another shudder and the train started moving again towards Pillau. The last fifteen kilometres went through sandy dune country heavily defended by German soldiers.

Finally, the terminus at Pillau was reached. End of the line for this load of passengers. Like the ones before it, this train would now head back to Königsberg to collect more refugees. Transport would not stop until the inevitable defeat of the defenders of the city.

In the cold darkness, Franz and Helena joined the crush of humanity moving towards the docks.

Chapter 25

Von da mit einem kleinen Frachtdampfer.

(From there in a small freighter.)

H ere at the wharf in Pillau a unit from the Kriegsmarine (German navy) had been assigned to see to the orderly embarking of refugees on vessels when they became available. This unit was small, consisting mainly of trainee submariners, and the task gigantic for the refugee numbers were huge. Attempts to organise the frantic masses had at most times failed miserably.

To take all to safety was appearing to be well-nigh impossible. A priority schedule had been decided upon, but the young faces, even in a uniform of the State, failed to command the necessary authority required to enforce the schedule. Large signs had been erected to alert people to this procedure but they proved of little worth. For these refugees, there had been a change of attitude towards authority. For too long they had unquestioningly assented to its commands. The stakes were now too high for meek submission. Attempt at survival had become the prime motivation.

Pregnant women were given top priority. They were followed by mothers with young children, then children, wounded military personnel, older folk and lastly the other citizens. This all seemed logical and with smaller numbers could have worked satisfactorily. However, the situation was that thousands of people crowded on the wharf, each concerned mainly with his or her own life and those of their nearest. They fought for their places in the queues regardless of their priority ranking.

'What can be done Captain? Everything is getting really out of control. We've had too many deaths already.'

'Yes, we really need reinforcements, but with the state of the war as it is that is most unlikely. Fighting men are need elsewhere. We'll have to keep doing the best we can.'

'And how can we tell if the women are pregnant or not? Sure, with some it's very obvious, but for others you just have to take their word for it. If they are wearing a wedding ring and say they are pregnant how can we refuse their boarding the ships?'

'I even had one old Oma telling me she was pregnant. Mind you, she wasn't a slim lady,' added another young recruit. 'She insisted and kept pushing her way up the ramp. What could I do?'

'I would suggest you don't worry too much about cases like that. Just let them go whether you are sure or not. Don't forget, none of them wants to be caught by the Russians. The gentlest of people can change when they are caught up in a situation such as this.'

'And I saw a baby being thrown into the water,' contributed another young man.

'What? What on earth do you mean?'

'I'm sure it wasn't on purpose, but it did happen. It was on one of the smaller steamers. First the mother went aboard with her baby. Then she went to the side and threw the baby back to someone she knew on the wharf. This person would then pretend the baby was hers and so get on the boat this way. Apparently, it happens quite a lot. On this occasion, the woman was pushed off balance, lost her grip on the baby which ended up in the freezing water. No one was able to rescue it.'

'That just shows you how desperate the people are. They will go to all ends to get on the boats. Let's not judge them too harshly. Our job is to do all we can to help them.'

'And what about the wounded? That's causing a lot of problems as well.'

'Whether they are in the forces or not our doctor has to look at them and give an opinion. If the wound is minor they are allowed on board, but if the wound is serious and there is less hope of recovery, that person has to remain behind. There can be no exceptions. That ruling has come down from higher up. We are obliged to follow it to the letter.'

'That's pretty tough, isn't it, Captain? A chap fights for his country and then he's left behind to freeze to death.'

'I agree, sailor. It's a matter of space.'

And so the discussions continued in the Captain's temporary office. The men basically knew what they had to do, perhaps not always agreeing with everything, but they were trained to do their best.

Pillau, a small town of 12,000 people could not cope either. All buildings were occupied by refugees seeking shelter from the cold — schools, churches, naval barracks, warehouses, private homes. Food supplies had run out. The fabric of the town was breaking apart. Those who had succumbed to hunger, disease or the cold, were left piled in the cemetery, unburied.

Franz and Helena had spent the rest of a very uncomfortable night in a warehouse near the wharf. They had approached the building curious about the low thundering noise which was coming from inside.

'What on earth is that rumbling noise?' Helena wanted to know.

'No idea,' Franz was quick to reply.

Asking around those who had recently arrived on the same

train as they did, could deliver no satisfactory explanation. On entering the building, they soon discovered the reason for the strange noise. It was made by the thousands of people in the wooden-floored building stamping up and down trying to keep from freezing.

'I couldn't do that for very long,' Helena was quick to point out.

'Luckily those railway workers told us to put on as much clothing as we could. That should see us through to morning. Then hopefully the temperature will rise a little,' Franz replied as they moved to find a spare spot to put their belongings down. Then they sat down on their bags staying as close together as possible for warmth.

A long, cold, sleepless night becomes even longer as the temperature lowers, but a new day must follow. Morning eventually did arrive. Those on the wharf stared in amazement for looming through the sub-zero gloom enveloping the harbour was two-hundred metres of Nazi propaganda — the cruise liner *Robert Ley*.

A steward, immaculately dressed in black trousers and sparkling white jacket, rapped gently on a cabin door.

'Herr and Frau Schneider.'

'Yes, that's us.'

'The second sitting in the dining room will be available in five minutes.'

'Thank you very much. We'll get the children and make our way there straight away.'

With that, the steward walked briskly to the next cabin door to repeat his message to the guests there.

The Schneiders soon joined the eight hundred other passengers making their way to the dining room of this recently-built ship. The *Robert Ley*, together with her sister ship, the

Wilhelm Gustloff, were the pride and joy of a German organization called *Kraft durch Freude (KdF)* — strength through joy. The organisation was set up in the mid 1930s in an effort to combat growing disaffection among German workers. Trade Unions had been taken over by the State in 1933 and the Deutsche Arbeitsfront (DAF) had taken control. This body required increased output and complete dedication from the workers. As the leaders of DAF were seen by the rank and file as corrupt — growing rich on their subscriptions — discontent grew.

KdF provided sweeteners for the workers. A whole range of leisure activities was provided for them and their families. This included camps and holidays, outings to movies and the theatre, provision for sporting teams and gym training. All this and more was provided free.

Central in the program were the two ships. They were regarded as the first purpose-built pleasure cruise boats. Large passenger liners had existed, transporting paying customers between countries and continents. These however, were built purely for pleasure. The *Robert Ley* was named after the Nazi Head of the German Labour Front (DAF). He was a close friend of Hitler and in spite of the corruption he condoned, remained an important member of the Nazi hierarchy.

Mr and Mrs Schneider and their two children were some of the lucky ones who were selected to enjoy the colour and sun of the Mediterranean, a far cry from their worker's apartment in inner Essen. The blazing heat of the iron furnace was briefly forgotten in the friendly warmth of the Sicilian sun.

That was a week of happiness in 1936, eight years before.

War came and with it the disruption of the everyday life of the majority of European people. Who knows what fate awaited Mr and Mrs Schneider and their children after their Mediterranean cruise. Did they end their lives in the bombed-out debris of

Essen? War had also drastically altered the course once sailed by the *Robert Ley*. In 1939, she became a hospital ship. Its clients now were wounded soldiers being shipped back to Germany from Norway and the Baltic countries. The swimming pool was drained. The promenade deck largely unused and the sun deck abandoned. Pain had replaced pleasure.

Then followed a number of years tied up to a wharf acting as a floating dormitory for naval trainees. Now she, like Franz and Helena, was in Pillau. She was ready to be loaded with refugees like Franz and Helena. She would then take them to Kiel, to Hamburg, to wherever the authorities directed, to safety. It was ironic that a ship named after a staunch Nazi, someone who must share in the blame for the present predicament of the German people, should be undertaking humanitarian work.

The rosy rays of the January dawn which had momentarily highlighted the huge mass of the *Robert Ley*, had given way to the frozen mists of a winter's morning. The harbour scene at Pillau was one of sombre grey and dull white. The vessels were creating dark, ghostly passages as they pushed their way through the now ice-covered water. Their constant toing-and-froing compelled the freezing cold to relinquish its grip on the water. Ashore, the snow had lightened somewhat the dark mass of waiting refugees. The frozen stalactites hanging from the roof gutters threatened to impale unwary victims below. They were not glistening and sparkling with beauty as they would be in sunlight but were dull and foreboding — messengers of doom.

I looked, and there before me was a pale horse! Its rider was named Death, and Hades was following close behind him. They were given power over a fourth of the earth to kill by sword, famine and plague, and by the wild beasts of the earth (Revelation 6:8).

The pallor of death seemed to encompass this scene. But within all this there was the comforting sound of boats. Boats of all sizes and types had converged on the port to aid in the rescue, to ship the refugees out of the hands of the enemy. This was the Dunkirk of East Prussia.

There were tug-boats and fishing boats, passenger liners and cruise liners, torpedo boats and ice-breakers, coastal freighters and coal transporters. Each would take its turn to tie up at the wharf and be flooded with people. Members of the Kriegsmarine tried valiantly to stop the rush once a ship docked. It was an impossible as well as dangerous task. People were shoved into the ice waters to perish. Others were trampled underfoot. Children were separated from their parents. All this while from time to time enemy aircraft would swoop across the area shooting and bombing.

By mid-morning, Franz and Helena, whose ages had placed them high on the evacuation priority list, ended up on a small coastal freighter. The floor of the holds had been covered with straw which protected somewhat from the cold. They counted themselves lucky once again to be below deck, away from the icy blasts above. Many had to remain standing on the open deck, but even then, thankful to be off the land. Franz murmured a silent prayer of relief. Helena sobbed for her daughters.

A group of boats moved off together, accompanied by a couple of torpedo boats. Danger lurked on the waterways as well. Throughout the war large areas had been mined and the mines were still waiting, ready to attach themselves to a victim which came too close. There was the ever-present danger of being attacked by enemy submarines. Slow moving boats were easy prey for aircraft. Many escaped the icy chill of Pillau and the approaching Russian artillery to be drowned in the cold waters of the Baltic Sea.

Franz and Helena were again lucky. From Pillau they went via Gotenhafen to Swinemünde in Pomerania. But alas, the freighter could not dock there because the port had frozen and was closed. They were forced to return to Kolberg, a coastal town one hundred kilometres to the east of Swinemünde.

'Back to the east,' was Franz's reaction. 'Why couldn't we move further west, away from the Russians?'

Helena gave no response. In spite of her constant sobbing, she had drifted off into a fitful sleep. Franz was more alarmed with her condition than the direction their boat was headed. She had caught some sort of illness and even in the cold she was obviously running a temperature. But what to do? On the boat, nothing but comfort her. Perhaps when they eventually landed he could find some medical attention for her. They waited on the straw as the boat steamed eastward.

They finally sailed into the sheltered port of Kolberg. Not as far as they had hoped but still far from the shooting and bombardment of the eastern front. They had arrived there safely. Hungry and cold, but safe.

They, as well as the whole community, were soon reminded of the dangers descending on a nation becoming more and more defenceless against advancing, avenging armies. A few days after Franz and Helena had arrived in Kolberg the town was shaken by the news which arrived on another freighter which berthed there. The town was in turmoil. Sadness, disbelief and anger were widespread.

'How could anyone do something like that?'

'Why?'

'How could it happen? Didn't they have any protection?'

'Is our navy so helpless?'

'It can't be true. Ten thousand you say?'

'Oh, the stupidity of it all!'

These and similar comments were on the lips of all. They were heard on the streets, in the shops, in the factories, in the private homes throughout the city. The freighter, the harbinger of these strong emotions from the German citizens of Kolberg, had arrived with fifty survivors of the one-time cruise ship, *William Gustloff*, which had been torpedoed north-east of the city.

The *Wilhelm Gustloff* was the sister ship of the *Robert Ley*. She had been built in 1937 as a purpose-built cruise liner to provide periods of respite for German workers and their families. She, like the *Robert Ley*, had been named after a Nazi dignitary — in this case, the founder and president of the foreign branch of the Nazi party in Switzerland. Her history followed that of her sister ship. After serving the original purpose for a couple of years, she was taken over by the Kriegsmarine in 1939 to serve as a hospital ship. Following this, she was anchored, repainted naval grey, and served as a floating barracks in Gotenhafen. Then she took up duties to take refugees from the eastern areas to safety in the west.

On 30th of January 1945, she left Gotenhafen with an estimated 10,000 people on board. This number was made up of some Nazi personnel, officials and their families, naval trainees and civilian refugees including over 5,000 children.

The ship left Gotenhafen in convoy with the passenger ship *Hansa*, also carrying refugees and two torpedo boats as protection. A short time out the *Hansa* and one of the torpedo boats developed mechanical problems and the *Wilhelm Gustloff* continued alone. Her captain, apparently contrary to wiser orders, decided to take the ship further off-shore into deeper waters to avoid the possibility of hitting mines. There she was spotted by a Russian submarine. Three torpedos hit their target and in forty minutes the huge ship was lying on the floor of the Baltic Sea. The passengers, all except a fortunate 1200, were lost.

Only one life boat was able to be launched. The lowering mechanism of all the others failed to operate. They were frozen.

Survival in 4° water was impossible. At a time when ship carrying large numbers of refugees were being bombed and torpedoed, the sinking of the *Wilhelm Gustloff* represented the greatest loss of life in a single naval event.

Franz and Helena were caught up in the soaring emotions which were released when the news spread through the small city of Kolberg. As was their experience since leaving their home in Rucken, they were living at a time when some survive and others are less fortunate.

It soon became clear that Kolberg could not be their final destination. It had been declared a fortress city to be defended at all costs. This was no place for refugees. Reliable reports indicated that the Russian advances could not be stopped, and so it would be a matter of time before the front reached Kolberg. It would then be turned into a battlefield and suffer destruction. Eastern refugees were to be moved on as soon as arrangements could be made.

Chapter 26

Dann sind wir wieder im kalten Güterzug bis nach Neubrandenburg in Mecklenburg gefahren, wo wir ausgestiegen sind, weil meine Frau schon viele Tage krank war.

(Then we travelled to Neubrandenburg in Mecklenburg in a cold goods train again. Here we got off because my wife had been sick for a number of days.)

And the days in Kolberg dragged on. For the refugees, there was little that they could do. This meant long hours sitting, waiting, brooding, discussing, reminiscing, prognosticating, and worrying.

'But I can't go on, Franz.'

'You must, Helena,' urged Franz. 'We have come all this way, and we can't give up now. No way in the world should we stay here. The Russians will want to destroy Kolberg as soon as they can. They will be attacking all the German ports along the Baltic coast. It would be suicide to stay here, even if we were allowed to by the authorities.'

'I'm so tired. I can't seem to get to sleep. And when I do, I'm waking up all the time. And I'm so worried about the girls.' At this Helena burst into sobbing again.

'I know how you feel, my dear, but we have no way of finding out where they might be, or what might have happened to them.

I'm very concerned too; but worrying will not be able to help either them or us. Our only hope is to make sure we stay safe and keep going west.'

'But what if they were caught by the Russians? Oh, my poor girls!'

'You mustn't keep thinking the worst. We have come through everything quite well so far. OK, not so well, but we are still alive. Let's try to be positive about them too.'

But Helena could not be consoled. 'They are so young and they have never been outside of the Memelland. How will they know where they are going even if they are still fleeing?'

'They are not stupid, Helena, and they can ask people. There's two of them and they will stick together and help one another. They will be able to ask when they need help. Local people will be only too happy to help young girls fleeing from Russians. Our main job now is to think about ourselves. They will need us when we get to safety in the West as much as we want to have them back with us.'

'That's so easy for you to say.'

'But it's what we must do. As soon as we find somewhere safe to settle down away from the fighting and the Russians, we will contact your cousin in Hamburg. The girls will know to do that too. Until then, knowing the state of things in Germany at the moment, we really can't do anything.' Franz was trying to remain positive but firm in his idea of what they should be doing.

Helena was unconvinced that they should just be thinking about themselves and doing nothing which might help them find out about their two daughters.

'Well, I'm going to try,' stated Helena quite purposefully.

At this, Franz was taken aback. 'What on earth do you have in mind? What are you going to do here?'

'Well,' began Helena, 'we don't really know where they were

headed on that tank. That young Lieutenant said that they were to head for Braunsberg, but we don't know where they may have ended up. There were Russians everywhere and they may have had to change their route. The girls may have ended up coming here.'

'I hardly think so,' considered Franz. 'Even if they did head for the coast to try to get a ship to safety, there are lots of places before here where they would go.'

'Maybe, but I'm going to do something.'

'What for heaven's sake, can you do here? There's no place here taking the names of refugees who arrive.'

'Well, I'm going to ask around,' relied Helena resolutely.

'You're going to do what?' asked her astonished husband.

'I am going to go to the various places where they have housed refugees and ask if anyone has seen our girls. I'll ask those good people who dish out the soup. I'll go to the army kitchens. I'll ask the pastors in the churches. At least I'll be doing something. I just can't keep sitting here doing nothing.'

'I really admire you for wanting to do this, but do you really think that you will find them? If we knew that they were coming here, yes; but as it is, they could be anywhere in Germany or Poland. And what about you? You haven't been feeling very well, have you?'

'Oh, that's nothing. It's only a bit of a pain in the stomach. I'll soon get over that.'

'Really,' said a sceptical Franz. 'I've been watching you the last few days, and I think it's more than just a little pain in the stomach.'

'No, I'm okay, and this afternoon I'm going to go to that school back there along this road.'

'Well, seeing that you are so determined, I don't think that you should go by yourself. I'll see if I can find someone to look after our belongings so I can come with you.'

Later that day with maternal determination, Helena accompanied by a slightly reluctant Franz, left the shelter of the grain warehouse where they had found shelter. They walked some way up the street and entered the school complex which had become a refugee station. They immediately approached the local volunteers who had been handing out hot food to the cold and hungry refugees. To their queries concerning the girls, they received sympathy but no success.

'My eyes are on the ladle, the soup pot and the plate. Mostly I only have a fleeting glance of the person I am serving,' remarked one of the helpers. 'I would have trouble remembering any of the faces that have filed past me. Two young girls together? I certainly don't remember any two teenagers together by themselves.'

Other helpers nodded in agreement. That was the experience of all of them. Asking from room to room received similar responses. Uninterested eyes had become quite unobservant to the passing parade of despondent refugees. Without some extraordinary characteristic, a person became a small indistinguishable part of a crowd rather than an individual. The teacher who previously could hold the attention of, and entertain a motley group of fifty pupils, walks alone, unknown. The cheery shopkeeper who had a friendly word ready for each of his customers, now greets no one. The dedicated mother who had nurtured her four children to adulthood sits idly, staring into a vacuum. Personalities have been put aside. They have been stripped from the human being by the threat of doom. The teacher, the shopkeeper, the mother, stripped of their essence, are now simply faceless refugees.

Returning slowly to their quarters that afternoon, Franz and Helena looked back on an unsuccessful day. It yielded no information or clues as to where the girls might be.

'We must not be too disappointed,' commented Helena. 'After

all this was our first day and we came into contact with only a few hundred of the many thousands of refugees in the city.'

'Yes, I suppose you're right,' conceded Franz. 'And it did keep us occupied for the afternoon. Otherwise we would have been sitting feeling sorry for ourselves. And you are still feeling ill, aren't you?'

'I admit I'm a little tired now after walking all afternoon.'

'That's what I've been telling you. You must take it easy and look after yourself or you will get worse. Tomorrow I am going to find someone who can work out what is wrong with you and help you recover.'

At that moment, they met a group of about thirty people, loosely organized into three columns being escorted along the side of the road by four soldiers. They were not marching, merely ambling, and speaking a language that was clearly not German. Looking more closely, Helena noticed that they all had a patch with a 'P' fixed to the right-hand side of their clothing.

'Who are these people?' she wanted to know.

Before Franz could suggest an answer, a clue came from one of the German soldiers accompanying the group. 'Hey, Polski! Get a move on and keep up. I've got better things to do than to herd you lazy blighters around.'

'Oh, what a rude soldier. Why is he talking like that?' Helena was very upset by what she had heard.

'That's what war does to people, Helena,' replied Franz. 'If it's any consolation the man probably didn't understand a word he said. I think they must be a group of Polish forced labourers being taken back to their compound.'

'Prisoners of war, do you mean?'

'No, not prisoners of war. There's women there too. No, these would be Polish citizens who have been rounded up from where they lived to work here on the wharves and in the factories.'

'But, that is horrible! Do the German authorities here really allow that to happen?'

'Helena, my dear, it's the German authorities who do the organising. Back on the farm in Memelland we were kept away from things like this. We did not really know what was happening in other parts. I am sure that there is so much that we haven't been told about what is really going on in this war.'

'Look at how miserable and unhappy they look,' Helena couldn't get her mind away from these sad-looking Polish forced labourers.

'Unhappy! That's putting it mildly. Who wouldn't be unhappy? You are quietly going about your work in some Polish town when suddenly a German army truck pulls up and starts rounding up people to be taken away to slave camps. Here they have to work long hours — probably seven days a week — for little reward. Would that make anyone happy?'

'Can't they just leave and go back home?'

'You just saw a group. What do you think? How far do you think they would get? Hunted down in no time. No, it looks like they just can't wait to get back to the compound, lie down and rest for tomorrow. Running away would merely get them shot.'

'Franz,' sobbed Helena, 'how horrible everything has become. Is there nothing beautiful and cheering for us to look forward to?' Franz was a realist. He and his good friend from the neighbouring manor house back in Rucken had been at one in the condemnation of the National Socialists who had gained total control of Germany. They had drunk many a bottle of beer and skolled quite a few glasses of Hr Habedanck's premium schnapps while sitting condemning war and its repercussions.

There they lived in an area where racial tensions had been bubbling for decades. There were many, Germans and Lithuanians alike, who wanted nothing more than to live happily beside one another. But there were always those who were not content. They would exhibit varying degrees of prejudices towards one another.

Individuals and groups would set up a defensive wall around themselves, alienating themselves even more from one another. All this tended to set up situations which impacted on the humanity of their perceived opponents. In a situation such as this it was difficult to be fully human oneself while violating the humanity of others.

Prejudice and hatred result, and this takes away the joy of life. Franz and Helena were now experiencing the final outcome of racial prejudice and hatred — war; all consuming, total war.

'Happy?' Franz picked up on one of his favourite topics as they were approaching their shelter for the night. 'War brings no one happiness. Just look around us here. Are we happy? Is any refugee happy? Is anyone at all happy? We've lost practically everything. Two of our sons, our homeland and now our two girls are goodness knows where.'

At which point Helena began sobbing once again. She ran to the edge of the footpath and began coughing up. Franz regretted having mentioned the two girls and went over to comfort his wife who was obviously ill as well as being so upset about the two girls.

Her illness epitomised the condition of the society at that time. All elements of German society were fractured, restless, suffering, unhappy. The forced labour groups were clearly restless and bleeding. Since their city had been designated a Fortress City by the military powers, the local citizens could only envisage a gloomy future. They would have to leave before the advancing Russian and Polish forces bombarded their homes to pieces. The German soldiers also knew that defeat was imminent. That would mean death or capture; perhaps capture and then death.

The once pleasant Baltic resort town of Kolberg was now a centre of sadness and worry, of hatred and tension. The beach baskets which had lined the sandy shores of the Baltic were long forgotten. No longer could the laughter of children splashing in the cool waters of the Baltic on a hot summer's day be heard. The resort hotels had been taken over by military forces. The cafes on the market square had disappeared. The bells of the cathedral of St Marien were sombre. War had altered cities as well as citizens.

It was approaching the middle of February. The number of refugees entering the city kept rising, boosted both by those from the East who kept arriving on boats and German nationals from the surrounding districts who feared the advancing Russian army. The temperature however remained low. January is statistically the coldest month followed closely by February. February has an average minimum temperature of -2° and an average daily maximum of 3°. Now with the temperatures wavering around zero, Franz and Helena were told to go to the train station and be ready to move further west on the next train. This was headed for Schwerin.

There was no time for further enquiries about their daughters, no time to search out medical attention for Helena, when the opportunity to move came, it had to be taken. Now together with many others they boarded a train which would move them further into safety.

Deep cold had settled over Pomerania and the temperature remained below zero throughout the day. Even though they were huddled in the shelter of an enclosed wagon on the goods train the cold attacked from every direction. This discomfort was discounted somewhat by the thought that they were heading towards a city which would be beyond the Russian advances. Schwerin was well within the German heartland and if the rumours were to be believed, the Americans were advancing towards this area in Northern Germany. Franz and Helena hoped that they would find respite there.

The train moved at a steady pace through the towns and villages towards the large city of Stettin — Treptow, Greifenberg, Naugard, Gollnow. These were the names that Franz saw through the cracks in the goods wagon. They were names that he did not know, but names that were one by one, distancing them from the terror sweeping from the East. Who was to know what fate awaited these towns? It probably lay in the hands of the German High Command. If a defensive line was established near or in them then destruction would follow. If not, then the mood of the advancing Russian forces would determine their future.

And the train kept moving; through this landscape of black and white. Winter snow blanketed the open fields while villages and forests loomed dark in the distance. This rural winterland disappeared as the train moved into the town of Altdamm, across the Oder river from Stettin. Here it stopped. There had been intermittent stops on the journey from Kolberg but they had been of short duration. This time the train remained standing.

The passengers became restless. Shouting began. 'What's going on?' 'Why aren't we moving?'

Eventually rail officials walked the length of the train explaining the situation. 'Attention! Attention! There will be a delay of at least two hours due to circumstances ahead.'

'Circumstances. What sort of circumstances?' various individuals wanted to know.

'Everything should be rectified within two or three hours,' was the official reply. 'Anyone who wishes may alight from the train. Be ready to board again once it is announced.'

'Same as bloody always,' was a comment from Franz' travelling companion. 'Always ready to tell us what to do but never giving any explanation.'

'We'll just have to wait,' replied Franz, not committing himself to any rash statement to someone he did not know.

'Well, I'm off for a walk, and see if there is any food available on the platform. Anything I can get for you and your wife?'

'Thank you very much. You are most kind. I'm OK and my wife is not feeling too well.'

With that the man was gone and Franz left with his wife and his thoughts. Two hours sitting on the floor of a cold carriage with nothing to do passes very slowly. It passed even more slowly and more uncomfortably for Helena, in spite of Franz trying to comfort her. The third hour passed even more slowly, for it was three hours and more, before whistles were heard warning passengers to board the train to continue the journey.

Franz was a little ashamed of himself when their outspoken travelling companion returned with a large mug of hot soup which he offered to Helena. Such was the situation at this time, and for the previous years in Nazi Germany. Trust was forgotten and so often good intentions were left unrealised.

'Bless you,' were Helena's words of thanks.

The journey continued, without any information given them as to the cause of the holdup. Most realised, however, that with the war being lost, the transport infrastructure of their country was collapsing. They were simply happy to be on a train taking them to safety.

Their route went over the two main branches of the Oder river, passing to the south of the main city of Stettin. They were now heading towards the large regional centre of Neubrandenburg in the state of Mecklenburg.

Those torturous two hundred kilometres proved to be too much for Helena and she could not possibly stay on the train until they arrived at Schwerin. They had to leave the train when it stopped at the main station of Neubrandenburg. Shivering with cold, very fatigued and frequently bending over double with spasmodic stomach pains, Helena was helped from the train. Their newly found helper, who proved to be from Tilsit, carried the luggage. He accompanied them to the station's waiting room.

He left them with 'Good-bye, and may God go with you,' proving that there were still helpful, considerate people in Germany.

Chapter 27

Ende April mussten wir wieder bis Schwerin flüchten.

(At the end of April we had to flee again, to Schwerin.)

It was late on that cold February night when Franz and Helena found themselves in an unfamiliar town.

'Where are we, Franz?'

'This is Neubrandenburg.'

'Where?'

'Neubrandenburg. It's a town in the state of Mecklenburg. At least we are now getting into traditional Germany territory.'

'Will we be safe here?'

'For the time being; but for how long I really have no idea. But we have to stay here until you are completely recovered.'

'But what are we going to do now in this cold railway waiting room? It's as cold here as on that train.'

Franz was just looking around to see what they might do when help appeared in the form of a uniformed railway official. He clearly saw that the two worried-looking passengers who had alighted from the refugee train needed advice. He proved to be understanding and helpful, responding immediately to their need.

'What I suggest is that you stay here at the railway station tonight. Bring your stuff with me into the office where it is much warmer than here. There is something there for you to rest on for the night. In the morning, I will find someone to help you.'

Without any more ado the three of them moved from the chilly waiting room into the smaller, warmer office. Here was a couch on which Helena could settle down while Franz made himself comfortable in an armchair.

'You two stay here, and don't let anything, or anyone, bother you. There will be other trains of one sort or another coming through during the night so I hope the noise and goings-on won't bother you.'

'You are most kind. I hope our staying here is OK and won't get you into trouble.'

'Don't worry. In these times, anything goes.'

In the warmth of the office and the embracing comfort of the armchair and couch Franz and Helena were able to have much needed rest. For the first time in many weeks they were able to rest in peace. This peace was broken sooner than they would have really wanted. Already at an early hour next morning the station was alive with action. The helpful railway worker of the previous evening was nowhere to be seen and in his place there were a number of men moving in and out of the office, but paying no attention to their two half-awake guests. Outside was a scene of noise, shouting and bustling activity.

One of the officials stopped by Franz when he noticed that they were awake. 'Good morning. I'm Alfred. Martin from last night told me to look after you when you woke up this morning. How are you feeling after your night in Hotel Bahnhof?'

'Good morning. Franz Natalier, and this is my wife Helena. We are so grateful to you both, for Helena was very ill last night and had to get off the train which would have taken us to Schwerin. That's where we had planned to go.'

'Yes, Martin told me all about it this morning before he left. But first I'll find you something hot to warm you up inside. After that we will see what can be done to help your wife.'

'Thank you very much,' replied an appreciative Franz, 'but tell me, what's all that activity outside? Is this station always as busy as this?'

'It's just that a military train has arrived in. When that happens, we keep our distance and let them take over. They use a group from the prisoner-of-war camp to unload it. There is usually a lot of shouting of orders from the officers and slow-reluctant work being carried out by the men. But don't worry about them. Now let's see what we can get for you.'

With that he strode off whistling an indistinguishable tune. Franz relaxed for here, next to shouted orders and reluctant servility, there was a person seemingly unaffected by the consequences of war happy to break into his daily work routine to help someone in need. Surely this was an attitude a society should be seeking rather than the one on display only a few metres away.

Later, well rested in the softness of the armchair and fed by the generosity of Alfred, Franz was anxious to start finding help for his wife. An evening's rest on the warm couch had certainly improved her condition but she was still suffering and obviously in pain. Alfred then appeared with one of his co-workers.

'OK, then. Here's what I think we should do. St John's church is just a little way down the main street which runs from here. Heinz here says that they have a centre there which looks after refugees. We will take you both and your belongings down there and hand you over to the Pastor and his helpers. They will be in a better position to get medical attention for your wife than we are.'

'How can I ever thank you enough for all your kindness? We would be completely lost without someone like you. If they are anything like those we met in Königsberg I'm sure they will be able to help us. We are ready to go as soon as you are.'

'The Pastor and his helpers should be there by now, so let's make our way down to the church.'

They were moving towards the front entrance of the railway station when a loud 'Halt!' stopped them in their tracks. They turned to be confronted by two armed soldiers and a German officer who addressed the railway employees.

'Who are these two people and where are you taking them? This area is to remain secure when we are operating here.'

'Yes, Captain, I know all about that. This lady, who is very ill and her husband are refugees from the East. They had to get off the train going through to Schwerin last night. She must now be taken to receive medical attention.'

'That might be the case but you still need my permission.'

'That is the case, Captain. Can't you see that she is suffering? Her only interest now is to get to some help as soon as possible. So do I now have your permission?'

'One day, Sir, you will push me too far. At the present time, I have more important matters to attend to than spend time on you. Now move on. Take those two out of here before I change my mind!'

The four then moved out of the building into the square in front of the station. Looking forward they could already see the tall spire in the centre of the red brick church of St John.

'What was that all about?' Franz wanted to know when they were well out of earshot. 'Why were those soldiers so officious?'

'That's mainly because they are in charge of that work group from the prisoner-of-war camp which we have here in Neubrandenburg. Now with things going so badly for our German forces the prisoners are becoming more and more hard to control. The soldiers on guard are always on edge.'

'So all those men doing the work were prisoners of war?'

'Yes. It is a very large camp with thousands of prisoners who are scattered all over the countryside around here. It seems they know how the war is faring. I bet they are listening to their hidden radios as much as possible these days.'

They walked past a parkland area and the town's medieval wall, before arriving at the church. As Alfred and Heinz had suspected, there was already activity at the church. They delivered their two souls to the help centre, wished them all the best and headed back to the station. Here at the church, Franz and Helena were once again met with friendly warmth.

'Is everyone here so friendly and welcoming?' Helena was impelled to comment.

'What else do you expect in Neubrandenburg?' one of the ladies jokingly replied, and then continued, 'Actually, you were lucky to have met those two who brought you down here. Good old Alfred and Heinz. Both very kind men. Unfortunately, there are many others who would not have been so friendly. It's that big prisoner-of-war camp nearby. It's caused everyone to be on edge. But I shouldn't rattle on so much. How especially can we help you.'

Franz explained their predicament and the urgency of Helena receiving medical attention. He was wanting to continued but the chatty lady wouldn't let him get any further.

'I knew it. As soon as I saw Alfred bringing you two here I thought to myself, 'That woman doesn't look very well'. You poor dear, being chased out of your home in this weather would have to be really awful. No wonder you are not feeling well. Herr Pastor,- now calling across the room-this poor lady needs to go the hospital or a doctor. Can you come over here for a minute and we can work out what is the best. Don't worry, my dear,- turning once again to Franz and Helena who were just standing there,- the Pastor will know someone who will be able to help you. He just never stops. He is helping people all the time. Why only yesterday there was this couple who had come from... from... oh dear, let me think. Naugard? No, that wasn't it. Frau Schneider, you remember those two old people who arrived here yesterday, with that big red bag. Do you remember where they came from? It wasn't....'

'Thank you, Frau Weyer,' interrupted the Pastor. 'How can we help these two people?' With that he introduced himself to Franz and Helena.

Franz explained their situation once again and it was clear that this man of God was practised in emergencies. He immediately outlined what he believed should be done.

'Frau Weyer, if you are not needed at the moment could you please see if you can locate Hans Hoger and ask him to come in here. Last I knew he was out in the garden cleaning snow off the paths. And Frau Schultz,' he continued, turning to one of the women arranging clothing on a table, 'do you still have that attic room spare where these two good people could stay while they get their good health back?'

Mrs Schultz indicated that the room was available to them. She came over and made herself known to Franz and Helena saying that she and her husband would be pleased for them to stay while Helena recovered. In the meantime, an overweight, puffing Hans Hoger came in from the garden, sweat running off his brow.

'You want me, Pastor?'

'Yes,' replied the Pastor, 'but tell me, has the weather warmed up? It was so cold when I came in this morning and here you are sweating as though it's the middle of summer.'

'It's only warmed up for the poor beggar like me who has been shovelling snow off the footpaths.'

'Good man. But there is something I would like you to do. Frau Natalier here needs to get medical attention as soon as possible. So could you get my car and take them down to the clinic in Pfaffen Street and find help for them.'

'That shouldn't be too hard,' replied a cheerful Hans.

'And then,' the Pastor continued, 'take their belongings around to Frau Schultz's place. They are staying in her attic room until they are ready to move on.' Hans looked at Frau Schultz and she nodded. 'Yes, Hans, Harold is home today. There were no deliveries to be made at the warehouse. He will let you in and help you take their belongings up to the attic.'

Both Franz and Helena smiled their appreciation. This, he thought, is a Germany which they had not experienced for some time. Here was a place where people are happily going about their everyday activities, pleased to help those in need. But how long would they be able to continue this way of life? Advancing armies would soon break into their present existence. Who would arrive in Neubrandenburg first? Would it be the Russians who were moving very rapidly from the east or the British and Americans who were advancing from the west? The answer to this race could determine the fate of many of the cheerful, helpful citizens of the city.

Whatever the answer, Franz was firm in his resolve that they would move further west as soon as they were able. Right now, however, his sick wife needed attention and in no way could they keep moving.

The doctor diagnosed an upset stomach brought about by eating poor food, over exertion and anxiety. He prescribed some tablets which he said would settle her stomach down and advised that she should rest for a number of days.

'You can't keep going on like you have been, Frau Natalier, or you will end up in a much worse situation. No, I know it would be pointless and silly for me to tell you to stop worrying. We are living in times when everyone is plagued by anxiety. Only peaceful times will cure that. I can however, encourage you to eat more regularly and try to rest more. You have somewhere to stay? Good. Go there and recover.' Hans then delivered them to Harold Schultz, who was expecting them.

A few days rest in warm, comfortable surroundings with adequate food and soon Helena was on the way to recovery. But Franz was becoming increasingly unsettled. The evolving war situation was one concern, but at that time even more nagging was the fact that they were living with Herr and Frau Schultz, who were not well off, and contributing nothing. Throughout his life Franz had never accepted assistance that he could not repay. Now here was a situation forcing him to do just that, going against all that he had lived by.

He brought his concern to his wife to gauge her feelings on the situation. Helena could certainly appreciate his dilemma, for she knew her husband. She, however, did not feel as strongly as he did. She saw it as something they would willingly do if the situation was reversed. After all she reminded him, they did have three children from Berlin staying with them for a number of months to escape the bombing there. They did that, she reminded him, with no thought of payment.

'Yes, I can see that Helena,' stated Franz one evening when they were discussing the situation, 'but those kids did help around the farm, and in a way, did earn their keep. But there's not really anything around the house here that I can help with.'

'If it's worrying you so much, you should ask Harold if he knows where you might be able to do something to earn a little money to repay them,' Helena suggested.

'I've been thinking along those lines myself,' admitted Franz. 'As it is OK with you, I'll speak to Harold as soon as I get the chance.'

Franz probably knew that this conversation would take place

on the following day. They had now been enjoying the healing hospitality of the Schultz family for a week and had also been enjoying their company. Franz and Harold had much in common in their attitudes towards politics, the war, religion and life in general. They appreciated the time when they could sit and discuss topics of mutual interest. It was not difficult at all for Franz to bring up the probability of his finding some paid work around the town.

'That's not at all necessary,' was Harold's immediate response, as Franz knew it would probably be. But when Franz insisted, Harold did come up with a suggestion.

'There are times in the warehouse where I work when we could use an extra pair of hands. The Boss has been short staffed for some time now. He's a decent chap and refuses to take forced labour and so we are left with doing more than possible at times. Tell you what; I'll ask the Boss tomorrow and see what he thinks.'

'Be sure you explain the situation. I am not as young and fit as I used to be and the last few months have taken a lot out of me, but I will still be able to hold up my end.'

True to his word Harold did approach the Boss and it was agreed that Franz would be called upon to give extra help when needed. He would also be paid for the work that he did. Harold also assured Franz that the Boss wouldn't really miss the few Deutsch Marks he would pay. He had done very well out of Government and military contracts. It was agreed that Franz would help in the delivery department when needed. But Franz had barely become used to walking up to the warehouse in Speicher Street when circumstances dictated a change in direction for him.

The Russians were coming. These were more than rumours. No longer did anyone believe the propaganda being broadcast that they German army would hold off the advances. They had been fed these lies throughout the last year but the enemy kept moving forward. It was the middle of April, 1945, and it was clear that the end of the war was fast approaching. A sense of urgency had invaded the city. Anxiety was heightened when definite new came through that Stettin, less that one hundred kilometres away, had fallen and the Russian forces were preparing to advance on Neubrandenburg.

It became clear that this was really happening. The prisoners-of-war were being marched away from the Stalag, marched westward away from the advancing forces. This was a sure sign that the military command knew that the city would soon be in the hands of the enemy. There seemed to be no indication that attempts were being made to halt the advances. Everything had fallen apart. All was lost. Germany had become a defeated nation. Franz and Helena were still in danger of being in the midst of what they had always dreaded.

Franz was adamant. 'We must move away from here. If we stay and the Russians find out that we have come from the eastern regions we will be either sent back to prison or shot. And I have a very good idea which it would be. We must go now while we still have the chance to travel!'

'But how, Franz? How? And where to?'

'It will have to be by train. We couldn't possibly walk like the poor prisoners-of-war. It will have to be by train to Schwerin. The news has been saying that the Americans will have taken Schwerin by the end of April. If that is the case we will be safer there.'

'Will we be able to get on a train. Won't the whole town here have to evacuate like Tilsit and Kolberg and all those other cities in the East?'

'I don't think so. Because this has traditionally been German territory the people feel that they will be treated more humanely then we would have been. Especially now that the war is basically over.'

'Oh, I hope so,' said Helena. 'They have been so wonderfully kind to us.'

'We must be prepared to go. The Schultzes agree that we must not stay here. Harold will take us and our few things up to the station tomorrow. We will be there waiting and hope that those good men who met us there a few weeks ago will be able to get us on a train going to Schwerin. Or at least somewhere else in the west.'

Now with April drawing to an end, with spring in the air, with new life appearing in the fields and on the trees after the death of winter, Franz and Helena found themselves crammed like sardines on a goods train heading for Schwerin. They were crammed in a carriage with German soldiers. These soldiers were no longer being ordered to fight. They were heading for an area where freedom would be less dangerous. Franz and Helena also were hoping for a brighter future.

Chapter 28

Cricket

The 1946/47 ashes tour to Australia had been going poorly for the English cricketers. Looked at from the other end of the pitch, it had seen the Australian test team doing very well. England's woes had begun at the Gabba in Brisbane when they were embarrassingly beaten in the first test. Sure they had to chase Australia's huge first innings total on a pitch which had been deluged by a tropical hail storm, and this made the task difficult. The bowling of Lindwall and Miller on this rain-affected pitch made it virtually impossible.

The tour continued without the English professionals being able to build up any momentum. The Australian public was enjoying this. The hardships of a long, bloody war were forgotten. Cricketmania was sweeping the country. At lunchtime on all the school playing fields around the country little Bradmans were striding out to the wicket to imitate their hero. Then at the desk in the afternoon many a sum would be incorrectly added up because the mind was on the cover drive which ended up in Charley Schimming's lucerne patch. Roaring around the playground as Spitfires and Zeros, playing hide-and-seek in the school trenches was abandoned.

In factories, farm sheds, barber shops and home kitchens, wherever there was a radio it would be tuned to the ABC with eager ears listening to Alan McGilvray, Vic Richardson and company ensuring that their listening public did not miss a single ball. The nation was now captivated by the battles being fought on the ovals at the MCG, at the Sydney Cricket Ground and at the Gabba.

For many in Australia VE day and VJ day were events consigned to the pages of the history books. This did not lessen the reality however, that for many others the battles fought in the skies over Europe, in the deserts of North Africa and in the jungles of New Guinea were still being fought daily as they sought to rectify lives disrupted by violence and horror. But how wonderful that people could open their daily newspapers and read, **NOT OLD DON, BUT HE'S STILL THERE**, on the front page. How wonderful that the photographs were not of bombed out cities and struggling, suffering soldiers.

Frank and Henry Natalier, and the others in their community also shared in the joy of peacetime. The previous decade had brought uncertainty not only in the world political arena but also to their individual farming life. During these years their region, as indeed the wider area of eastern Australia had suffered from intermittent drought. But the rains had recently returned to their normal, expected pattern and the countryside was once again smiling, anticipating a greener future. With the rains had also come violent storms and damaging hail. Lives can be cut short not only by enemy bullets in battle but by unfortunate accident. Whereas joy and happiness can be experienced in the midst of horror and death, so also can sadness and loss be found where peace and prosperity prevail.

Henry Natalier had gone to town to see how much his batch of fat pigs would sell for. Numbers were down on the usual numbers for a Monday sale. Probably because of this, the bidding by buyers was brisk and he came away very contented with the price he received.

'That was a good pen of pigs you had there. You should be

happy with what they fetched.' Henry turned around to see his brother Frank.

'No, I can't complain,' replied Henry. 'I was a bit worried, for prices were down quite a bit last week. I think a lot of farmers must have held off sending any in for today's sale. So the bidding was very good. You didn't have any here today, did you?'

'No,' complained Frank. 'I was one of those who held off. But I'll have to bring them in next week.'

'Well, I hope the prices don't fall back,' said Henry. 'Oh, before I forget. Have you or Annie heard from Aggie about next Sunday?'

'Next Sunday? No, I haven't and I don't think Annie has either. She hasn't said anything to me. Why, what's happening next Sunday?'

'Ned is coming up with a couple of his kids and we thought you and Annie might like to come for dinner and have a chat with them as well.'

'I'm sure that would be okay. The women can work something out. I would like to catch up with Ned and see how things are going. We haven't heard from him for ages.'

After a little while talking about farming matters the two brothers went off to finish their business in town.

'Kamikaze. That's what they were called. Kamikaze. Bloody maniacs. That's what we called them. They would line up our ship and come straight for us. The poor gunners had to shoot like blazes and blow their planes out of the sky before they got you.'

They were sitting around the Sunday dinner table at Henry's place and Mick, one of Ned's sons, was entertaining everyone with stories of his time as a young sailor on a warship in the Pacific. He often had them in stitches but one did not need to delve too deeply to see the great danger in his experiences.

'Did you ever get hit?' Ron wanted to know of his cousin.

'We got strafed often enough but no plane ever blew up on our ship. I probably wouldn't be here if one did. Some came mighty close though. And we were right beside the *Australia* when she got hit. There were a lot of casualties but that one hit didn't sink the ship. That was in the Philippines somewhere.'

After dinner, the young people went down to the horse paddock to catch a couple of the riding horses. Mick and Noreen had come up with their father, Ned, from Brisbane and seldom had the chance to go riding although they enjoyed it so much. The parents went into the lounge room.

'So how are things going, Ned?' Frank asked his brother-in-law. It was coming on three years now since he had lost his wife, Emma, after a long illness. Left to look after four adult children while having a job which took him away from home during the week was not an easy task.

'It's hard, Frank. You don't know how much you depend on a wife until she is no longer with you. But we all pitch in to do our best. I have to rely on Noreen so much to do those things around the home which Emma used to look after. Don't know what I'd do without her. But I hear that Roy has had some sort of an accident?'

'Yes,' replied Frank. He fell and jagged his leg on a steel stake. The wound became infected and they are having a devil of a job containing it.'

'So is he home yet?' asked Aggie. 'I knew that he had to be taken to the Ipswich hospital for treatment.'

'No,' replied Annie. 'He's still there. We have no idea how long he will have to stay. And we just can't get down to see him as often as we would like. What with petrol rationing we can't be driving down there every day.'

'That's terrible,' said Ned. 'They will be able to fix it all up, won't they?'

'We certainly hope so,' replied Frank. 'The way it was going at first, it seemed as though he might lose his leg. Now they are treating him with penicillin, but it's too early to know whether it will do any good.'

'It's funny,' remarked Henry, 'we've just been through a war where countless people have lost their lives. So many families have been torn apart by the loss of loved ones. All three of us here have escaped losing someone in the war, but we have all had our own sad loses here, miles away from the battle front.'

'Yes,' agreed Ned. 'And Henry and Aggie, I was so shocked to hear of Terence's accident. I'm sorry that I couldn't get up for the funeral. We should be asking how you are coping with it all.'

'We still find it hard to accept that he has gone. And it was such a simple accident. It is not as though he was riding so fast on his bike when he fell. And the rock had to be just where his head landed. But it all happened and we can do nothing about it.' Aggie had tears in her eyes.

'Just look at us all,' and Henry waved his arm over the other four present there. 'We come together for a family dinner and end up being so morbid. I've lost Emma, my young sister and Terence, my son, and I grieve for them very much. But I suppose it does us all good to talk about our losses. And we are all family, after all. But for all that, we are much better off than those who have lost much more than we.'

'Fair enough, Henry,' Frank somewhat agreed. 'But who exactly are you talking about?'

'Well, I could mention those poor beggars in Japan who got wiped out with those atomic bombs that the Yanks dropped on them.'

'But they were the enemy,' objected Ned. 'I'm lucky that their kamikaze pilots didn't hit Mick's ship and kill him. No, I don't have much sympathy for them.'

'Enemy, yes, but human beings just the same. They would have loved ones just like us. And what about all those in Germany. Just think Frank, if our Dad had stayed in Germany and not come out here when he did, goodness knows what would have happened to us and our children.'

Ned didn't give Frank the chance to reply. 'Emma never really talked about it to me, but do you know of any relatives still back there? I remember that when we were first married she jokingly said how I was probably shooting at her relatives when I was over there in 1918.'

'Funny,' said Frank. 'Henry and I were just talking about that some months back, before the war was over.'

'And?' Ned wanted to know.

'We don't know of any for sure. But we are pretty certain that there must have been some. Dad left quite a few relatives behind when he came out here,' explained Henry.

'I wonder how they got on?' queried Annie, and she continued. 'My dad had also mentioned how they left behind a lot of Manteuffels over there too. Are they still our enemies? And what has become of them?'

'We will probably never know,' concluded Frank.

And the topic of conversation turned to other matters. 'Did anyone catch the stumps score from Sydney yesterday?'

Chapter 29

Nur was ich an hatte und den Krückstock habe ich gerettet.

(I saved only what I was wearing and my walking stick.)

Click-clack, click-clack, click-clack. The regular beat of steel wheels on steel tracks was reassuring to Franz and Helena as they sat huddled together in the corner of the goods' van. They felt their journey was nearing its end. There was also a guarded light-heartedness among the German soldiers who were also crowded into the same space built for boxes and produce and not for people. Fighting for them was over.

In this last week of April many German commanders on the battlefields, recognising the inevitable, had surrendered to the victorious forces. A raging, unbalanced Führer may have labelled such actions cowardice and treason, but to those with closer knowledge of the actual situation, it was common sense. As a result, during this week and the next until victory in Europe was declared by the Allied Forces on 6th May, 1945, millions of German soldiers placed their fate in the hands of their conquerors. What specifically would happen to them was as yet unknown but it seemed a better option to surrender than to die fighting for a hopeless cause.

One further thing was also generally acknowledged. Better to end up in the hands of the victors coming from the west than be taken by the Poles and Russians coming from the East. This was why Franz and Helena's travelling companions, who had recently been dreading facing a superior Russian force, were relieved to be heading into the waiting arms of American forces.

Schwerin had suffered only minor damage from the bombing raids which had wreaked destruction on other towns such as neighbouring Hamburg. Now with the cessation of hostilities the city was occupied by the Americans without opposition. The romantic Schwerin palace, the old city centre with the red, Gothic cathedral, all remained for future generations to appreciate.

The citizens of Schwerin would remain living in their city, albeit with a foreign overlord. The soldiers on the train accepted that they were travelling towards a willing surrender. That was the choice their commanders had made for them. Franz and Helena had become well aware of what they were fleeing from, but were unsure of what the future held for them. They were still travelling into the unknown.

'What now Franz?' Helena asked while they were still travelling on the train, but was really referring to when they would arrive in Schwerin.

'That is a difficult question to answer, my dear. There are so many unknowns. We will be in the middle of a real bloody mess.'

'What do you mean "a real mess"?'

'I don't mean a battle field. That I hope is behind us. But we have to realise that Germany has been destroyed. We have been a bit lucky in that we have been able to keep ahead of the real destruction. The fighting hadn't yet reached Neubrandenburg and the soldiers say that Schwerin was occupied without any fighting. So many other places have been shot and bombed to ruins. We are lucky in a way to be in an area where the invading armies from the east will meet those coming from the west.'

'Well, I hope they don't start shooting at one another with us in the middle,' joked Helena.

'That's hardly likely, unless they start fighting over which part of our country they want for themselves. I think the first thing we will have to do is to contact your cousin in Hamburg. That probably won't be as easy as it sounds either. Everything in the country is in disarray. And we will have to find some permanent place where we can be contacted. We must not give up hope that the girls are also safe somewhere and will be able to get into contact with Hamburg as well.'

'And what about the Americans soldiers? How will they treat us?'

'It will be interesting to find out. Better than the Russians, that's for sure. But how much better, I really have no idea. Don't forget that they have seen all Germans as Nazi enemies for the last years. No doubt they have been taught that a German is a Nazi, and that's all there is to it.'

'Surely they would know better than that,' objected Helena.

'I should certainly hope so, but in this war everyone has been taught to hate. This is what drives battles. Even with peace the hatred and urge for revenge are not easily forgotten,' replied her husband.

'Pray God that all will go well with us.'

'Amen to that,' concluded Franz.

They had been travelling for a number of hours. In war-time, one hundred and fifty kilometres can be a long distance. Progress had been slow. Why? No one could offer any suggestions. Each unscheduled stop was nerve-wracking. Cooped up in a box car, stuffy, dark, not knowing what might be happening outside was a claustrophobic, worrying experience.

Once again, the train halted but this time everyone soon realised it was the end of the line for them. The voices shouting outside were not speaking German, but English.

'Raus! Raus! Everybody out! Get off the train! This is it. This is as far as you are going.'

The doors were opened and armed servicemen stood outside waiting.

'Raus! Line up. Everything on the ground behind you. Five paces forward. Move now!'

Confusion reigned for some time. Eventually the bewildered German soldiers understood what they had to do and displayed no resistance. They moved forward leaving their kitbags, rifles and other belongings behind them.

'You too, old man,' a young soldier directed this to Franz and Helena.

'What's he saying?' Helena asked of Franz.

'I don't know, but I think he wants us to leave our belongings on the ground and move forward with the rest. We will have to do that for we are in no position to argue.'

'Can't we find someone who speaks German so that we can tell him that we are not soldiers and this is all we own and we need it.'

But they were moved forward with all the others leaving their meagre belongings behind. They stood while the Americans came through and searched everyone. The soldiers were marched off while Franz and Helena were left standing. What were they to do? They turned to go back and collect their belongings but an American shook his head and pointed in the other direction. It surely was clear that the two older people, one being a woman, were not part of the military. The Americans would not be moved, even though Franz went up to an officer and tried to talk to him.

He only shook his head. 'No Deutsch,' and pointed them in the other direction repeating, ' Swear in, swear in.' They could do nothing but follow his directions.

'It appears that he wants us to walk to the centre of Schwerin which is in this direction,' Franz explained to Helena, as they moved off leaving the last of their possessions lying on the ground.

'We have escaped the Russian hordes, my dear, but we have lost everything we had. Here we are surrounded by defeat. Unable to speak to those around us telling us what to do. Helpless. After months of fleeing, helpless. Look at me. My walking stick. That's all I am.'

And he put his head on his wife's shoulder and wept.

Chapter 30

Helenas Vetter in Hamburg schichte am heiligen Abend zu Ostern 1945, eine Depesche das die Töchter sich gemeldet hatten; da war die Osterfreude gross.

(Helena's cousin in Hamburg sent word on Easter Saturday 1945, that our daughters had made contact with them. Our Easter joy was complete.)

Ruth and Edith had escaped the hustle and bustle of the market square in the Thuringian town of Arnstadt and were sitting in a back pew of the Bach Church. The quietness inside the church was a welcome change to their troubled experiences of the last four months.

Away from the church, the town, the district, a vicious war was still raging. Germany's enemies were tightening their stranglehold. The bloody battles being fought in all four corners of the nation and the demoralising bombing raids on major cities were hastening the country's defeat. The march towards defeat could not be reversed. The majority of German citizens were quietly wishing for a quick return to peaceful times.

For a number of minutes, the girls sat quietly admiring the simplicity of the three tiers of the church which surrounded them. Ruth broke the silence. 'Do you realise, Edith, that this is the first time we have been in a church since back in Rucken on the day before we left?'

'Yes, you are right, Ruth. And before you mention it. Yes, God has protected us. I wonder whether he has been as kind to Mama and Papa.' Edith was finding the separation from their parents harder and harder to accept.

'You know that I cannot tell you for sure, as much as I would like, but I keep telling myself that they are safe.'

'Isn't it nice just sitting here? One can just sit here, close one's eyes and pretend nothing awful has happened in the last months.' Edith appeared relaxed.

'I'm so pleased Manfred suggested we come down here. He is right. I don't think we would have been happy in Erfurt. It was too big and we are used to living in a much smaller place.'

'Yes, Ruth, I am too. And let's hope that he has found that friend he was looking for. At least those people in Erfurt were able to help him.'

'Did you know, Edith, that Bach played the organ in this very church when he was just a little older than me?' Ruth had completely changed the topic.

Edith looked at her sister speechless, and then after a moment said, 'How are you to know that? We had never heard of this town called Arnstadt until yesterday, let alone this church.'

'It says it here in this brochure I picked up at the entrance,' replied Ruth. ' It was his first job and he was organist here for four years from 1703 to 1707. It has only been called the Bach Church for ten years. Before that it was simply called the New Church.'

'The New Church!' remarked Edith picking up on the name. 'You could have fooled me. Looking at it from the outside it seemed anything but new to me.'

'And further,' continued Ruth reading from the brochure, 'the first church ever built on this site was consecrated way back in 1333.'

Edith interrupted. 'Was that called the Old Church? But you had better stop Ruth for you are beginning to sound like Papa. Remember how he would always be telling us about everything as we were....' and then she began sobbing.

Suddenly they were startled by the organ which started playing above them. They sat and listened for a while, captivated by musical sounds which they had not heard for months. The sounds echoed through the empty church. It created a whole new atmosphere for Edith and her sobbing stopped. She smiled as she looked at her sister. 'I wonder if that is Bach come back to do some organ practice?'

Ruth's scowl turned to understanding before she could say anything to further upset her sister. Then she said, feigning seriousness, 'Shall we go up there and find out?'

It was the Pfarrer who was somewhat surprised by the appearance of these two rather scruffy girls. He stopped playing, turned to them and said, 'Hello. Do you like the Toccata and Fugue in D minor?'

'Hello, Herr Pfarrer,' replied both girls together. and then Edith continued, 'That's nice music that you were playing.'

'Why, thank you, young lady,' smiled the pastor. 'That was Bach's famous Toccata and Fugue in D minor. I've been trying to play it properly for goodness knows how long.'

'Oh,' replied Edith, now quite embarrassed. 'I didn't know that it was called that and that it was composed by Bach. The music sort of reminded me of church back home.'

"Why? Does you organist like playing Bach?'

'Probably, but I don't really know. I think he just plays the hymns for our Sunday service.'

'If he does that then I'm sure he would also like playing Bach's music. All organists can play pieces composed by Bach. You know, he was very famous around here. He probably composed that piece I was playing in this very church. He was organist here for a number of years. That was about two hundred and fifty years ago and I am still trying to play it.'

Edith began to smile and then started to giggle. The pastor looked at her with a frown and asked, 'Do you find my playing so amusing?'

'Oh, I'm sorry. It's not that at all. I think your playing sounded so lovely. No, it's just that you started to remind me of my Papa.'

The Pastor looked puzzled and then asked, 'Is it my bald head?'

'No, Papa still has plenty of grey hair. It is because when we would go anywhere he would always be telling us all the information about where we were. And you were doing that with Bach. Just a little while ago my sister was reading to me from the brochure and she sounded like my father as well.'

'Is your father here with you in Arnstadt?'

The girls then related to the Pfarrer their predicament while he listened carefully and sympathetically. Bach had been forgotten. His organ practice completely abandoned. Most importantly, as far as the girls were concerned, he offered the possibility of help. He also suggested they stay in the vestry of the church until Sunday.

'It's much warmer there than in the church here. By Sunday I hope I can arrange somewhere more comfortable for you to stay.'

The girls looked at one another in amazement and thanked the Pfarrer profusely. He then continued, 'I will send one of my daughters around at about 5 o'clock with something for you to eat and a few blankets to keep you warm. Now make sure you don't run away and I will see you on Sunday at the church service, if not before.'

The Pfarrer was true to his word and spent time the next

day organising help for these two girls who had turned up on his doorstep. He knew whom best to approach and these had found it hard to say no to their Pfarrer. By Sunday he was able to tell the girls what was possible for them.

Mrs Heise and her daughter were living in a small apartment with a built-out attic area and they agreed that the two girls from the east could stay there. Mr Wandel was part owner of a stone quarry located at the edge of the town and was happy for the girls to turn up there every day and do various jobs to earn some money to keep themselves alive. In less than a week after arriving in this town, Ruth and Edith had been lifted out of their worries and feelings of hopelessness by the love and care of the Pfarrer and his congregation members.

Ruth and Edith were sitting in their own little room, feeling safe and warm. They knew that in the immediate future they would not starve or be attacked. They were thinking about their last four months.

'It hasn't been easy,' was Ruth's assessment.

'It was horrible,' was Edith's response.

'It could have been worse,' Ruth countered.

'It was horrible.' Edith could not think of anything worse to say.

'Yes,' agreed Ruth. 'I can't disagree with you about that. Now that we are sort of settled we should write to Hamburg and let them know where we are staying. Perhaps they have already heard from Papa.'

'Oh, yes. We have to send a letter away as soon as possible. We can still send letters in Germany, can't we? Or has the German Post stopped operating?'

'I'm sure the mail will still get through.'

That settled, Edith changed the subject. 'What do you think about Mrs Heise and her daughter?'

'I think that they are great. And not just because they agreed to have us live here with them. We must do everything we can to help them. They have suffered a lot during this war as well. It's not just us from the east that have suffered.'

There was a pause as Edith looked questioningly at her sister. Then Ruth continued. 'Didn't you hear that woman telling us that both Mr Heise and their son have been killed somewhere in Italy?'

There was a normalcy in the daily existence of Ruth and Edith for the following weeks. For six days a week they would walk to the quarry, work all day and then walk back to their attic, dirty and tired. But they received a small payment for their efforts. Except for a small amount which they kept for their own personal needs, they handed the money over to Mrs Heise who provided them with food.

On Sundays, they would accompany Mrs Heise and her daughter, Inge, to the Bach Church. Then they would spend the rest of the day relaxing with Inge, walking around the town or simply sitting quietly reading books in the house. If it were not for the knowledge of what was happening not far away, the aura of uncertainty that hung over them and the fact that they had heard nothing as a result of sending the letter to Hamburg, life was not unpleasant. The people in Arnstadt struggled in these times of war and most had been personally affected in one way or another. Fighting had not invaded their town. The atrocities which they had heard about on the radio and which were written about in the newspapers had remained distant from their little bit of peacefulness in Thuringia.

In early April, American soldiers marched into the town. Warily, with their rifles at the ready, their backs weighed down with backpacks, they made their way down either side of the main road which lead into the town centre. No shots were fired.

There was no German army presence in the town to deny them entrance. The local citizens came out of the houses and huddled in their doorways quietly watching as the victors kept coming. They did nothing that might be construed as aggression. For most it was probably a relief to know that the war was grinding to its inevitable conclusion.

'What will we do?' the girls asked Mr Wandel at the quarry. 'Will we be safe to go home to Mrs Heise's place?'

'I'm sure you will be as safe as anyone else,' replied their Boss. 'But why do you ask? What is worrying you?'

'They might find out that we are from East Prussia and will want to send us back to the Russians.'

'You needn't worry about that. You are here now. The Yanks have arrived and any danger from the Russians is only in your imagination,' consoled Mr Wandel.

And it proved to be just as Mr Wandel had predicted. A company of US soldiers did set up camp in the town but did not worry the local people at all. They went about their daily business. Ruth and Edith kept walking to and from the quarry every day and were soon relaxed once again.

Things did not change for a couple of weeks and then one evening the local people were curious about a convey of covered trucks which drove through the town centre to the American camp. Next morning the word was spreading that some had seen faces peering out of the back of the trucks. Later that day groups of non-American troops were patrolling the streets.

'Who are these soldiers? They are not Americans. Why are they here?'

'They are speaking in some foreign language and it's not English. Some say it is French while at other times it doesn't sound at all like French.'

'French? Are they part of the French forces? They must come

from the French colonies in North Africa. Are they Algerians or Moroccans?'

The mayor of Arnstadt soon ascertained that they were Moroccan troops assigned to the Americans in this region. They were to help in containing areas captured by the invading forces. The whole atmosphere of the town soon changed with the arrival of these African troops. The men of the town saw them as bullying and unfair. They were continually ordering local men to do jobs which were pointless merely to exercise their authority. It was the women however, who felt most threatened.

'They leer,' was the feeling expressed by many. ' I don't feel safe here any longer.' Ruth and Edith also felt threatened going and coming from their jobs at the quarry.

It was only a few day later as they were walking up their street in the fading light when they noticed soldiers and police in front of Mrs Heise's house where they lived. They were stopped from going any further.

The policeman was firm. 'You are not allowed to go on.'

'But why? This is where we live.'

'You live here? Where exactly?' the policeman wanted to know.

Ruth explained. The policeman at first said nothing but merely looked at the girls. Then he muttered, 'Wait here,' and went off towards the front of the house. He returned a little later with a senior police officer and an American army officer.

Ruth had to explain once again who they were and how they came to be living in this house. Her explanation seemed to satisfy the officers. Edith who all this time had been standing looking around at all the activity now asked, 'What has happened here?'

The police officer explained. 'Both Mrs Heise, who you know lives here, and her daughter have been taken to hospital. Three soldiers broke into their flat today and assaulted them.'

'Assaulted? You don't mean that they were...' Ruth was lost for words. 'How are they? Are they seriously hurt?'

One of those horrible sides of war, which these two farm girls from the Memelland had heard from their cousin, Katie, those many months ago, had now arrived on their own doorstep. They felt that they now had the opportunity to help those two who had suffered at the hands of undisciplined soldiers. When Mrs Heise and her daughter were discharged from the hospital they did all they could be make their life more pleasant.

Their nursing however was not to last for long. Finally, that letter which they had been wishing for every day finally arrived. Ruth held in her hands a letter from Hamburg. 'Oh, how I hope that it contains welcome news, good news, news that my parents are still alive and are safe somewhere,' she thought.

'Edith,' she shouted. 'It's arrived. We have a letter from Hamburg. Come quickly and we will open it together.'

Mrs Heise and Inge could see the contents of the letter written on the faces of the two girls as they read it. They could see what it contained by the way Edith was jumping up and down and then hugging her sister. Mrs Heise turned to her daughter and said, 'I have the feeling that we will not have our two girls with us for much longer. I'm sure that they will be anxious to make their way back to their parents.'

Chapter 31

Zuerst Ami, dann Tommy und zuletzt Ivan.

(First Yanks, then Pommies and finally Russkies).

Disappointment and relief, helplessness and frustration, uncertainty and longing, despair and hope, terror, anger and sadness: these were some of the mixed emotions which had converged on Franz and caused him to release his pent-up feelings in a flood of tears. Throughout the last six months, these and many others had never been far from his mind, but the necessity of his being there for his family, of wrestling with decisions which needed to be made, kept them at bay. Now, with his nation's battles nearing an end, finally arriving in an area occupied by a friendly foe, his mind was free and for a moment he withheld nothing.

Helena was understanding, knowing how her husband had unselfishly shouldered the responsibilities throughout their flight. Now she also burst into tears. Tears of joy but also of sadness. The two of them had arrived at a relatively safe location, but the present circumstances of their two daughters, Ruth and Edith, remained unknown. But that was only part of the grim reality they were now facing. The battle to stay alive was over. Now began the battle to keep living.

They were but two of the many millions of German citizens who, at this time, were facing the same challenges. With their cities in ruins, their homes destroyed, livelihoods in tatters, families decimated and the food supply practically non-existent, hope evaporated at last. Many unknown thousands, whose strength and resolve had been shattered by long years of conflict and subservience to an evil power, opted to take their own lives. Suffering for them was over.

This option was not even contemplated by Franz and Helena. Their Christian beliefs would have vetoed this path had it arisen. They had lost all but still had much to live for and saw their continued survival as important for the well-being of their family. Not only were the girls to be considered but Helena's two surviving sons were also part of their closely-knit family.

Her oldest, Fritz who was a soldier, by last reports had survived the fighting. He had been captured somewhere in north-west Germany. However, being a former member of the SS he would certainly come under close scrutiny by the allied powers. He would need their support. Erich, the youngest son, saw out the war as a lorry driver. He and his wife continued working throughout the years of conflict and could be considered some of the lucky ones. Even so, family remained important to them.

Apart from family considerations, Franz and Helena never considered that at some time in the future they would not be able to return to the Memelland, restore their farm and continue life as before. They still regarded their flight was a tragic, brief necessity which had been forced into their lives. It was the immediate present which now had to occupy their attention.

'So what now, Franz?' Helena repeated the concern she had expressed on the train a few hours ago.

'Well, it appears the Americans are not really interested in us. They are more concerned with the German soldiers who have surrendered. And I can't see that we are in any real danger from them. What we need to do is to find someone, somewhere, who is able to give some aid to refugees. There must be places which are set up to do that. We need to walk into the centre of the city now and see what we can find out.'

Franz and Helena made their way slowly towards where they believed the centre of the city lay. They hoped that they would find help there. To some people who watched them ambling along, they could be two middle-aged folks going for an afternoon stroll. Other local inhabitants would dismiss them completely uninterestedly as refugees, many of whom were flooding into their town. Only the two sad souls themselves knew the exact reality of their situation and the true depth of their sorrows. Hunted from their homeland, recently stripped of the last of their possessions, they were now alone in a city which until recently they had hardly heard of.

But it was German. It seemed to be safe and if some of the inhabitants were as kind and helpful as those whom they had encountered in Neubrandenburg then they could dare to imagine things improving. This thought made their tired walk bearable.

It was the end of a freezing cold winter, nearing the end of a bitterly fought war, but even this could not hold back the coming of spring. The blossoms of April spoke of a happier future. The tentative foliage of all those sturdy species which sought refuge from the frosts and snow by a protective hibernation were signalling brighter times. Franz and Helena, in spite of their predicament, were not unresponsive to the beauty emerging from the death of winter. After all they had lived in a region where the winters were always extreme and where springtime was always eagerly awaited.

The sun shone brightly on the blue waters of the *Pfaffenteich*, the birds were busy in the branches overhead, a warmth surrounded the two lonely refugees, as they walked slowly towards their future.

'Just look around here, Franz. Who would think that there

was a war going on. The people are going about contentedly. There is no damage that we can see. The trees are starting to flower. It's quite lovely.' Helena seemed at peace with herself.

'Yes,' agreed Franz. 'It all seems so unreal to what we have been used to. Look over there. There are even people sailing on the lake.'

They continued walking.

'I wonder is that Arsenal Street up ahead? The man back there said that we would have to go to the left if we wanted to get to the centre of the town and the cathedral.'

'We will soon find out,' returned Franz. 'At least the walk has probably been good for us. It was good to stretch our legs after being crammed up in that cattle wagon for so long.'

'And to get as bit of fresh air,' Helena added. 'I'm sure some of those soldiers hadn't had a bath for a month.'

'Don't blame them too much, the poor beggars. There is no doubt that they would have rather been doing something else than fighting. And I was about to say, it's good to see that nature's beauty has not deserted us or our country. The beauty returning to our land will certainly give us hope.'

Except for the groups of American servicemen standing around, the city centre of Schwerin did present an atmosphere of normality. German citizens were hurrying to and fro seemingly going about their everyday business. Shops were open. People were purchasing. This scene which burst upon them when walking along Bischof Street camouflaged to a great extent what would be their immediate experience.

There were friendly, helpful people who put themselves out to help Franz and Helena. The majority, however, struggling to get their own life back on track after the adversities of wartime, saw the eastern refugees as a hindrance. The whole country was lacking most of the basics needed to pursue an every-day life.

The norm was to battle for one's own existence at the expense of helping those in dire need.

Franz and Helena were given a few basic requirements at the welfare organization associated with the council. They lived in temporary refugee shelters until transferring to a more permanent place in the barracks once occupied by groups of forced labourers from Poland. Spartan, it was, but it was a roof over their heads. The daily meal was obtained from the community kitchen.

Idle days were long, with constant hunger making them even longer. With so much unoccupied time on their hands they became despondent with their minds unable to imagine anything positive. Helena would become inconsolable in her sobbing for their two daughters. Nothing Franz was able to say could ease her pain.

Then the relief, the joy unbounded, when a telegram arrived from Hamburg telling them that the girls were alive and well in Thuringia on the other side of Germany. As arranged before they were separated from their parents those many dangerous months ago, they had made contact with the relatives in Hamburg. However, with the state of communications in Germany at that time news travelled slowly and only after an unbearably long time did the good news eventually arrive in Schwerin.

With the arrival of this information Franz and Helena viewed their future more positively. Their situation had altered little but their newly regained positive attitude could see past present hardships.

Then the Americans left Schwerin. Oh, how rumours fly when no one knows for sure what is happening.

'Why are the Americans leaving?' Helena wanted to know.

Franz had heard many rumours while talking to other refugees. 'It seems that the leaders of our victors had met months

ago working out how they would divide Germany up after they
defeated us.'

'Who do you mean?'

'Well, I suppose England, America, Russia and France. They
were the main ones.'

'What do you mean, divide Germany up?'

'We can't do anything about it. We no longer have a
government and someone has to make sure things do not get
out of hand. Each of these four powers will take an area and see
that it gets running again.'

'And the Americans? Why are they leaving here?' Helena
queried.

'I've heard,' Franz replied, 'that they are taking an area in
southern Germany, and so we are not in their area. Someone
else will look after this part.'

'Oh, dear. Who will that be?'

'There are rumours that it will be Russia.'

'Oh, no! That can't happen.'

'Well,' said Franz,' they are not so very far away. I've heard
that shortly after we left Neubrandenburg, they came into the
city and burnt it down. That was just a few days before the war
ended. Remember all those beautiful old buildings — the city
castle, the old town hall, and the churches? Everything was burnt.
For nothing.'

'And our good friends there?'

'Who knows what happened to them. But things have
quietened down a little and they are not committing the atrocities
they were before.'

'Please God they won't be coming here,' Helena concluded.

Her fears were allayed when a convoy of British soldiers
arrived in the town at the beginning of June. Things improved
slightly for them too. The British seemed concerned that the

refugees should be looked after a little better than they had been. Their food supply increased in quantity and quality although still only representing starvation rations.

Finally, after weeks of waiting, Ruth and Edith arrived from Thuringia. What in normal times would have involved a few train trips, transformed into a mammoth effort in war-ravaged Germany. But the family was reunited and this brought great comfort to all four of them.

Then at the end of June the unthinkable occurred. Russian forces arrived in the town and the British prepared to leave.

No! How could this happen to them? For nine months, they had been fleeing for their lives, determined to keep ahead of the Russians and now, in the supposed peace after the war, the victorious powers had simply ruled that this part of Germany should be controlled by Russia.

What would now be their fate? How would the Russian military commanders treat those refugees who had escaped from the eastern sections of the German Empire? For Franz and his family, it was a frightening prospect.

Chapter 32

Wir waren heilfroh den asiatischen Horden den Rücken gekehrt zu haben.

(We were jolly glad to have turned our back on the Asian hordes.)

The worst fears of what it might be under the control of their Russian conquerors were allayed. It soon became clear that the inhumane excesses which had been perpetrated on the German civilian population while the war was drawing to an end had been curtailed. Wholesale persecution did not occur. Indiscriminate vindictive punishment was a rare occurrence. Those known to have been associated with the German armed forces, especially with Nazi affiliations, received little mercy. Imprisonment and executions were wide spread.

The civilian population, while still being molested, were not constantly fearing for their lives. All were aware however, that they were not a free people. The iron grasp of the eastern victors gradually imposed its authority. This was an authority that tolerated no dissension. The wisest choice of the majority was to go about their daily business without attracting the notice of the controlling forces.

Life was difficult for everyone. For homeless, powerless, penniless refugees from the east it was especially difficult. Work was almost impossible to find. Food was scarce. Life for Franz and his family in Schwerin seemed to be locked in a slow downward spiral. It had reached a crisis point.

'What can we do?' asked a desperate Franz of his family. 'We didn't come all this way, we didn't suffer all those months of flight, for nothing. The war is over. We are still alive but I feel so helpless.'

'Papa, dear, you mustn't get so upset. Our present problems are not because of you. Most refugees are in the same position. If it wasn't for you we would have all died somewhere in the frozen lands of East Prussia,' consoled his elder daughter, Ruth. The womenfolk in the family had become his strength.

'Some of the others have been going out into the villages. There seems to be a better chance of finding work there,' put in Edith. 'Maybe we should do that too.'

'But where?' asked her father. 'We know nothing about the area or where we might be able to find a place to live. And what about work? We need to earn some money.'

'We shall ask around. Some of the farmers at the markets might give us some ideas,' Ruth suggested.

After a week, they could make some definite plans. The closest villages around Schwerin offered no possibilities. They would have to move further afield. Moving was possible provided they stayed within the Russian Zone and the authorities were notified of their movements.

Everything went to plan and now with winter approaching — it was now twelve months since they had to leave their homeland — the four Rucken refugees were living in an attic room in a small village thirty kilometres north-west of Schwerin. Here by harvesting wild berries and fruit, by gleaning wheat and potato fields and by doing as much paid labouring as was available, they eked out an existence.

It was a bare existence. A life now, it was true, free from the death and atrocities of war, free somewhat from the harshness of the weather, but not without its worrying uncertainties. The village was some distance from the small town where they could buy their everyday necessities. The fifteen-kilometre trip was fraught with danger, especially for the girls. Groups of occupation soldiers would drive around these isolated country roads. Accounts of rape were not uncommon. Their leering and the suggestive intonation they put into their unsolicited comments were particularly frightening.

Added to this were the frequent home invasions. From time to time a group of Russian soldiers would demand entry to their home. Ostensibly they were searching for Nazi sympathisers, but in reality it was a tactic to upset the local people. Living under these conditions was becoming more and more stressful for all the family. It became ever clearer that their flight to safety and freedom was not yet at an end.

At the beginning of 1947 news was circulating that the English Zone was still accepting eastern refugees. Franz had no hesitation in registering his desire to move away from where they were.

At the end of January, they once again experienced the discomfort of being jammed into a rail goods wagon like herring. This time, however, they hoped it would be the beginning of a more pleasant chapter in their lives.

After suffering once more the indignity of being thoroughly searched by the Russian border guards, they arrived in the English Zone. The welcoming smiles there suggested a happier future.

Eighteen months of deprivation, of loss and horror, of suffering and anxiety, were now overshadowed by the promise inherent in their friendly welcome.

However, as with so many other refugees here at this time the family found it very difficult to live through the scarce times of post-war Germany. Franz, finally yielding to the constant pleading of his daughters, looked further afield for help. With the aid of the Red Cross this was found in distant Australia. More than fifty years after saying goodbye to his Uncle Fritz, Franz was delighted to see contact restored between his family and that of his favourite uncle.

Chapter 33

A Letter from Germany

Frank Natalier was sitting on a block of wood in front of his tool shed having afternoon tea when brother Henry drove up. He watched with curiosity as Henry got out of the old Buick and came towards him with some papers in his hand.

'Good day,' he greeted. 'What brings you here at this time of day? No afternoon tea at home?'

'Hello Frank. You won't believe what came in the mail today.' Henry seemed quite excited as he waved the papers around.

'A cheque for a hundred pounds?' suggested Frank.

'No. Look at this.' Henry held out an air-mail envelope for Frank to see.

'An air-mail letter. Who do you know who would be sending you an air-mail letter?' said Frank as he took it. 'It's addressed to you, but what strange hand-writing. And — as he read Deutsche Post on the stamps — it's from Germany. Who on earth? Don't tell me it's from some Nataliers over there.'

'It is,' confirmed Henry. 'It's from someone called Franz Natalier. That's what you were christened. It's a coincidence, isn't it? Remember when Ned was up about a month ago and we were talking about possible relatives in Germany, and what might have happened to them? You said then that we would probably never know. Well I have the feeling that we are about to find out.'

'Have you read the letter?' Frank wanted to know.

'What do you think? Like you I've forgotten all the German I ever knew. I looked through it but couldn't make head nor tail of anything.'

'So what will we do?'

'I've been thinking. Pastor Koehler would have had to learn German when he was at the seminary studying to be a minister. We will have to take the letter over to him and see what he can make of it all.'

'Good idea,' agreed Frank. 'Let's go over in the morning. He's not likely to be out anywhere. Why don't we take the letter in to show Annie now. She won't be able to understand it either, but would be interested in seeing it.'

So Frank picked up his few biscuits, left his mug of cold tea half drunk and headed with Henry to the house to share the news.

Next morning the Pastor could well understand the brothers' excitement. This excitement was dampened somewhat by the contents of the letter for which Pastor Koehler was able to give an approximate translation.

'The trouble,' he said, 'is that my German knowledge is very bookish. I would probably do a better job of translating some of Martin Luther's theology than this letter. But I think I've got the main gist of it.'

'Well let's hear what it says.'

'As I see it,' began the Pastor, 'this man, Franz Natalier, had to flee with his wife and two daughters from a place called Memelland. They are now in the British sector in the north of Germany, but have lost everything. They have little food or clothing and desperately need help. He says he remembers his Uncle Fritz coming to Australia and hopes there are some relatives here who might be able to help him. That's about it.'

'He said his Uncle Fritz came to Australia,' Henry picked up on this name. 'That would have to be our dad. If our dad was really his uncle that would make this Franz our first cousin.'

'Well I never,' was Frank's reaction. 'I wonder what other relatives we might have over there that we have never heard of.'

Here was a situation which gave rise to a whole range of emotions for the Australians. There was the excitement of discovering new relations, but sadness that they had lost everything in the war and were now struggling to survive. There was concern about how they might go about trying to help. After all, Germany was on the other side of the world.

The wars had not been unkind to Frank and Henry Natalier's families. The last six years had had their hard times but their farms kept operating as they normally did and income kept coming. They were not rich landholders with vast amounts of agricultural or grazing land. They both had small mixed farms on which they ran a small dairy herd and where they grew saleable crops of vegetables. But they were certainly in a position to help their distant relatives who were in need. Henry was nominated to write back to cousin Franz in Germany.

'So what are you going to say?' asked Henry's wife, Aggie, who was leaning over his shoulder as he was thinking about what to write.

He looked up at her. 'I think at this stage I should keep the letter short.'

'Yes,' she said. 'I believe you will do that. When have you ever written a long letter?'

'Ha! Ha!' he replied, but in a pleasant way. 'When have I ever had to write a long letter? No, I'll tell this Franz who we all are here. That Frank and I are his first cousins and that there are also two girl cousins. How we were surprised and excited to get his letter and that we would certainly be happy to help them.

Then I will ask what they specifically need. That should get the ball rolling.'

'But how do you know that he will be able to read English?' asked Aggie.

'I have no idea whether he will be able to read English or not, but I'm sure he will be able to find someone who can.'

And Henry wrote a letter to his cousin which restored contact between these families who were on different sides of the world, spoke different languages, were on different sides during the recent world war, and had vastly different experiences during that war. Franz Natalier, who as a small boy loved his Onkel Fritz dearly, was now for the first time in contact with his uncle's two sons, Frank and Henry. Frank was certainly named after him and Henry named after Onkel Fritz's brother, Heinrich, who had died during the flight. A family bond had previously existed between them and it could now only grow and be strengthened. A new chapter in the lives of these families had begun.

Postscript

Morgen, oder vielleicht übermorgen, scheint wieder die Sonne.

(Tomorrow, or perhaps the day after, the sun will shine again.)

The war was over. Living for many was very difficult, especially for the refugees from the east who had arrived with nothing in a devastated nation. After the Nataliers in Australia were surprised by that very first letter, contact was renewed and continued.

Extract from a letter written by Franz Natalier to 'Henry and Family'.

Buchholzermoor, 15th September, 1947
Before the elections we were promised to get compensation. After the elections, everything remained as before. Up until now we have received nothing other than the monthly beggar's payment. Many are going from home to home. Some call it foraging, others begging. Until now I have never done either.

Now, my dear relatives, that I had the Red Cross find out where you were, was a result of my daughters. They wouldn't give me any rest, for many others found out the addresses of their relatives in this way. In my whole life, I have never asked for help if I couldn't repay it. For the reasons I have explained here, I cannot promise if I will ever be in a position to repay you. If you send anything it will be accepted with many thanks but you will have to regard it as a loss to you.

....

This year was a severe drought and only half the crops survived.

The (English) Zone is over-crowded and without help we will die of starvation. Over the years we have forgotten what it is like to eat meat. But there is a daily lack of fat as well as flour and sugar. As far as under-wear, clothes and shoes are concerned, we basically have nothing. Wool is also desperately needed. All the women can knit and my wife spins. She only has a pair of material shoes and they are worn out. Her foot size is 38½ or 25½ cm long. Ruth almost always has work and desperately needs shoes and stockings. Her size is 39 or 26 cm. For her we ask if possible that the heels be not too high. Edith has almost the same shoe size as my wife. Both require winter coats, not as necessary as Ruth. I don't get around a lot and shoes are not so necessary. My shoe size is 45 or 35 cm. Fritz has a somewhat shorter foot but high instep. My winter jacket is still OK but I have nothing for the summer, but it has now passed. For myself I ask for a cap size 55 cm, a pair of braces, perhaps some fur for a fur collar and a small tobacco pipe. I've made my own tobacco. It's mostly to get over the hunger. And a head scarf for my wife, not a hat. Ready- made things for me would probably fit badly; as long as they are the same size and can be altered.

And so my dear cousin, our wish-list is very long. I ask only for the most desperate...

Extract from a letter to 'Cousin Henry and Family' from Franz Natalier.

Buchholzermoor, 22nd August, 1948.
This is now our writing paper that we get to buy from time to time in exchange for handing in old paper. Here everything is so dear and poor quality.

Dear cousin, you write whether my daughters would be able to migrate to live with you. I will not pressure them one way or the other. I will leave it to them and my wife to come to a decision. Is it possible for German girls without any experience to get ahead over there? Ruth meets a lot of new people in her work, but that is not the case with Edith and in her present condition she is just not able to do any hard work. Ruth is now working in a bathing resort but she will probably have written to you. Edith is taking English lessons a couple times a week but she hopes soon to have a job through the Work Office.

I've heard that young men from our homeland have immigrated to Australia, but the government have paid their way. How much would such a trip to Australia cost? In US dollars for I do not understand English pounds. We have no money whatsoever and if we do not receive any compensation will remain penniless. I am now 68 years old and probably do not have much longer to live and I would be happy to know that they were in your care...

Extract from letter to 'Uncle Henry and family' from Ruth. Wangerooge, 14th December, 1950.

...From our dear father, your cousin dear uncle, you will receive no further letters for he has died in June so far from his homeland. He died quite suddenly from a stroke and was buried on Pentecost Saturday. He wanted so desperately to return to his homeland once again, and he wanted so much to be assured that we two girls were provided for; but such was not granted him. He had to leave us so early.

We were very sad and upset but our work left us no time to brood about it and really helped us overcome our sorrows. Father could no longer do the work he loved and had a lot of time to sit and think. He just could not get over the fact that after a rewarding life of work on his own beautiful farm now in his old age he had become as poor as a beggar. All of this accompanied him to the grave. His one regret at death was that he could not properly care for Edith and me. But we are both young and healthy, are able to work and will be able to fend for ourselves.

As to our coming out to Australia, when things became serious and I had forwarded the necessary papers he wasn't at all enthusiastic. He really wanted us to stay here in Germany and my mother had the same wish as well. So, although I really would have like to come out there I have given up the whole idea on account of my parents. I shall now have to accept that and perhaps think about it sometime in the future. I am sorry to have put you to so much trouble for I know that you were doing it for our best. I personally am very disappointed to have not continued but I did it out of love for my parents.

Extract from letter to Glen from Ruth.
Hamburg- Harbing, 26th October, 1954.

I am still sorry that we did not come, but it was not my decision for I would have really liked to come. But I loved my parents too much and my sister was not so keen. But I am still lonely and alone without any family, as if I were in Australia. My father has died, my mother lives so far away that we only see one another once a year. I haven't seen my sister for two years. She has married well, has an apartment already. Her husband works in a bank and she is also still working. They are doing quite well.

Extract from letter to Glen from Ruth.
Hausen, 7th December, 1965

It's now over four weeks since I received your letter. It arrived on my birthday on the 4th November and was a big surprise. We had just moved into new accommodation on November 1st, a beautiful three roomed apartment with kitchen and bathroom. Until we had everything just right I didn't have time to write. I had been wondering why you had not written for so long.

I have now been married for almost five years and our son, Gert, will be four years old in January. We are living not far from Frankfurt in the same town where my sister Edith and my mother live. They have had a one-family house built where mother also lives. Edith has a young daughter who will soon be five years old.